MORNING TIDE

NEIL M. GUNN

———◇———

MORNING TIDE

SOUVENIR PRESS

First published by Faber and Faber Ltd.
This edition copyright © 1975 by
Souvenir Press and John W. M. Gunn
and published 1975 by Souvenir Press Ltd,
95 Mortimer Street, London W1N 8HP
and simultaneously in Canada by
J. M. Dent & Sons (Canada) Ltd,
Ontario, Canada

Reprinted 1977, 1982

*The publisher acknowledges the financial assistance of
The Scottish Arts Council in the publication of this volume.*

ISBN 0 285 62191 2   casebound
ISBN 0 285 62201 3   paperback

Printed in Great Britain by
Fletcher & Son Ltd, Norwich

TO JESS

PART ONE

I

The boy's eyes opened in wonder at the quantity of sea-tangle, at the breadth of the swath which curved with the curving beach on either hand. The tide was at low ebb and the sea quiet except for a restless seeking among the dark boulders. But though it was the sea after a storm it was still sullen and inclined to smooth and lick itself, like a black dog bent over its paws; as many black dogs as there were boulders; black sea-animals, their heads bent and hidden, licking their paws in the dying evening light down by the secret water's edge. When he stepped on the ware, it slithered under him like a living hide. He was fascinated by the brown tangled bed, the eel-like forms, the gauzy webs. There had been no sun to congeal what was still glistening and fresh.

A faint excitement touched his breast; his lips parted; his eyes shot hither and thither. He began rooting at the bed with his boots, stooping every now and again to examine the head of a tangle. At length he found one with a small delicate limpet stuck in the cup of its head; a young one because its round stem was slim and not two feet in length. As he snicked it free its leathery tail-frond flicked sea-mist to his face. His teeth began to water. He cut the brown stem two inches from the shell with his pocket knife, which had one strong sharp blade. As he pared off the claw-roots

9

that curled round the hollow where the shell was, he was very careful not to remove the shell. The shell was the jewel in its head, importing tenderness and sweetness. It was also something to "show off". He put the tangle head in his pocket and lifted the folded sack that had slipped from under his arm. Then he went on rooting amongst the bed until he had found two more tangles with shells. But neither was so delicate, so thin-skinned, as the first. The first was a beauty! When he had dressed them and stuffed them in his pocket, he gave an involuntary shiver; his teeth clicked and he brought the back of his hand to his wet nose. His nose was colder than his hand. His body twisted and wriggled inside his clothes searching for warmth. But his round dark eyes were on the boulders down by the hidden sea-edge. It was time he got his "baiting".

Below the high-tidal sweep of tangleweed the beach sloped in clean grey-blue stones rounded and smooth, some no bigger than his fist, but some larger than his head. As he stepped on them they slithered and rolled with a sea noise. The noise rose up and roared upon the dusk like a wave. All around no life was to be seen, there was no movement but the sea's. It was too lonely a place to make a noise. He was relieved to come on firmer ground where the boulders began. He went out among the boulders quietly until he came to the mussel bed. Then he folded back the bag, squatted down, and began tearing the clusters of mussels from the ground.

Sometimes stones stuck to the roots, but these he caught and tore off easily. Many of the mussels were very small, and a small mussel made an insufficient bait. But fat mussels were what were needed. It took the same labour to shell a big mussel as a small one.

Indeed it was easier, because the two sides of the small mussel were so close-shut and delicate that the knife-blade would not go in between them, and so was inclined to slip and cut the ball of the thumb. It was very vexing to cut a thumb when working in salt water. Besides, the salt water was great for making the cut keep on bleeding. And then, as everyone said, it was a difficult thing to get an open wound to heal readily in cold or wintry weather. Peter Navook had said that last night. He had a loud voice that would go suddenly serious: perhaps because he came from up the glen and so had to give the news of people who were ill or who had had misfortunes. Really he had three voices: a poking, joking voice; a sensible, manly voice; and a serious voice (which always made you notice his eyes, because they grew serious too, although they were small). It was in the manly voice that he had said, "When the frost gets into the cut it's the fair devil an' all;" adding, of course, "just the fair devil an' all". But when you looked at his face as you plucked mussels in the cold ebb, one thing that was clear was that his skin was like the skin of a pig. When a pig was scalded and had the bristles shaved off. . . Peter Navook killed pigs. He went about from one place to another sticking them. Not many people could kill pigs. They pretended not to know the way. The knife went right into the throat and out at the other side, and the blood ran down off the point of the blade for a long time while the pig kept squealing. You could hear him squealing a mile away. It was a terrible thing! . . . The knife had to find a vein, they said. And Peter Navook knew exactly where it was. When a pig was squealing like that, one pretended not to mind. One laughed and shouted, "Are you hearing yon? Ha! ha! ha! Peter Navook is killing Dan

11

Ross's pig. Listen! . . . Boy, isn't he squealing?"
And all the time one's heart was beating and ready
to jump at nothing.

The boy lifted his dark head and looked about the
boulders as though his thought might have been overheard. There was an uncertain defensive smile on his
face, which faded immediately he was sure he was
alone. His hands were now bitterly cold. He could not
feel his fingers. There was a drip of water to his nose
which he brushed slowly away with the back of his
hand, at the same time pressing the hand hard against
his nose as though to warm the point, pressing it
harder still, till his whole body quivered with the sus-
tained effort to draw heat from inside him. But no
heat came, and as he straightened himself his teeth
chittered. Then he began smartly slapping his arms
across his breast, as his father did and the other fishermen. But the clip of his finger-tips against the curves
of his back was painful.

He kept up the manly exercise for a little to satisfy
appearances, but he knew he wasn't really letting his
hands slap properly. It was too sore. The cold had
now chilled them to the bone and the fingers were
growing painful. He put them under his blue jersey
and knuckled them against his stomach. He drew
them forth again, closed them into squirming fists,
cupped and blew on them, pressed them against each
other. In a sudden frenzy he began slapping them
round his sides again, but now in real earnest, not
caring for the pain.

Gradually the heat began to come. The tingling of
it grew. The arrowy stabbing in the numbed fingers
became unbearable. They began to burn in agony. He
looked at the reddened swollen tips, holding them
claw-upwards in an utterly helpless gesture. His body

12

writhed and little dry sobbing sounds came from his throat.

But he would not cry. He only pretended to cry in order to ease the anguish. He could have cried readily enough. His body twisted and doubled up, but he daren't touch anything with his fingers now. Something inside was trying to force its way through them. The tingling flesh was swollen and wouldn't let the thing pass. Then suddenly the pain reached a point from which it had to recede or he would have cried.

With the throb of the pain dying down, the relief was exquisite. He even pressed the thumbs hard against the finger-tips to make the pain sting a little, as though he were catching it up and hurting it before it slipped away altogether. Now his hands were in a glow. He felt exhilarated. From his pocket he drew forth the young tender tangle, and scraping the transparent skin off its end with white even teeth, he bit on it exactly as a dog bites on a bone. The tangle was not so hard as a bone, but very nearly. Saliva flowed into his mouth, and with wet red lips and sharp teeth he sucked and gnawed, moving the tangle-end this way and that until his stretched mouth ached in the effort to give the crunching molars a real chance. But the bit he broke off was sweet and tender to his palate, and its salty flavour excited a greater flow of spittle than ever, so that his mouth moved richly and he swallowed many times. A tangle was always a little disappointing in the first minute, as though the memory of it contained more food. But once you started gnawing you could not stop.

With a final look at the shredded end, he stowed the tangle in his pocket. If he didn't hurry it would soon be dark. And his father would be waiting for the

13

bait. And, anyway, he would pick up another young tangle with a shell on his way back. He would keep it whole to show off, because the other boys were playing football. He himself liked playing football better than anything. First of all he had said to his mother that he wouldn't go to the ebb. The mood had come on him to be dour and stubborn. It was a shame that he should have to go to the ebb, with the other boys playing football. The injustice of it had hit him strongly. His father had said nothing. But if he didn't go then his father would have had to. And by two or three in the morning his father would have to be aboard. It must be terribly cold in the dark out on that sea; out on that sea in the small hours of a sleety morning, or on a morning of hard frost, with a grey haar coming off the water like ghosts' breath.

The loneliness of the bouldered beach suddenly caught him in an odd way. A small shiver went over his back. The dark undulating water rose from him to a horizon so far away that it was vague and lost. What a size it was! It could heave up and drown the whole world. Its waters would go rushing and drowning. He glimpsed the rushing waters as a turbulent whiteness released out of thunderous sluices. "But you can't," he half-smiled, a little fearfully, glancing about him. A short distance away, right on the sea's edge, he saw one of the boulders move. His heart came into his throat. Yet half his mind knew that it could only be some other lonely human in the ebb. And presently he saw the back bob up for a moment again.

Yes, it was a man. Seeking among the boulders there like some queer animal! He looked about him carefully. There was no one else. There were just the two of them in the ebb. Here they were on this dark beach,

14

with nobody else. A strange air of remoteness touched him. It was as though they shared this gloomy shore, beyond the world's rim, between them. There was a secret importance in it. He stooped and began filling his bag with mussels, picking big ones in a manly way. The water was now merely cool to his burning hands. He worked with great energy, a red sea-anemone stopping him for less than a minute. This one had feelers out that quietly retracted to his touch. Whereupon he squeezed the red jelly with a knack that sent a little spirt of water out of it. As he swished some bloated weed away below the red anemone, he disclosed, however, a pocket of dulse. This had the unexpectedness of a pleasant find. He had quite forgotten about dulse. He ate some of the tenderer fronds, and shaking the water from the rest of the bunch, stowed it in his pocket on top of the tangles until his pocket bulged and overflowed.

When he thought he had gathered sufficient mussels, he stood up and tested the weight of the bag. Then he said he would gather twenty more to make sure. He gathered twenty-five and then three more for luck, and then made it thirty, adding one after that to make dead certain.

As he came erect, the man who was also gathering mussels in the ebb straightened himself and put his hand in the small of his back. His back curved inward. So it was Sandy Sutherland. Swinging his bag onto a boulder, the boy got under his burden and started off towards Sandy, but yet slanting away from him a little to make his approach not too deliberate.

"Is it yourself, Hugh, that's in it?" The note of surprise in Sandy's voice was pleasant and warm. His face was whiskered, his ways quiet, his eyes dark-shining and kind.

15

"Yes," said Hugh, pausing, and tingling a little with shy pleasure.

"Getting your father's baiting, I see".

"Yes".

"Aren't you cold?"

"Oh no."

"Well, you're plucky," said Sandy. "And it's your father that's lucky. Here I have to be down myself." He said this with no grudge in his voice. It was half a joke. "And my back has got the cramp in it, sure as death." Though he was over sixty, his whiskers were black with a very white hair here and there. He took out his pipe. "Was your father at the line when you left?"

"Yes. He had just cleaned it."

"It would be fair stinking, I suppose?"

"Yes, the bait was rotten. You could smell it all over the house," said Hugh, smiling, a faint flush on his face.

"I'm sure," nodded Sandy. "It's hard enough work baiting the line. And then to have to take all the bait off again without using it is—is enough to try the patience."

"It is that," said Hugh. "It's been a big storm."

"It was blowing as hard the night before last as it blew this winter. Indeed there was one gust that woke me up. I thought the roof was going."

"The roof of Dan Ross's barn was torn off, and a screw of Totaig's hay was blown into the burn."

"So I heard. Totaig wouldn't be pleased at that!"

"No."

"I could see him spreading it out yonder all day!"

"Yes!" Hugh gave a small laugh. Totaig was cross in the grain and mean. Sandy gave a chuckle also.

"Well, I'll be coming with you, if you wait till I

16

gather one or two more. What sort of baiting have you yourself?"

"Oh, I think I have plenty." Hugh dropped his bag on a boulder and caught Sandy's eyes measuring the quantity in a secret glance.

"Perhaps you have, then."

"Oh, I think so," murmured Hugh.

But there was a faint reserve in Sandy's voice, as though he didn't like to suggest that the boy might not have gathered a full baiting.

It was a delicate point. Hugh saw that if Sandy could find a hidden or off-hand way of adding a few, he would do so.

"Perhaps you have, then," Sandy repeated. "Though you could gather one or two more for luck if you like while I'm finishing off. It would save you to-morrow night maybe."

"Father isn't wanting a full baiting," Hugh explained. "There's not much short of half one at home."

"Oh, that makes a difference! To gather more would be waste. Indeed, I'm thinking you have a full baiting there as it is, if not more." The voice was amused rather than relieved. But Hugh understood perfectly.

"I think there's plenty," he considered, as if now a trifle doubtful.

"Plenty? I should say so! Do you think I have as many as you myself?" He measured both bags with an eye. "I should say nearly."

"You have more, I think," judged Hugh, politely.

"Well, if you say so. But remember, it's you I'll blame if I'm short! It's a cold place this, anyway." He lit his pipe, sending great clouds of blue smoke about his head. "We'll chance it. So let us be going." He shouldered his bag cheerfully and they both set off.

Besides the sea's breath, there was no wind, and

17

the only sound was the wash among the boulders, with a deeper note from the rocks beyond the beach where the quietening water swayed sullenly in a murmurous *boom-oom*.

The light was now more than half gone, and the figures of the man and the boy, bent a little under their burdens, gathered as it seemed all the eyes of that place upon them as they walked away. Heads stooping forward, backs slightly arched, dark stumbling figures, moving up from the sea. Sparks of fire suddenly came from the old man's head. Each spark shone distinct and round, sprightly and mocking, gleaming wayward moments of an intenser life. The defeated water choked among the boulders. Through a rocky fissure a lean tongue thrust a hissing tip—that curled back on itself in cold froth.

They won clear of the weeded boulders. They approached the foreshore. Their fists gripped across their breasts upon the ends of their sacks. The twist of canvas bit into their shoulders, bit the boy's neck, as they stumbled up the slope of grey-blue stones. The stones rumbled and roared, carrying each foot back to the sea. But foot went before foot, and soon they were on the high-tidal bed of weed. Treacherously it slithered under them, and when the boy stumbled the man cried to him to take care. Soon they were over that, first their legs disappearing beyond the crest of the beach, then their bodies, and finally their heads. An eddy of darkness like a defeated wind swirled in among the boulders. There was nothing left for the watching eyes to see beyond that crest but the first pale stars in heaven.

II

As the man and the boy went on they spoke together companionably. The creek or harbour was on their right hand. Between them and it were three boats that had been hauled up and lashed with ropes to driven piles. No highest storm could touch them there. When a boat is hauled to its last mooring it gives up its spirit, and its head-rope becomes a sagging halter.

On their left hand, in the middle of the brae-face was a line of thatched cottages. Yellow lights gleamed in the little square windows. There was still sufficient daylight left for the whitewashed walls to gleam also, but with a whiteness that came against the eyes in a ghostly way.

"Is the bag heavy on you?" asked the man.

"Oh no," said the boy.

"You'll be going to school every day?"

"Yes."

"How old are you now?"

"I'll be thirteen next birthday."

Sandy almost stopped.

"Go' bless me, you're a big boy for your age!

Hugh smiled shyly. He was tall for his age but thin, and could if necessary twist his legs like a tailor. His elbows and his knees did not stick out, and he could run on his toes. Only sometimes, and privately, did he feel himself too light, did he know himself less weighty than one or two boys of his own age, a something light and airy that could be bruised with a stocky fist and knocked off his balance. Sometimes he regretted this very much, and longed for a fist that would sheer through hands and arms as through the leaves and twigs of a tree. But only for moments, his body was so lithe.

One or two men passed, calling greetings. Magnus Sinclair, a member of his father's crew, stopped before them. His voice was loud and windy.

"Only now taking home your baiting, Sandy?"

"Yes," said Sandy. "I was down at the sale in the forenoon. But the prices weren't great."

"Did you sell your cow?"

"No then, I didn't." After hesitating a moment, he added, "I don't think the wife would like to see her go. And the year is coming. We'll see."

Hugh grew afraid for a moment that Magnus might say something too obvious to Sandy, who now had said everything. For Sandy was delicate in his mind and wise, and his body was like a clasped knife. Magnus's body was made of fibre, coarse-woven, but regular in its pattern and useful. When defending or offending, his raking voice would blow itself over the edge of decency. He was an upstanding reddish man, but there was a lack of quiet sense or manners in him which the other fishermen often played on. That it was not always noticeable made the sport uncertain and interesting.

But all that Magnus said at the moment, in a voice thoughtful as spite, was:

"We could do with some money."

"That's true," agreed Sandy, who, after all, had a cow to sell. Magnus lived in one of the whitewashed houses on the brae-face where there were no cows.

"Ay." Magnus turned deliberately to the sea. "The glass is moving up."

"That may be wind. I don't like the look of the

20

water," Sandy remarked. "I didn't like it at all when I was down there in the ebb. There's something unsettled somewhere."

"I don't like the smell of it myself."

"All the same," and Sandy cast a look at the sky, "I think we're going to the sea in the morning."

"We'll have to go, and that's short."

"I don't want to clean off a second baiting myself."

"No," snorted Magnus. Then he looked at Hugh. "Who's this you have with you? Is it the skipper's son?"

"Don't you know Hugh?"

"God, his father's lucky!" said Magnus. "I wish I had someone to do something for me. My bairns can do nothing but cry for their meat." Though he laughed shortly, the harsh grumble came through.

Hugh's mind might have been the anemone on the rock, the way it drew in. Yet there was a certain pleasure, too, in the implication that he was doing a man's work while other boys of his age went crying about their mothers' skirts. He wished, however, that Magnus would go. He hated him when he tried to be jocular, because at any moment something ugly might spirt out. That would make his present companionship with Sandy very uncomfortable. Camden P.L.

"I have a good night's work before me yet." Sandy smiled. "And that's maybe more than you have."

"But I haven't a cow," retorted Magnus.

"No, that's true," murmured Sandy.

"It's only too true."

"Though maybe a cow doesn't exactly live on air!"

"Yes—fine day!" Magnus laughed. "I know you!" He turned away. "Half-past two in the morning, and see you're up in time."

Sandy and Hugh crossed the foot-bridge over the

21

river. Neither of them made any reference to Magnus, who remained in Hugh's mind as something he had escaped from. When Magnus lifted his head as if he was somebody, his throat became sinewy. There would be whipping sinews in the place where a hidden kind mind should be.

"Can you shell the mussels, too?" asked Sandy.

"Oh, yes. I'll start in when I go home. Father will be at the baiting by now."

"You must be a great help to him. What would you like to do yourself?"

"I don't know."

"You wouldn't like to go to sea?"

"I don't know," murmured Hugh. But he knew in his heart that he wasn't going to sea. The idea of it was so remote that it hardly touched him. He could look on himself as another boy going to sea and fall into reverie. But he woke up always with a quiet thrill, secretive, without meaning, having to do in the deeps with life unexplored and strange. On his face the queer faun-like smile would linger. For his eyes were a deep brown flecked with tiny dark spots and his face was thin and attractive under its dark hair, the smooth pale skin being faintly shadowed by the weather.

But now as he walked along the road with Sandy he might well enough be a man going to sea. Some of the importance of this manliness set him apart from boyish things for the moment. Their voices were reasonable and unhurried. The night set them apart. The bag on his back, the bag on Sandy's back, their hands gripping over their breasts, walking on, talking to each other with a quiet confidence, their heads stooping forward, the two of them.

"Well, I'll leave you here," and Sandy drew up.

Hugh felt a little shy.

"How's your mother—how are they all at home?"

"Very well, thank you." Hugh wanted to ask how Mrs. Sutherland was, but felt the question too important for one of his age.

"Good-night, then, Hugh. Tell your father I'll be looking for him in the morning."

"I will," Hugh answered readily. "Good-night."

"If I come down past your way, I'll throw a stone at his window, tell him," called Sandy out of the gloom.

"All right!" called Hugh, laughter in his tone. As he went on alone he felt confident and happy. For a few steps he ran, but the bag bumped and slewed round, nearly choking him. He would drop it presently when no one would see that he had to take a rest.

With loud chatter, some boys loomed round a bend. The Seabrae boys going home from football. Hugh walked calmly, like a man.

"Ha! ha! here's Hugh!" cried Rid Jock, son of Magnus.

The other boys also cried the same thing.

Hugh's manner was quiet. "Coming home from the football?" he asked.

"Why didn't you come? You said you'd come in the morning."

"I said I might," corrected Hugh mildly.

"You didn't. You said you would," corrected Jock positively.

"Yes, I heard you," piped little Dannie. And the others piped the same thing. "I heard you say it! I heard you say it!"

"You didn't," said Hugh.

"Am I a liar?" asked Jock.

"You are, if you say that," said Hugh.

23

"Oh, I am, am I?" asked Jock. "Ho! ho! I'm a liar, am I?"

"You are," repeated Hugh, who had not yet raised his voice.

"Say that again," threatened Jock loudly.

Hugh, ignoring him, took a step on. Immediately his bag was tugged from behind. He swung round. Dannie scampered off, and from a safe distance shouted, "Does your mother know you're out?"

The other boys laughed loudly as they backed a step or two.

"His mother wouldn't let him to the football—in case he would fall!" All the boys laughed and jeered, repeating the final insult in sing-song. Hugh made no move. This inaction at once frightened and goaded them.

It was nothing that this very morning at school he had been on easy terms with them all. A roving homeward band had happened on a solitary doing something different from themselves, and their minds immediately became excited and cruel. Moreover, this solitary did not belong to Seabrae. He was a bee from another hive, a gull from another rock.

"Mamma's pet!" shouted a voice, and encouraged by the sally, Jock suddenly hit Hugh's unprotected face.

In the same instant the bag dropped and Hugh sprang at him. Self-consciousness got blotted out in fury. He saw nothing but the blur of Jock's face and lashed at it. Nothing would stop him so long as he could see and stand. His fury was destructive and primal. Blows rained on his own face. They merely made his fury red. Something had to give way. It was Jock, because Jock, though a good fighter, could not be possessed by a demon.

The little band with their leader broke and fled, shouting insults. Hugh leapt after Jock and tripped him as he ran, so that Jock fell headlong on his face. Hugh sprang on his back. Jock covered up his face and squawked his fear and rage. Hugh, pinning down the neck with his left hand, walloped the head with his right, shouting, "Get up! get up!"

Some of the other boys came back.

"Get off him!" they yelled threateningly. He ignored them. One boy tried to kick him. He leapt from Jock's back. A stone hit him on the breast. All the boys, including Jock, retreated. Stones fell around him, where he stood stock still on the middle of the road, quivering.

"Never mind; you blooded his nose!" said a consoling voice in the distance to Jock, whose face was damaged more by the gravel of the road than by Hugh's fists.

Automatically Hugh's fingers came up to his nose and touched there the slime of blood. He peered at the reddened tips. He now felt the blood running down his upper lip. It was also trying to slide down the back of his throat. The taste of it was salty and sticky in his mouth. Drops fell on the back of his hand. They had been falling upon the breast of his jersey. He pressed his knuckles against his nose, and his throat swallowed a lot of the blood before he could stop it. He held his head back, and then the blood went down his throat freely. You always have to hold your head back when your nose is bleeding. It's the only way to stop it. But you should always at the same time hold something cold to the back of your neck.

He stumbled over the edge of the road holding his head back, over the grassy bank and down to the edge of the river or burn. He was not thinking of anything but the blood. All his flesh was trembling. He was not really frightened of the blood. Here he was with his nose bleeding after a fight, and he was calmly stretching backwards against the bank and pressing a cold stone to the nape of his neck.

He lay quite still, his eyes to the pale stars. There were not many; one here and there. The sky was very very far away. It was quiet, too. It was high and dark, and the stars were lonely in it. He had to swallow every now and then. The blood was stopping. It was strange and lonely on your back, looking at the stars, down by the burn. He was doing all this by himself. He had fought Jock—the whole of them—and sent them flying. His teeth closed and his face went cold. His face felt like a cold wedge and his eyes glittered relentlessly.

One could weep through sheer rage. But not even that would he do again. No matter what happened to him in the world, never would he cry more. He had conquered—and sent them flying. Everyone knew that the fight with Jock had to take place, and now it was all over and he was lying here. His nose had been blooded, but—that often happened at a fight. He had seen it happen once with grown men. But when a grown man had his nose blooded, he did not stop fighting for that. Only boys stopped fighting when they saw blood. Once Fred Munro was winning a fight when someone cried that his nose was bleeding. When Fred saw that it was bleeding, he started howling and weeping and running away. Everybody laughed. Fred was only eleven past, of course, but still. . . And once a piper's nose had started bleeding. It was at the Games. The blood kept trickling down on to his white front. Everyone was silent, looking at the trickling blood with twisted faces. Then the judge had gone forward and stopped him. The piper was astonished, and did not know his nose had been bleeding. He got third prize. Some said he got it for consolation. But Hector the Roadman, who was the finest piper in the district, said that the man had shown by the bit he had played that he was the best piper there. "I knew it by the way he tuned his pipes," said Hector. So it was good of the judge to give him third prize. He needn't have given it to him. It was fine, therefore, of the judge that he did.

It was nothing to have your nose blooded—once it had happened. They couldn't crow over him for that. He had sent them all flying. The whole of them. He fought them with his nose bleeding—and sent them flying. Swallowing, he found that there was nothing more to swallow. He waited for a little longer to make sure, then very carefully sat up with a finger lightly against his nostrils, waiting. No blood came. He breathed slowly, mouth shut. The inside of his nose was cold and stiff. Still keeping his head tilted, he went to the water and very carefully began washing himself. They would not need to know at home.

Voices came from the road, and footsteps. Listening, he remembered his bag of mussels. It must be right in the way. Lightly he climbed up the bank. A man and a woman were close at hand. The black hump of the bag was lying by the edge of the road where the man was walking. Unless the man was looking where he was going. . . The woman laughed. It was the voice of his sister Grace. At that moment the man tripped on the bag and kept himself from falling flat by splaying his hands on the road. "Blast it!" he said. As he rubbed his hands free of gravel he kicked the bag. "Who left this lying here?"

Hugh went forward a step or two uncertainly. You could hardly make out anyone's face clearly, because it was so dark.

"So it's your bag, you little devil!" said the man.

Hugh knew who he was, but he did not know Hugh, who was waiting for his sister to say something.

"You shouldn't leave a bag lying like that, you know," was what his sister said. Her voice was not angry. Yet its gracious reproof was curiously cold. In a moment Hugh understood that she was not going to know him, because she was with this particular man.

"Oh, it's nothing," the man said. "But don't you do it again!" He chuckled. His voice was rather kind, after the surprise of the first moment.

"Yes, but it was silly of him leaving it there," said his sister as they moved off. The reproof was still in her voice, but it was laughing and kind under the man's.

"Oh, I don't know. . ." The man's chuckling excuses faded out.

Tears welled up into Hugh's eyes where he stood. His jaws were shut tight, but the tears brimmed over and ran one after another down his cheeks. His eyes floated, his sight grew blurred. Still he made no move. Behind his clenched teeth his throat choked—and swallowed tears that were hot and raw. His misery became too much for him. It rose up and up in a swelling spout, drowning even the clenched teeth. Stumbling, blinded, he dragged the bag off the roadside and threw himself down over the crest of the bank. Crushing his face into the grass, he sobbed harshly. His shoulders heaved, his body writhed. He was defeated utterly.

The agony of the defeat passed into a profound

misery as his sobs died down and his eyes grew hot
and burned. It was not what had been said to him—
that was nothing; it was the two who had said it.

Not now that he minded them. He cared for nothing
now. Nothing in the world mattered. There was no
good doing anything more. He would lie out here in
the dark. Lie for hours until the cold froze him, until
he grew stiff perhaps and dead. They would find the
bag—and then him lying here dead. His father would
be amazed at seeing the bent body lying with its
white dead face on the grass. His look would grow
wild and scared, and his voice would come quick and
queer, as he stooped and picked up the body. Then
his mother would give a little husky scream that was
like something clutching at your heart, and the scream
would go searching round like a moan, as she herself
went searching round, not being able to stand still.
Oh-h-h-h. . .

One or two tears came again and he swallowed
them quietly. But not before he had seen, behind his
mother, the white scared face of his sister Grace, and
the wondering face, serious and a little scared too,
of the man who had been with her.

He sat up and slowly rubbed his eyes with the back
of his hand, faintly embarrassed by his vision. The
crushing of his hand against his eyes was like the half-
shy crushing of himself away from his embarrassment.
It had hardly been right to see his mother like that.
Only once had he heard her cry—quick and husky-
sharp as from a stab by a knife—going on, twisting
on itself, as though the knife wouldn't come out.

He was a little ashamed of thinking it over again.
A judgment might come on him. And not only on
him·

Slowly he looked around at the deepening night,

at the uncaring sky. Nothing cared. What if a judgment did come on him? Well—let it!

But in his defiance was a suppressed fear. His teeth chittered and he shivered all over. If it wasn't that his father was waiting for the mussels, he mightn't go home at all.

With a dour grace he got to his feet. A hand struck against the tangles in his pocket, but he ignored them. The memory of the fight came upon him with satisfaction but no warmth. He felt cold towards the boys concerned, cold and hostile. He would not get hot with fury if he was fighting Jock again. He would fight him, cold as death. He would meet him with a smile of disdain. Jock—who was Jock? To think that he had often trembled in secret at the thought of the unavoidable fight with him! He could always beat Jock now. And Jock was thirteen and a half.

He shouldered the bag with such violence that he staggered, and then went evenly on his way. Two men approached, and as they passed one said cheerily:

"Hallo, boy; are you getting home?"

He did not answer.

"Who is he?" one asked of the other.

"I'm not sure, but I think it's a son of MacBeth." The voice rose loudly for Hugh to hear its amusement at his surliness.

His ears tingled. It was not his nature to be surly. But he knew who they were. Jim Dallas and Donald Campbell from Seabrae. Donald was Dannie's father.

Into his loneliness entered a secret pride. There was no need for anyone to remember him. When they asked at home, "What kept you?" he would answer, "Nothing," and go about his business of shelling the mussels in a quiet way. He would take no notice of his sister Grace, would never show that he had met

30

her on the road, no matter how nice she would be. He would not be dour. He would be pleasant, but in a reserved way.

At this his heart became uplifted in a cold happiness. A man swung onto the main roadway.

"Good-night."

"Good-night," answered Hugh, his heart suddenly beating. It was the man who had been with Grace, and he was going now in the direction of Barrostad House, two miles inland and on the other side of the glen.

The man's name was Charlie Chisholm. He wasn't over thirty years of age and owned Barrostad with its sheep farm. His father, they said, had bought it for him, and had sent him here to keep him out of mischief. Though there were many stories about him, of course. Queer stories. Some said he drank, and some said it had been women. And once Bill Keith said that Charlie Chisholm had been cheating at cards. But likely that was the sort of thing that Bill had got out of a paper. In any case, when someone had said to Bill that he had got it out of a paper, he denied it. He said he hadn't got it out of a paper. But that was merely because someone had seen into him. For when he was asked to say:

> *Sure as death,*
> *cut my throat and*
> *burn my breath!*

he refused. "Why should I say that to please you?" he asked. But if it was true about the cards he would have said it like a shot. And everyone knew that.

Yet it was queer of him to think about the cards—and terrible, too. For there was a reckless laughing way about Charlie—and his gay fair face could grow in a moment still and sarcastic—with fine manners when he liked—like a secret hero. To accuse him of cheating at cards!—well, he might have done it because it was such a terrible thing to do, but he wouldn't have done it because it was cheating.

Hugh thought of Charlie, and took all the graces of the man unto himself. And the first thing he did when he was Charlie was to come into his own home and say to his mother, "Here you are, Mother; here's a little present." It would be rather an embarrassing moment for them both while his mother stood helpless with the hundred pounds in her hand, but he would laugh it off. Then he would make an arrangement about the future. . .

Engaged in this self-conscious pastime, he came in sight of his home. Its yellow light kept going out and in as he wandered up through the whin clumps, but he didn't play a winking game with it to-night. Nor did the darkness half frighten him nor wild figures lurk behind black clumps. True, he cast a sidelong glance now and then and his ears were very open. But the virtuousness of his present task comforted him and set him in safety. Moreover, there was ever at the back of his mind the glory of his victory over Rid Jock and the tribe of the Seabrae. It had been behind his tears, making their flow a sweet bitterness on the altar of valour. The inside of his nose was still stiff. All his body was indeed a trifle compact and queer, and could be looked at secretively as if it were moving beside him with the finger of valour upon it.

But to Grace and Charlie, who did not know of the fight, he had not been a warrior, he had been a little fool. But they would come to know yet. He wished ardently that they would come to know. But never from him. To-night he would go on working quietly, speaking only when he was spoken to. Grace would wonder. She would not be sure. She would look at him with her dark eyes and secretly try to smile at him. But he would not see her. . .

From the last clump of whin a figure noiselessly stepped out in front of him.

He just stopped the cry in time.

It was Grace.

"Is that you, Hugh?" Her voice was soft and husky, yet quite clear. She caught his arm and a faint scent of violets drowned his body. Her head stooped slightly and her friendly hand kept insinuating its way under his arm.

"Are you cold?"

He did not speak.

"Dear boy!" There was a sweet compassion in her voice; yet it was friendly and laughing as though they were equals. So he could not speak.

Her other arm came groping across his breast.

"How cold your hands are! she murmured. She slipped a coin into one of them, then held it shut tight with a warm pressure.

The violets clouded his senses. The soft fur she had round her neck brushed against his face.

"Dear Hugh!" she murmured, caressing his cold hands as they gripped convulsively into the twist of canvas, the round hard coin against a palm.

He wanted to repudiate the money. He wanted to cry, "No, I don't want it! I don't want your money!" But he hadn't sufficient control of himself. He knew his voice would break if he opened his mouth. But— deeper than that—was the notion that he would be a boor to hurt the feelings of this gracious woman.

Yet he imagined he saw perfectly clearly in his own mind why she was doing it. She was doing it "to make up." She denied him down by the burn and now she was making up.

"Come on!" she said gaily, and impelled him forward with the hand that was under his arm.

And then, as on an afterthought, as if out of the amusing intimacy that was between them, she added:

"Don't tell Kirsty that you saw me with Charlie Chisholm, will you?"

A pale light went over Hugh's mind. Kirsty was his other sister. Kirsty and Charlie Chisholm had often been together before Grace had come home.

"Why don't you speak to me?" asked Grace lightly, as they went on. In her voice was friendliness, a frank curiosity, that held in it something entrancing as the violets.

A few paces from the door, Hugh stopped and held out a hand.

"I don't want it," he said.

"Don't be silly!" She laughed, pushing his hand playfully from her and squeezing it shut.

He could not persist in refusing because somehow he could not say more. She opened the door for him and followed him into the lighted kitchen.

III

His mother, who was bent over the kitchen fire, turned round without straightening herself. The lamp was not on the mantelshelf over her head as usual, but on the edge of the dresser to the left against the back wall. He was conscious of her examining him rather curiously as he turned to the lamp. There was a lovely smell of fried steak and onions coming from the great pan over the fire. The sizzling had been a cry of welcome immediately the door had opened. The ardent smell of it stung his eyes. His stomach flattened in a lean hunger.

Yet the importance of his entrance was impressed upon him by his mother's gaze. Here was her young schoolboy of twelve coming home with his baiting like a grown man.

But his step hardly hesitated as he turned to his father, who was sitting with his back to the kitchen, baiting the line. Right under the corner of the dresser, so that the light from the lamp shone down upon it, was the wicker creel or skoo—shaped like a great scoop. Into the back part of the scoop curled the line, while in front, row upon row, were placed the baited hooks. There were six hundred hooks on the line.

There was just room for Hugh to pass between the corner of the great boxed-in bed and the herring basket that held the line. The bag of mussels dropped with a squashy sound on the blue stone floor.

"So you've got back, boy?" said his father quietly. His voice was companionable, as though he were talking to another man. His face as it half turned had a kind smile. His eyes were dark, and when he was pleased they flashed. There were points of resemblance between Sandy and his father; only Sandy was slower; not so daring when roused, perhaps; nor so vivid in his affection. Not that his father ever expressed affection—except with his eyes and his quick smile and the lines on his face; as if it came from him without his knowing, flashing from a quickened heart. Then in a moment he was calm again.

But now his whole manner was quietly friendly to

Hugh. His calmness was almost austere. There were only the two of them doing this work. A tacit partnership against the unhelping world. His father added handsomely, "You made sure you'd take plenty, anyway!"

"I think so," murmured Hugh, not yet turning round.

"I am nearly out, boy."

"I'll start shelling for you," said his son in an even voice. He half turned. "Where's the knife?"

"Hugh," said his mother, who had not taken her eyes off him, "what's happened to your nose?"

He started. So this was why she had been gazing!

"Nothing," he mumbled, his eyes glinting as they searched the dresser for the knife.

"You've been all bleeding," said his mother. "There's blood on your wrists and on the breast of your jersey."

"Nothing." He was unable to spot the knife anywhere.

His father gave him a hidden look.

His mother came a step or two towards him, her open face penetrating and anxious.

"Can't you leave the boy alone?" demanded his father.

"I don't see the knife," mumbled Hugh, going slowly towards the dark back-kitchen, looking as he went.

"Hugh!" called his mother.

"Watch the pan, woman," said his father, "or it's on fire it'll be."

The crisp onions were making a great crackling, and on a cold night the smell was enough to draw water out of dead teeth.

His mother swung the crook with the pan hanging

to it out from the blaze a little. After turning over the thin tongues of steak and shreds of onions with the knife that was in her hand, she straightened herself and asked her daughter Grace:

"Where did you meet him?"

"I met him on the way home," said Grace innocently.

"Didn't he say anything to you?"

"No. He never said a word. I didn't notice in the dark."

"He's been fighting with some of the Seabrae boys," said her mother. "That's what it is."

"I'll go and see," said Grace.

But in the darkness of the back-kitchen she could not see Hugh. She called under her breath. She groped forward. When she touched him she divined that he was crying. She had seen from the dark lines round his eyes that he had been crying to-night already. His mother had seen, too. Her guilty heart overcame her. Her hands caressed his arm, his shoulder.

"What was it, Hugh? Won't you tell me?"

"Leave me alone."

Hugh was not crying. But the violets came about his nostrils again, unmanning him. The soft warmth of Grace and the scent brought a great lump into his throat.

"Go 'way!" he muttered harshly.

"Hugh!" she appealed, as if he had hurt her.

"Want . . . wash . . . " said Hugh, stirring.

Grace slipped into the kitchen for a candle. Hugh dashed a hand against his eyes, his teeth grinding shut in a burning face. But holding his breath, he listened for anything that would be said about him in the kitchen.

"Poor boy!" Grace murmured in a humoured pity. She was an excellent actress.

"I'll poor boy him," said his mother in a voice meant for him to hear, "if it's fighting with the Seabrae boys he's been."

"How do you know that he's been fighting?" asked his father. "Perhaps he fell, for all you know, in the ebb. It would be full of tangleweed anyway."

Hugh made a noise with the basin, as though he were not listening.

"Perhaps he did," Grace agreed. "For when I was coming up the road I was looking for him, and I saw his bag by the roadside. He came up from the river. I thought he had been taking a drink."

"I thought you were at Ina Manson's?"

"So I was," Grace answered lightly. "But I wanted to take a turn down by the braes on the way back— just to see if Hugh was coming."

And in no time she was standing in the back-kitchen doorway, her face all lit by the candle she held before her. Her face was pale and dark-eyed and beautiful. And what lured in the beauty was its smooth grace. Nor did one think of the face as being pale. It had the warmth of a sympathy that caught its gleam from hidden feelings. Yet it was faultless and poised.

Her dark head stooped to him.

"Come on, Hugh!" Her low voice laughed. "Look!" She lifted a pail of water and poured some into the tin basin. "Here's the soap." Then, under her breath, her voice losing its slight "English" inflexion altogether, "Ach, never mind them, man!" She gave him a nudge with her elbow. "Come on!" She squared him to the basin as though it were a game.

Then she turned away to the rope against the wall on which a towel hung. She flipped it off. Before she came back to him, she paused a moment and con-

38

sidered the slow way in which he was rubbing the soap on his hands. Her eyes embraced him in a curious thoughtfulness.

Humming softly to herself, she pretended to be doing little things, until he had got the length of washing his face. Presently she said, with the fun of the game between them, "Let me see. . . Ah, that's better. Here's the towel!"

The face he rubbed with the towel made it clear that there was no need for her to wait; she could be going in. It did not laugh and the hands moved slowly.

Dipping an end of the towel in the basin, however, she caught at the breast of his jersey and began rubbing it. She laughed softly at the colour of the towel, then washed it in the basin.

"What happened, Hugh? Won't you tell *me*?"

It was a secretive appeal.

Perhaps that was why he could not tell her.

She got a broken bit of comb from the little shelf below the cheap mirror. She began combing back his hair.

"That'll do." His forehead moved impatiently, and he stood back, waiting for her to go in. Her eyes gleamed beneath their lids. She went up to him.

"Hugh," she asked gently, "why are you angry with me?"

". . . not," he muttered.

"Hugh." She put an arm round him. She drew him up against her. She stooped down to his face. "Did anyone do anything to you? Surely you'll tell your sister Grace?"

"Nothing!" he muttered, struggling from her scented embrace.

She stood away.

"All right," she said, with quiet sorrow. "Are you coming in?"

He did not speak.

The table legs clattered on the kitchen floor. His mother's voice uprose:

"Are you coming in, there?" And continued to his father, "You can stop baiting and wash your hands. And be quick—or it'll be cold."

Hugh wished passionately that Grace wouldn't stand there another minute. He would search in his pockets as if he were wanting something. He found the dulse and the tangles with the shells. When he had put them in a corner and turned round, Grace was gone.

He breathed deeply, his lips coming a little apart. Taking up the chewed tangle, he bit on it. The hard sound of the biting cleared a way through his emotions. His father came in.

"Well, boy; have you washed yourself?"

"Yes," said Hugh, putting the tangle away.

"Be going in then to take your tea. I'll be back in a minute." He opened the back door and went out.

Hugh waited until he heard his father returning, then he went into the kitchen.

His mother took no notice of him. Nor did Grace, who was now in her jumper blouse with its fine stripes and its low ring round her neck, which when it slipped a little showed a skin fresh as new milk.

Grace had been telling her mother with amusing mimicry what Ina Manson had been saying. But, the topic being feminine, she turned it off, when Hugh came in, into something quite different. This permitted her to go on as if she had not been interrupted. Perhaps her mother thought it was hardly worth while deceiving Hugh with such art, for she went to the frying pan at once and began dishing the steak and onions. Hugh slowly examined the skoo and judged that more than half the baiting was yet to do. Then his father came in, stamping his feet and saying mildly:

"It's cold, cold." As he rubbed them together, the skin of his hands made a loud noise.

At that moment his mother poured a little hot water out of the kettle into the pan. The fierce sizzling made everyone start.

"Sit in," she said. Lifting the pan from the crook, she poured the gravy onto the plates. "If it's not tender," she added, "I can do no more with it. Ask the blessing, John."

Her husband lifted his left hand to his brow, which he smoothed for a moment. Then he pronounced the grace that was in the Shorter Catechism. There was a living note of intercession, and his open hand kept moving over his forehead and his closed eyes. His face was spare and pale, and for the moment, losing its normal human quality, became austere and strong. Only where the skin of the forehead ran into the roots of the grizzled hair was its pallor worn by his sixty-three years.

Hugh's mother, who was five years younger than her husband, sat with her hands on her lap, her full body upright, her head bowed. It was a comely attitude, and her eyes were wide open and steady as though staring far into her mind. The fine skin was smooth, the forehead wide and not very high, the features symmetrical and calm. She could get up and lift a boiling kettle from the fire while her husband was saying grace without destroying the moment's harmony, as if wisdom dwelt also in her movements.

Grace's shoulders were bent as well as her dark

41

head, the body being innately more pliant than her mother's. Hugh, who had his cold hands clenched between his knees, saw within the focus of his stare her eyes slant a look at him. But he took no notice. Grace was twenty-three years of age, and nothing that she wore suited her so perfectly as her name.

The first person to break the involuntary silence that followed the blessing was his mother. Any one speaking before her was inclined to do so in a whisper, for urgency of personal indulgence after communion with God was not seemly. Yet the momentary silence was never obtrusive, and the mother always broke it naturally and cheerfully.

Then they started into their meal while she poured the tea.

The smell of the food had been exciting from the beginning. It was rich and good and full of promise. It made hunger merry. It made craving a joy. The rare memory of it would come into lean weeks for long after.

Hugh noticed that his mother had given him the onions that were done brown. He liked them like that. His father preferred to crunch them half raw, and had them according to his taste. His father whipped a forkful into his mouth audibly and solemnly. His jaws worked plenteously, and for a moment his head was still and his gaze fixed and dreamy.

The mother passed the cups of tea. She had the natural air of dispensing life's mercies. Her movements were soothing and sufficient. She was the starting point of a circle that finished in her. Within that circle were their faces and their thoughts and their hands. The paraffin lamp, which was now on the mantelshelf, shone down on them its soft light.

She waited for the first mouthfuls to be tried, and

42

when Grace admitted that the meat was a bit tough, she said:

"It's not fair—after paying that good money for it." Her tone was grieved; her whole mind was resentful. "Are you sure you told him it was frying steak you wanted?"

"Yes," answered Hugh.

"It's not that bad," said her husband. "Where did he cut it off?"

"The hind leg," replied Hugh.

"It is tough," said the mother, trying her own small piece.

"It's not so very bad," Grace said. "Did he give you good weight?"

Hugh looked at his plate. "When he weighed the slice, it was just a little heavy against the pound."

"What did he do?" prompted Grace.

"He didn't know whether to take a bit off or not." Hugh became self-conscious, as though he were giving away his restraint by so much talk, but he couldn't resist the impulse. "He went over for a bit of paper, and by the time he came back he had made up his mind. He rubbed his nose, and then he cut a wee little bit off."

"He mightn't have bothered himself," said his mother.

But Grace laughed softly. She saw the old butcher snipping off a red corner that would curl from the knife like a tiny tongue. Then he would scrape it along the hacked board, pick it up on the blade, assisted by a finger-tip, and place it on the heap of other tiny tongues. You always watched him do this with close attention. That's what made him rub his nose.

Hugh's sharp teeth bit into the meat. It was tough, but it was good. He would swallow the soaked bread and onions and still have the meat in his mouth. After a time there was no taste left in it.

When it got like that, the plan was to let it slip over in a lump. You were always a little surprised to find it going down easily, if slowly. Then you were all ready for a new mouthful. With the meat, the tea had a sort of oily brown taste that melted and was not too good, but it was hot and curled its warmth inside you. The gravy made you eat a lot of bread, and soon your happy belly began to fill up and spread its comfort over all your body.

When you had cleaned your plate, you could put butter on your bread and rhubarb jam on the butter. Then your mother gave you a second cup of tea.

The entrance of his sister Kirsty allowed Hugh to put thoughtlessly a lot of jam on his bread.

"Hullo!" said Kirsty. "What a good smell!" She stood a moment looking at them and smiling. The gladness of being in her own home sparkled in her eyes. "Were you at the ebb to-night, Hugh?"

"Yes."

"Wasn't I sure! I was looking down the sea road and saw a boy going down with something under his arm. I felt sure it was you. And did you take home the baiting?"

"Yes," muttered Hugh, embarrassed, not looking at Kirsty.

"My word, Mother, isn't your son growing up?"

She cast a look of much admiration at Hugh, tempered with affection. Her fair skin was touched to red at the cheeks and her eyes glistened as if she had come out of a clean frost. Her hair was the red-brown of autumn in a fine sunlight.

She was, indeed, the complete contrast to Grace.

Grace was dark, and her body was elegant and

44

attractive, like the branch of a tree in a warm wind.

Kirsty was red and direct, her body remaining straight until high action made it quick and vivid as a northern streamer. Her clear blue eyes could stand still even when emotion welled up—to show too profound an affection, an attachment too deep and too whole, for they were rarely concerned with the cunning of bodily appeal.

Now in Grace bodily appeal was an instinct, which she could express consciously with an artist's feeling or almost without warmth. She had seen it expressed very often in the course of her employment during the last two years in London. Mrs. Bentley was very rich, and Grace had become something more than her lady's-maid.

But Kirsty was only a dairymaid at the Home Farm, and, although the older by two years, could look upon Grace's dark refinement with a momentary wonder, a quick catch of admiration, a faint envy that made admiration complete. There was even Grace's small fine hand—compared with her own long one and its bony knuckles. Looking at Grace, she could feel the angles of the old drystone dykes of the north in her own joints, although her body moved freely, and she was slender and good-looking.

For Kirsty had the rare quality that is called imagination, and her eyes had often to remain steady in order to let her imagination go to work.

And there was something, finally, in Kirsty that was like story-telling in a saga. At great moments it came into her voice. Her love had to be for someone or something outside herself. Her love for any member of her family in peril had the simple awful note of the great hero-stories. This she inherited, with her colour, from her mother's people, for though her own

45

mother was dark, her mother's mother had been red.

And yet dark and red were here, sisters of the one family, and common to them were a hundred little invisible currents of the blood.

Now as her mother showed no enthusiasm over Hugh's growing up, Kirsty immediately understood that there existed a delicate tension. She smiled, glancing from face to face.

"How are you here just now?" her mother asked pleasantly.

"I thought I'd take a run over before the milking. I mightn't get later, because Elsie wants to go out. I said I'd wait in for her."

"Will you take a cup of tea?"

At first she refused, but then, changing her mind, said, "All right, I will," and sat down between Grace and Hugh.

While her mother got up for a cup of tea, Kirsty leaned to Hugh and whispered, "So you're going to sea now!" and then added aloud, as her eyes steadied on a reddish streak in his nostrils, "what's wrong with your nose, Hugh?"

"Just ask him that!" said his mother.

"But what happened? Did you fall?"

"He was fighting," said his mother, "with the Seabrae boys. That's what happened."

Hugh got up and went into the back-kitchen.

"Go' bless me," said his father, shoving his chair back, "can't you leave the boy alone?" And for the first time the irritation in his voice sounded real.

"You'll have another cup of tea," remarked his wife evenly, and began filling his cup.

He lifted his pipe off the mantelshelf, fumbled in his pockets, and then sat down. "I don't see why you need all be at him like that! It's not every boy that would take a baiting from the ebb at his age,"

"That's true," said his wife darkly.

"Why are you angry with him, Mother?" asked Kirsty. "Perhaps he couldn't help it."

"He could help it well enough," replied her mother. "If he's got to go to the ebb, that's no reason why he should fight in it."

"You sent him to the ebb yourself," said her husband strongly. "You know that. It wasn't me."

His wife spread butter on a small piece of oatcake. Her calm face was set, but quite expressionless.

Grace slanted a half-amused look which Kirsty insensibly answered.

But something uncomfortable was moving in Kirsty, and all at once she had an involuntary intuition of her mother's mind. It was not the fighting that mattered: it was the thought of this young son of hers going the way of the sea. She could not be reasonable with that fear clutching at her heart, because she would not give in to it. She had to hide her fear and bear herself calmly. Rather than see her husband go to the ebb, she had sent her son, because her husband would get little enough sleep as it was, and had to face the small cold hours in an open boat.

So Kirsty came to the surface dissembling cheerfully, and admired Grace's jumper. "It does suit you."

"Do you think so?" Grace smiled.

"Yes. Was it one of Mrs. Bentley's own?"

Grace nodded, with a careless sidelong glance at herself.

"It's good," said Kirsty simply.

"It was quite new. It didn't suit her."

"So she just gave it to you?"

"Yes."

47

"You're well off!"

Grace found herself looking inside Kirsty's open coat. "That dress suits you, too, doesn't it?" Her eyebrows lifted critically, pleasantly.

Kirsty noticed that her green dress was showing, so she pulled her coat still farther apart, and flushed, partly with pleasure, for any praise from Grace she found irresistible. "Do you think so?" It was also Grace's present. "I just put it on because—because I just thought I'd take a run over."

While admiring the dress, Grace knew from Kirsty's flush that she had hoped to meet Charlie Chisholm. Why else put on the dress before the milking? As though her conscience touched her for what she had done that night, she said on a sudden impulse, "I have something else that I might give you. It would go with the dress."

Kirsty's eyes sparkled. Their father got up noisily and lit his pipe, sending clouds of smoke about the mantelpiece. Kirsty looked at him suddenly and then regarded her mother.

"One minute—" Kirsty got up—"and I'll go and see Hugh."

"You needn't bother," Grace remarked.

Before Kirsty reached the back-kitchen, she heard the latch of the outside door rattle and Hugh go out. But she was after him in a moment, and caught him by the water-barrel.

"Hugh!"

"What?" he muttered coldly.

"Tell me; who were you fighting with?"

He gave no answer.

"Oh, Hugh, tell me. Was it Rid Jock?"

"Yes."

She put an arm round him, the strong arm of an

48

ally, and there was no delicate scent to cloud his senses.

"Did he—did he—?" Her eager doubt trembled.

"No, he didn't."

"Oh, Hugh!" She gave him a hug. "Did you—?"

"I walloped him."

"My darling boy!" Her low voice sang. She gave him an embrace that smothered his face. His heart stirred in him like a shout.

"There were five of them and—and they all took to their heels—and me after them," he said in a dour voice.

"Hugh, my hero!"

He could have cried because she was so glad he had won. He would have liked to embrace her also, but being a man he could not do that.

"They all started on me," he said. "And just by chance—Rid Jock—blooded my nose."

"Did he, the great big dunce?"

"It was just by chance," said Hugh again.

"He's like his father—nothing to him but an empty sound."

"It was—just chance," said Hugh once more. She did not seem to see the point.

"Never you mind," she nodded, "that was nothing. And you made him run, even with your nose bleeding —that was great." And added, "It was far greater than if it hadn't been bleeding."

Hugh made no reply. Kirsty could see through a thing at once. She was great.

"Come on in then," she said, "or they'll be wondering." Her companionable gaiety gave dignity to his silence. But as they moved towards the door, he said:

"You needn't tell Grace I told you."

"No," she answered, divining instantly where Grace had failed. "No," she repeated warmly.

At the door she paused.

"Hugh." Her voice held a curious suppressed note. "Did you—you didn't—see any one who—was looking for me?"

Hugh also had his moment of divination. A surge of emotion swelled up into his throat. The night grew large and still.

"No," he murmured.

"I thought—you might have—about the sea road." His throat choked.

As she leaned a little sideways, her hand to the door, he saw vaguely the flat of her face. Her eyes were to the night. Through the dark her cheek came pale with thought. He heard her hold her breath.

That lie hurt him. He wanted passionately to tell her the truth. He never told a lie. He hated a lie.

"All right," she breathed and nodded. "Don't say I asked you."

Hugh followed her in, closing the door slowly as though he were closing it on the lie in his mind.

The lie remained there through the evening. He could not get over it. After a time, however, it gave him a quiet strength, as if in that still moment by the back door he had looked on the pale glimmer that is the ghostly face of grown life.

Having promised Grace, he could never tell Kirsty where Charlie Chisholm had been that night. Never.

This denial moved in his mind like the sadness of an old tune. And after Kirsty had gone to her milking, he would look across sideways at Grace sitting by the fire opposite her mother. Then he would look back again at the mussel he held in his left hand, scrape its joint, and push in the knife.

IV

A little later, his brother Alan came in. He was eighteen years old, tall and well-made, and strong as a man. He brought a breeze with him, through which his voice called gaily, "Hallo!" He looked at his father's back and at his young brother shelling the mussels. His voice sharpened in mock surprise. "Goodness, Mother, do you mean to say they're at it yet?" Incredible! "And is it Hugh shelling the mussels?" That finished it!

Grace looked him over. He was rather a handsome fellow.

"Hallo, Grace!"

"Hallo, yourself!" she mocked.

But he did not hold her glance, as though he were still a little shy of this charming woman of the world, whom he had only seen twice since she came home a week ago.

"Come and sit down," said his mother. Her voice was bright and welcoming. "Take that chair. They must be nearly finished."

"And not before time, I should say!" He went and looked at the skoo.

"Is that you?" said his father over his shoulder. The tone was quiet and correct. There was no warmth in it.

"You've a good bit to do yet, man," said his son.

"We'll manage," said his father.

Alan, turning a knowing smile to the women, remarked in the same bantering voice:

51

"Geordie Macleod has finished long ago."

"Perhaps you helped him," suggested his father.

"Hmff!" smiled Hugh.

"What are you hmffing at?" asked Alan, catching him by the hair.

"Let me go!" twisted Hugh.

"Will you leave the boy alone?" said his father, giving him a sharp look before setting a baited hook in its place.

"And that's the way you shell mussels!" scoffed Alan. "Here, man!" He caught the knife out of Hugh's hand. "Get up!"

"Give me my knife!"

Alan lifted him off the stool.

"Run and warm yourself. There's a drop to your nose."

The line rattled out of the basket and across the oilskin on his father's knees like a flicked adder.

"Come here, Hugh, and get warm," coaxed Grace.

"Look, this is the way," scoffed Alan. "Watch! For one moment you see that mussel in my hand hale and whole. The next, ladies and gentlemen, and the blade slips in and up . . . round . . . back . . . crack! and one half of the shell drops clean as a new six-pence, while—swoop . . . scraap . . . plop! and the bait's in the bowl!"

Grace nodded to her father's back with a warning face.

Alan gave her a wink.

"I can do it quicker than that myself," said Hugh.

"Ah, but what a clever boy!" emphasized Alan.

"Someone would need to be clever," muttered his father.

Alan turned his head over his shoulder, laughing silently, his eyes dancing, while Grace made a warning

52

face and an attractive pout. The mother was knitting a sock.

"Come over here, Hugh," said Grace in loud innocent tones, as if there was nothing going on at their father's back.

"Have you done your lessons?" asked his mother.

"No," muttered Hugh.

"Well, it's high time you made a beginning."

"But he can't be farther down than the bottom of the class anyway, Mother," observed Alan.

The line rattled angrily and a chair leg scraped.

Alan's shoulders shook silently. He turned a wary laughing face. Grace's brows drew down in real reproof. Alan laughed mockingly at Hugh.

Hugh wrinkled his nose at him and said sarcastically, "I suppose you baited Geordie Macleod's line." Geordie was certainly a special friend of Alan's, but he also had a daughter named Cathie.

"What's that?" reprimanded his mother.

Alan laughed silently and turned away, saying in a calm voice, "If you would like to know, I baited half of it."

"What did you do?" asked his mother interestedly.

"I baited half his line," repeated Alan. "He had to give in."

"What's wrong with him?"

"I think it's the old trouble he had last year."

"I'm sorry to hear that, poor man!" said his mother. "Has he any pain?" Her face grew soft and kind; her hands fell in her lap.

"Yes. He was crying out with it. He had to go to bed."

"Dear me! They'll be in a state. Did they send for the doctor?"

"No. He said he thought he might get eased when

53

he got warmed up. If not, they'll send for the doctor before the night's finished."

"But he can never go to the sea in the morning?"

"No," replied Alan. "That's certain."

His mother murmured with pity, her pained eyes on the fire.

"And who's going to sea for him?" asked his father quietly.

"I am," said Alan, equally quietly.

All the kitchen went still, waiting for his mother's voice.

"Alan," came the voice at last, "you are not going to the sea in the morning." Her face was white; her eyeballs glistened, turning to him, as though they were strained.

Her son made no answer, his head over the basin of mussels, his fingers busy.

"Alan . . . do you hear me?"

"I promised to go."

"Then you had no right to promise. They'll have to get some one else. You're not going."

Her son made no answer.

"Do you hear me, Alan?"

"I promised to go."

"But you cannot go. You are learning the shepherding. You are with Willie Hendry of Carnfuar. You had no right to promise. You will tell them that to-night." Anxiety, despite her, was creeping into her voice. They all knew her feelings to the sea.

His father said no word, but there was now a smoothness in the way he baited the line. Suddenly a desire came on him to have a draw at the pipe. He wiped his fingers and put his half-smoked pipe in his mouth. "Can you give me a light?" he asked in gentle tones.

54

Hugh went to the fire and lit a piece of paper. It was not well folded, but his father caught it expertly and balanced its blaze on the top of his pipe. He smacked at the pipe loudly: then, settling down again, he lifted a bait from the plateful on his knees and with a deft twist hid the hook in it.

"Are you telling me that?" he asked humanely. "It's a sore trouble." And he set the bait by its neighbour on the green rushes.

"You heard what I said, Alan?" challenged his mother.

Alan did not answer.

"When did you say it came on him?" inquired his father thoughtfully.

"This afternoon."

"Uh-huh." His voice was friendly.

Grace stole a look at her mother's face. She understood the delicate opposition in the attitudes of her parents. It was elemental, like the wash of the sea— from which her mother recoiled, on which her father adventured. The fear of the woman: the quick pride of the seaman. She sided with her mother. Even the steak that they had had to-night, hadn't she herself provided it? And to think that this fine fellow Alan, this Hugh in his sensitive boyhood, should become common . . . no! It was all right here—where everybody was the same. . . .

"You have shelled enough," said his father. "There's barely two rows to do."

"In that case, there's enough," agreed Alan, and briskly flicked the water from his hands.

"There's a towel on the back of the door," said Grace.

Alan got up, and when he had dried his hands lingered a moment watching his father. The fine glow that was normally on his skin had deepened to an awkward flush, a sort of half smile at humour's having to be suppressed. His dark eyebrows and thick shining dark hair, parted on the left and combed neatly back, were in agreeable contrast to this healthy colouring. Only about the light in his eyes did his real emotion harden—as if it were composed of little, perhaps invisible, lines running to each iris-point. The shadow of embarrassment assisted their concentration.

"Well, I'll be going," he said.

"Where are you going?" asked his mother, challengingly.

"To Carnfuar, of course."

Her face was pale and set as she looked at him. But he avoided her eyes.

"Well, if you are going, I suppose you'll be down about half-past two," said his father naturally.

"Yes."

"You might as well have stayed here for the night. It would have saved you the walk down."

"I want my old clothes, and I must see Willie Hendry."

"Alan, remember, if you go to the sea in the morning it's against my wish," rose his mother's voice.

Still he did not look at her.

"I promised to go."

"He shouldn't have asked you—."

"He didn't—naturally."

"Alan—." Her voice was bright with pain.

He made a quick impatient movement.

"What's the good of taking on like that about it? A night at sea won't harm anybody." Then his voice became firm and brisk. "Well, I'll be off!" He flashed a challenging smile about him. "So long!" And he turned for the door.

Grace got up and followed him outside.

"Alan," she whispered, "you've hurt her." She had him by the arm, and her voice in its reproof was intimate and laughing.

"Well, what's the good of her going on like that?" he asked. "Who else would go for Geordie? Dash it all, what else has Geordie to live on? and they haven't been to the sea for five nights with the weather."

"I know, Alan. But mother's thinking only about you. She was telling me to-day about the great storm of this time last year when your boat was broken up on the breakwater and you were only saved by a miracle."

"Oh, yes, but how often does that happen? Look at father there—at it all his life and he's still to the fore."

His tone, however, was more hurt than satiric. The truth was that, for all his years, he hated having to disobey his mother. Not that her order always appeared wise, but that his affection was so profound that it was felt only in exceptional moments. For much the same reason, her exceptional order was always wiser than it might appear. For she was the permanent centre round which they all revolved, and her order came from that centre with a life-warmth.

"Still, Alan, you might have been a little more reasonable. Why didn't you explain all that?" Her very reproof was insinuating and affectionate.

"What's there to explain? Mother knows all right."

"Ach, well, never mind! Look in to-morrow night and be naetral!" She squeezed his arm.

A little rush of affection went to his heart. Grace was so friendly and at ease. And the way she exaggerated the enunciation of certain home words was charming and laughable. She could give them a little

57

extra twist of mimicry, as though she were doing it in a play. Now her voice laughed softly as she hung on his arm. She made one think of having great bouts of fun.

"All right," he said. "She'll have got over it by then."

"To be sure! What other! Good-night, then, you great lump!" and she gave him a push.

He liked Grace. Dash it, she was nice! He began to whistle, but stopped to think about her again. It was a cold raw ugly night. Fancy having to go to sea in the morning! You would think he was looking forward to it by the way his mother spoke! So you would. He buttoned his coat round his neck. The wind had started sniffing here and there like a treacherous dog. Bedam, but it looked as if it might be a dirty morning! He began to whistle again, with his mind so cheerful that it could laugh at the way Grace pushed him. Poor old Geordie, too. He saw Geordie get up on his elbow in bed, his blue flannel shirt open at the neck so that his grey beard sank into it, and lean a little towards him, as he had done when Cathie had left them alone in the kitchen that afternoon. Geordie's face twitched into a smile of humour and pain: "Your water comes through you like a—like a red-hot needle." Alan sucked in the cold night air with a hiss of pain. He hit his hips in short stabs with his closed fists. Oh lord, poor old boy! . . . Geordie's house loomed up, with its light in the gable-end. The light moved. Cathie would be carrying it through. . . .

Holding her breath, Grace had listened till his footsteps died away; then shuddered at the night that had swallowed him, and went in at the door with a little rush, blowing wind through her lips.

"It's a bitter night!" She stretched her pale hands

58

to the fire, looking at her mother with a half-inviting, half-coaxing smile. Her back arched as she leaned forward from her chair.

Hugh, sitting by the box-bed, had his school-bag on his knees. He was reading in a book with red covers. His feet were crossed under his chair, his back bent, his head drooping, perfectly still.

Grace touched her mother's knee, and with a pathetic expression drew her attention to the boy.

They both looked at the motionless figure. The face had gone pale and sensitive, as though worn a trifle by the day's doings. The eyelashes were long and dark. The body, the wrists, the fingers, were thin and immature. Yet the suggestion was fineness rather than thinness. The finger-tips were washed by the salt water to a torn whiteness.

Grace's dumb appeal made her mouth pout, her eyes glow darkly. But her mother said in a firm voice:

"You can put your books away. This is no time of night to do your lessons. You'll have to attend to them in the morning."

The figure unbent, the eyes flashing a quick look at the faces of the women.

He got up slowly, without a word, stuffed his book in his bag, and put his bag under the corner of the bed. Then he went towards the front door.

As he was passing out, he heard Grace murmur her sweet pity. In his mind, he saw her melting eyes.

He hesitated before pulling the door to, but his mother made only an indistinct sound. Yet he half-smiled at the sound, for her sternness he exquisitely understood. Real feeling has to be covered, as with a mask. In this play, he saw himself as a sort of martyred figure walking out of their hearts.

His eyes came up against the dark night as against

a wall. It steadied him and he stared into it, searching its depth and height. There was suddenly something moving and monstrous in the darkness that he could not detect. But he was not frightened of it. In this mood of importance that had come to him out of the hearts of his mother and sister, he kept himself knit and tall. He walked lightly on feet as sensitive as hands towards the end of the house. At any moment he could draw back or leap. For the darkness as he moved pressed up against his face. He felt it like a band against his forehead.

There were no stars now. The sky was blotted out. The wind moved on the ground rather than in the air, and as he rounded the corner of the house, hit him on the legs. A little scraping sound was in the low stone wall in front of the house. Somewhere a gate-hinge creaked mournfully and intermittently. He thought for a moment he knew where it was, but as he listened it sounded farther off and in another direction.

Standing by itself, the house drew all the water it required from a well some distance away. In such places children come to use the hidden parts of the world for their private needs. The instinct is at once cleanly and secretive. The natural functions of the wild animal are rarely enough observed, and its love-making hardly ever. Only the domesticated animal has lost its pride.

This last particular minute before going to bed gathers within it a still alertness, the head up, listening. Breathing is suspended.

All that had happened throughout the evening flashed through Hugh's mind, not so much in vivid images as in a vivid impressionism. The spirit, the essence, of the happenings. A man's work, the victorious fight, the attitude of his sister, of his mother, the endurance and lonely dignity with which he had borne himself. And the fight!—the fight!

So concentrated became the impressionism that it drew his suspended being to a quivering ecstasy. The moment surged up—and over into a profounder consciousness of the night. He felt the darkness forming into something just behind his head—into a spirit— or a veiled face—or a monstrous something getting ready with a vast claw-hand.

The act finished with an involuntary shudder and the suck of breath in the teeth. The body doubled up and trotted off with a shiver of delight.

V

Hugh's mind leapt awake, and in the roar of the wind about the house tried to catch the high forlorn cry as it died away. He was just too late. Nor could he be quite certain whether its last echo had been heard in sleep or in the instant of waking. Out of his taut body his eyes stared into the dark. The house trembled under a great bout of wind. When the bout passed, the wind cried and whined. But almost immediately the whine began to work itself up into a threshing anger that launched its violence in another bout. The walls shook. Then the torn, baffled wind began to whine again . . . to snarl . . . to work up. . . .

The front door smashed open and Hugh heard Kirsty's voice cry aloud. So intently was he listening now that he could hear the door being pushed against the wind, although no sound was made until it finally rattled shut. Then in the lull he was sure of the voices of Kirsty and his mother, though he could not make out what they said.

Their voices had the high sad quickening of fear. A sense of mortal loss came upon him. The cry he had heard was a drowning cry. Tossed arms and black tumultuous seas. The cry was now on the wind like the cry of a spirit eddying for a moment about the house before streaming far onto the lost moor behind.

He got out of bed and, groping his way to the door, opened it upon the top of the steep wooden stairs. His mother and Kirsty had passed into the kitchen.

"What is it, Mother?" he called down in high tones.

His mother came towards the stair-foot.

"Don't you hear the storm?"

There was something quiet in her voice now, like the emotion that acknowledges doom, yet is not defeated. Its quietening came upon him like a dreadful hand. His skin shivered all over. His mouth closed tight and he began to breathe quickly through his nostrils. The door opposite opened, and Grace came out slowly, saying in a husky frightened voice, "What is it? What is it?" She came up, groping for his arm. "Hugh, what is it?"

"It's the storm," he said, in a voice like his mother's.

He felt her head turn away and listen. A soft whimper stuck in her throat. Her fingers dug into his arm.

All his body began to tremble, partly with the cold, for he had nothing on but his shirt. Grace was clothed in a long white nightdress.

"Who—came in?"

"Kirsty."

"Has—anything happened?" She could hardly speak.

"They're on the sea."

At that moment the house shook.

"Hugh!" she moaned.

"It's all right," said Hugh. "Don't be frightened. You'd better go back to your bed." As he turned into his own room, Grace called wildly, "Mother!"

Groping for his trousers, he heard his mother answer:

"Do you hear the storm that's in it?"

And then Kirsty's cry:

"Oh, Grace, they're on the sea in that!" And in the brave cry was the note: They cannot live through it.

When he had got all his clothes on and went downstairs, he found Grace pale and pale-lipped in the kitchen, her coat with the fur collar over her nightdress. Kirsty had an old fawn-coloured coat buttoned tight round her throat, and a small hat from which her red hair straggled in wisps. Her cheek bones were whipped red and her eyes glistened. All three women looked at him silently as he came in, so that he did not meet their eyes but began casting about for his boots in a preoccupied way, his brows drawn.

A common instinct made the three of them forbear speaking to him, and Kirsty continued to tell Grace how she had wakened and, as the storm increased, couldn't lie in her bed any longer. She had meant to have gone straight down to the shore, but had thought that she had better first come and tell them, so that they would know that someone was down.

His mother, it appeared, had not slept that night, and was dressed when Kirsty had cried at the lighted window.

"You should have wakened me, Mother," said Grace.

Her mother did not answer. She was standing quite still again and listening. Grace began to listen, too; and it was as though by listening they brought the demon of the storm within the kitchen. Grace cowered, her dark eyes growing larger. Her cheeks were blood-less.

Hugh, having knotted the laces on his boots, straightened himself and from a nail on the corner of the box-bed lifted down his cap.

"Are you coming, too, Hugh?" asked Kirsty in a small voice. Courage always thrilled her.

"Yes," said Hugh.

"But—I can go alone. You needn't come."

He didn't answer. After twisting a grey woollen scarf round his neck, he was shoving the ends of it beneath his jacket, when the door burst open with a terrific crash, the wind invading the kitchen and making the flame leap inside the lamp globe.

For a second they all stared towards the door, waiting for what had to enter. Then the flame leapt to the mouth of the globe and disappeared.

In the darkness there was a scurry round the bed, under the table, along the walls. Things swung and rattled and quivered, straining at their ties. The tongue of flame on the smoored peat, which the mother had taken out of the grey ash and broken, darted and flapped, so that the demon leapt around on bat-wings.

Grace's abject terror died out in a moan. Kirsty said, "Oh, Mother!" The mother fought her way to the door, her voice rising to an awful, challenging, "Who's there?"

They heard the door being crushed shut, then into the kitchen from the dark passage there came a silence that was so terrible that it could not be borne. And Kirsty cried aloud:

"Mother!"

There was movement near the door and feet coming back. Their mother's voice said:

"It could only have been the wind."

At that they all listened to the wind outside and heard the whine and snarl in its throat, but also they heard, streaming away into the moor, the cry of anguish, of the unutterably lost, that was at its heart, that is always at the heart of great violence.

They did not move while their mother lit the lamp. In the light Grace was seen huddled in a chair, her lips apart, her eyes distended. Hugh knew that her legs had given way because his own were trembling so much. He also knew that he could not have gone to the door. Terror had in one moment paralysed him. He wanted to sit down now. If only, though, he had gone to the door! For nothing had been at the door. What could have been? What?

Kirsty seemed to be listening with her glistening imaginative eyes. She swallowed hard, and said in a haunted tone:

"Mother, do you think it was a sign?"

She regretted the words at once. Yet they held a dreadful fascination.

Her mother answered:

"We cannot say. It is not in our hands."

The fear that was at her heart inspired strength and calm. And in a brave way that could have brought tears, her motherhood touched each of them.

Grace drew in a long breath and looked from face to face. A faint strained smile came about her lips. Her coat had fallen open, her breast was bare. She gave a little shiver and drew her coat close about her.

"We'd better be going," said Hugh, turning from her to the door.

"Yes," said Kirsty; "we'll be going, Mother. You needn't be frightened for us." In her fear for others she was fearless. Lightness glanced in her tones.

"You'll take care," said her mother, calmly.

"Yes."

Kirsty hesitated, as though searching for some final word. Hugh turned round from the gloom by the door and saw his mother's eyes following him.

He made for the door-knob.

"Come on!" he called. Her mute eyes moved in him. It was time they were going. Oh, come on! He felt his mother's body coming up behind, and then her voice:

"Remember, whatever happens, you will not go near the harbour wall. You will go to the other side, straight to Morag Fraser's. She will be up. They will all be up."

"All right, Mother," said Kirsty.

The mother took the knob from Hugh's hand. "I'll close it after you."

The wind roared in their faces. Kirsty grabbed Hugh's arm. Their mother's voice was drowned. Kirsty called back, "What?" Then the night whirled about them and the door closed.

VI

They were blown against the wall of the house. Kirsty had a firm hold of Hugh's arm. "It's getting worse!" she cried at the top of her voice, and Hugh, after shouting "What?" put together what she had said. When they cleared the house, the wind made

Kirsty run, her clothes slapping and bellying as if they were on a rope. Hugh lay back on his heels. It was pitch dark and they stumbled frequently.

Once Hugh fell, and Kirsty's cry in his ear, as she grabbed him again, "Did you hurt yourself?" made him shout, "No!" abruptly.

He moved more reservedly than ever, refusing to run or act otherwise than in the way a man might upon whom is the responsibility. Lean fingers of broom suddenly whipped him across the eyes. "Look out!" he shouted, and caught her by the arm for the first time. They had missed the path altogether. "Follow me!" he cried, and bored his way amongst the bushes. "Take care!" he shouted. "Look out!" She got entangled, the bushes spiking upward into her clothes. Groping round her skirts with his hands, he broke back the withies. "Now!" he called. "Keep close!"

When they got clear, he was all aglow with a happy resurgent emotion. He felt daring and competent, like a fighter, and therefore more reserved than ever. Instinct told him, too, that at the moment his sister no longer mothered him; rather she respected and depended upon him. He could have called to her that it was all right, that the storm was nothing! She clung to his arm, her voice smothering in an intimate way. He could have bared his teeth and shouted at the black demon that lashed the night into iron shreds.

Presently they were sucked into the shelter of a stone wall.

"Wait," said Kirsty, and began to feel about her clothes. He turned his back to her.

"Oh, Hugh!"

He swung round.

She was quite still and straight now, her shoulders huddled a little.

67

"What is it?"

"Hugh—I'm frightened."

Her voice affected him in an instant. He blinked. He gritted his teeth. He made himself feel impatient.

"Oh, Hugh—they'll never come home—through this."

At that moment Kirsty had for Hugh the born voice of the story-teller and the story-teller's imagination. Her tone was not mournful: it was sweet as the honey of woe; its intimacy went down through the personal to the legendary where the last strands of being quiver together. Beneath these strands there is black nothing.

"Be quiet!" said Hugh.

"I know," agreed Kirsty; then broke the loaded silence, "it's Alan. Mother told him not to go."

Misery encompassed Hugh; held him fascinated. He could not move.

"It would be a terrible thing if anything happened to Alan. Just the one night—the one night he had to come down. It would be a terrible thing—if it was fated." The wind screamed through the crannies in the wall, swept over them in a solid curve, a living canopy. "And mother told him, too. If he was . . . this one night."

Hugh swallowed, his back teeth close shut.

"It's so often the way," she finished.

Hugh felt that in another moment the emotion she created would rise and drown them. He cleared his throat. He pressed his quivering lips together to steady them.

"No good thinking that," he said gruffly. He was mad at the way his eyes stung.

"But perhaps he'll come through it," she said suddenly on a hopeful note, relieved by having spoken her vision. She snuggled his arm warmly. "Will we go?"

Without a word, he swung with her out into the wind, a high misery at his heart, a dumb resentment. In time they reached the highway, and having followed it for a little, they branched to the left down the road to the sea. The river was now on their right and added its fitful undernote to the high violence of wintry trees. The trees were old and gnarled, and though they could not be seen they could be felt in a way that made the body cower, an apprehensive prickling between the shoulder blades. Nothing can be seen so clearly with the inward eye as the streaming contortions of trees lashed by a storm.

Kirsty's arm clung to Hugh's. Every now and then he felt an extra pressure, an access of nearness, an impulsive friendliness. He bore with it. It was as though Kirsty was capable of flying too readily from one mood to another. Yet it had its effect on him. And the earlier resurgent elation came back, but on a stronger, grimmer note.

These attitudes were marked when first the noise of the sea rose above all other sounds, rose high up over the earth from a far booming source, a thunder of doom.

Kirsty stopped, as if suddenly she had come face to face, as if even her vivid imagination had not prepared her. Here was—the thing itself. The solid earth trembled.

"Come on!" cried Hugh.

She went with him. But every footstep brought them nearer this danger, which now threatened themselves. It was too universal to be avoided, to be bounded by a sea beach. The footbridge across the river swung and clanked.

"Come on!" Hugh pulled her.

"I can't see," she cried, terrified by the swinging of the bridge, whipped by the spindrift. Gripping the twisted iron rope, she slithered foot before foot on the planking. "Hugh!" she shouted.

His voice came back thin and eerily, "Come on!" torn by the wind mockingly. Down below the black water seethed and hissed in a private storm of its own. The tide was coming in.

"What were you frightened of?" he shouted to her as she stepped off the planking.

She caught his arm. "I thought there might be a hole in it!" panted her voice in his ear.

"Who would put a hole in it!"

But she had him for manliness and he had her to lead. So they were both comforted and encouraged.

There were lights here and there in the Seabrae houses. Steady lights on which wind or sea-drift made no impression. On this black morning, they stared strangely, a little uncannily. Then one swung into motion, advanced—and disappeared as if by magic.

In the shelter of the ruined net store, Kirsty drew up.

"That was someone with a lantern," she panted.

"Yes. It got blown out."

"A lot of them are up."

"Yes."

With a startled, hindlike motion, Kirsty raised her head.

"Did you hear yon?"

"Someone shouting—down at the beach."

They strained their ears to catch again the high curving cry, but could separate nothing from the sound of ten million stones crashing together as the comber broke and receded.

70

"Let us go," said Kirsty, on a quick breath.

"I don't think there's a light in Morag's," Hugh said as they started out.

That Morag actually wasn't up came as a great surprise to them. Her window was dark. Her husband, Alastair or Alie, was of the same crew as their father. When Kirsty half-turned her head to listen, a lump of froth as big as a hen's egg hit her cheek. She gave a tiny scream, smacking the cold feathery thing away as if she had been stung. Her tongue coming out with her quickened breathing found her lips salt.

"What is it?"

"Foam," she answered, with a broken laugh. "Where can Morag be?" She knocked at the door. The wave thundered and receded. She went to the window and tapped the pane with her knuckles. From far away a thin aged voice cried:

"Who's there?"

"It's me, Kirsty MacBeth."

After listening and hearing no more, Kirsty turned to Hugh, and stooping secretly to his ear, whispered loudly, "She was in bed!"

"No!" and Hugh twisted his head seaward in a monstrous half-fearful humour.

The wind carried the fine spray as a stinging rain. When each wave broke, the heart caught up the trembling of the ground underfoot. The human body was a frail thing with no more than a hand-grip between it and the hammers of doom. And Morag in her bed.

There was a stone wall running in front of the houses and this broke the pressure of wind on Morag's door, which all at once began to open grudgingly.

"Are you there?" screamed a thin voice.

"Yes," said Kirsty.

"Come in, then!" The door opened wider and Kirsty

slipped through. The door was almost shut when it opened again and Kirsty called, "Hugh!"

But Hugh wasn't going in. He disliked at any time entering strange houses. And he wasn't going in to hear Morag's palaver now—while she got her clothes on!

"I'll wait for you!" And he moved off, ignoring a further shout altogether. Alone, the desire came upon him to get down nearer the sea, to find what voice had cried so forlornly from the beach. And because this implied danger, he suddenly had to do it. His heart began to beat and he became excited. All his senses grew very alert. He found he could now vaguely make out things near him when he stared long enough. And this was no fancy, for the darkest hour of the night was at last dying.

VII

Having shut the door, Morag took Kirsty into the kitchen. A red eye looked at Kirsty from the fireplace, otherwise all was pitch dark. She stumbled over a small wooden chair.

"Watch yourself!" said Morag, breaking the continuous lament in her voice for the awful night that was in it. "I'll get a light."

Kirsty stood still, listening to Morag's mumbling voice and sniffing the close atmosphere through sensitive nostrils. She felt superior to the den in a humoured way. This engaging of her attention brought a momentary relief from the dread of the storm. She tried to follow Morag's movements curiously. When Morag got down on her knees and began blowing on the smoored peat's red eye, she almost smiled. Morag would be saving a match! Morag kept blowing for a long time before the piece of paper caught fire. And then by the time she had lit the wick in the little lamp with the red glass bowl, the flame had burned to her finger-tips. "Fitch!" she exclaimed, and threw the paper from her.

In the globed light, she turned to Kirsty, her old face wrinkled up in a smile, her eyes kindly and welcoming.

"You' weren't frightened, lassie, to come out on a night like this?"

"Oh, no!" said Kirsty readily. "Why would I be frightened, with them on the sea?"

"Indeed you may say it." Her voice grew mournful again.

"Weren't you frightened yourself, Mrs. Fraser?"

"I've been lying listening to it ever since it started. And it's here we hear it."

Kirsty's lashes veiled a bright sceptical look.

"I thought I would have found you up," she said lightly.

"What would have been the good of me being up?" asked Morag. "It would only be adding to it by burning the oil."

But Kirsty could not see what deeps were revealed by such an awful economy. She doubted the facility of it. In her own home, life was a flame. The wind blew in at the front door and out at the back. Poverty there might be, and misery too—but the mournful saving note, never. To this house there was no back door. The years had come in and stayed; and at the end of a lifetime nothing new can happen but death. Stared at long enough, even death loses its novelty, and all

73

that is finally left is the voice weaving its mournful inevitable trapping.

Morag was only seventy, but her body looked shrunken within its pink flannel nightgown, as she turned towards the wooden bed. "I'll be putting my clothes on me," she said. "Though it's dark enough yet."

"I think we should be out."

"Ah, what good can we do out, lassie?"

"No, but—to see. . . ."

"There will be nothing to see yet. Nothing. Though the day should be breaking soon."

"Oh, Morag—Mrs. Fraser, do you think? . . ."

"It's in the Lord's hands."

"Yes, I know. But. . . Do you think—do you think —they'll be all right?"

Kirsty now was all impatience to be out. The thunder of the sea was shaking her mind again. And Morag's tone was having its effect. It was like the beginning of a death service. She passionately rebelled against it. She despised the old woman, her slowness. She didn't believe in her grief, in her mourning sorrow. Yet there was some dark thing in it that she feared.

Morag put on a knitted woollen petticoat with scalloped foot. Its colour was the natural grey, and her fingers fumbled a long time fixing it. Footsteps passed the window, and men's voices shouted loudly through the storm. Morag put on a second petticoat of exactly the same material and shape, except that its colour was a dull red. Now she would be ready in a minute, thought Kirsty. Morag put on a third petti-coat, of a more washen red than the second, but this one would not fix without its safety-pin. With a hand gripping it behind, Morag came shuffling and peering towards the mantelshelf.

74

"Do you see a safety-pin there? Your eyes are better nor mine."

Kirsty immediately caught up the lamp. "Where? Here?"

"Yes. Just there on the corner."

"It's not here."

"Then it must have fallen down."

Kirsty, pushing a chair back, searched in and about the fender. She couldn't find the safety-pin anywhere. "I don't see it at all," she cried. Her senses were now beginning to go outside the house. Her impatience increased. As she stood up, Morag took the lamp from her, saying, "It must be there," and she stooped slowly to the floor. Kirsty's quick eye caught the gleam of the pin on the seat of the chair. "Here it is!" She dived for it, nearly upsetting Morag and the lamp.

"You won't be long now, will you? I'm frightened—for Hugh." Kirsty took the lamp from her hand.

"The boy should have come in," said Morag. She became slower than ever, as though her senses were numbed and under the dark world of the storm movement was futile. Just when she had fixed the safety-pin, the pounding of a great wave shook the house to its roots, and a maddened flurry of wind lashed the window panes with sea-water.

Morag's mouth opened to a dark hole in her wrinkled listening face. Then a low moan broke from her and her body moved upon itself. She was going to sit down.

"I must get out!" cried Kirsty, terror choking her.

"Yes, yes," keened Morag. "Oh, yes, yes. Oh-h-h." She fumbled at the place where her clothes lay, and lifting a petticoat of dark brown wool, put it on. The next one was of the same colour and shape.

"I'll be going!" cried Kirsty.

75

"Wait, lassie. I'll be with you," intoned Morag monotonously. "It's time enough; time enough."

Oh, it was time enough for where they were going. Ah, time enough, time enough. You did not need to be in a hurry to meet—what would come to you . . . what would come to you . . . what comes to us all.

Under this rhythm of the silent keen, Kirsty's emotion became unbearable. She choked her throat against screaming. Her hands clenched. Blood and pallor were in her face. Her eyes flamed. She stood sheer back into herself, every cell vivid and tense.

All races have their legends of lovely women. Deirdre and Emir and Fand. There are moments in eternity when one conceives them, moments of fire, yellow flames blown out of time.

Kirsty's uplifted head turned to the storm, turned from the petticoats and the smother of the keening, to the ravening world. A prickling and burning ran up her body, up and round, swathing her, passing up beyond her head. At that tip-toe intolerable moment, Hugh's face came flat against the unblinded window.

The face was cold and ghostly. The eyes were black. They wandered, seeking, about the kitchen, until they met Kirsty's. Then they held. Slowly, with a puzzled pained look, they withdrew, and the face faded.

Kirsty's body ran over cold as ice. A strangled scream died in her throat. Nor did she hear Morag's startled voice as at last she stumbled for the door. Blindly she wrenched it open; left it standing to the wind; wheeled for the window, and in the second stride hit into Hugh so that they both fell against the house.

"What's wrong?" cried Hugh, scared.

"Oh, Hugh!" She embraced him passionately. She kissed his hair. She could not get enough of him.

"What is it?"

"It's—it's—" Her voice broke on an excited laugh. "That Morag in there—she's—she's—. Oh, Hugh, you gave me such a fright!"

"How?"

"Your face. I thought—." But she could not say she had thought it the face of his ghost. She felt exultant. The storm was no greater than the storm in her own blood. She could see his face now and embraced him again, murmuring.

"I was wondering what was keeping you." His teeth chittered.

The day was breaking in a dirty grey light. Her arm about him, she looked over his shoulder strangely, from outline to outline. Hugh felt deeply attached to her at that moment. Her affection and her body warmed him. He did not break away at once.

"The wind is going down," he said.

"Did you see anyone?"

"Yes. A lot of them are down."

"There's no sign?"

"No. They say the boats can't manage it yet."

"Oh, Hugh—do they think?"

"They don't know. Father's boat is the worst. It's not decked at all." His teeth clicked again. "I'm not cold."

She took his hands and pressed them. She peered into his face. He avoided her eyes, but there was no impatience in his involuntary movement away from her. She understood and caught his arm. They walked along the front, and turning the corner of the waist-high wall went down to the sea.

The gale was certainly moderating. They had not to lean on it in the same way. Yet it seemed to them worse than when they left home, for here they came solidly against the terrifying violence of the ocean.

77

Out of the murk each roller came, a wall of water, deliberately gathering volume, massing itself, steadily advancing, gaining speed, curling all along the line to a smoking crest, onrushing, uprising, curving over— till its baffled speed thundered crest-first on the beach. Great feathers of spume flew through the air and the myriads of grey-blue stones were sucked seaward in a deafening roar. But already, behind, the new wave was gathering volume, massing itself, steadily advancing. . . . .

Hugh and Kirsty struggled along the path by the crest of the beach. To Kirsty the cruelty of the sea held no mercy. It was not merely deathly: it was ravenous. It was not merely ravenous: it was uncaring. In its colossal game men were no more than torn weed. It would smash their skulls and suck their black bodies down among the boulders like twisting tangle as it retreated to gather volume once more. And even if, far, far out, it had already tossed and choked and drowned, still it would come deliberately out of the murk, a wall of water, massing itself, steadily advancing, gaining speed, curving, smoking, onrushing, uprising—crushing.

But to Hugh there was also a terror which he kept to himself; for he had overheard a man say that his father's boat could hardly have lived through it; that she must have been swamped. For the violence of the wind must be breaking the seas far out. And great high seas did not matter—until they broke. So he piloted his sister past the corner of the shed where the men had spoken, and went on towards the harbour breakwater. In the lee of an old stone cooperage they came amongst a motley company. An old woman greeted Kirsty warmly in a sad high-pitched voice, and Hugh slipped along to the men's corner.

Two or three boys were there, and he recognised amongst them his last night's antagonist. One of the men spoke jestingly to him in a kind voice. The others took notice also. He distracted their attention. They asked him if he had come down alone. He felt their eyes linger on him, while he turned his head shyly this way and that, and he knew that they were saying within themselves that his father and his brother were on the sea.

The women were huddled closely together, and in the vague light looked mysterious and hooded. But the men kept restlessly moving in ones and twos round the corner of the wall in a continuous vigil. They would come back to stamp the ground and blow through their lips. Sometimes one would say, "Not a sign." Then they would all move and stamp the ground.

Hugh was conscious of Rid Jock on the other side of the men. Jock would now and then say something in a loud blustering voice to the two boys who were with him, as if Hugh did not exist. But Hugh knew that this was a sort of bravado, and did not mind. Indeed, that he had beaten one who could be so confident surprised him a little. There was a thin pleasure in it that passed coldly over his face and lingered secretly in his eyes. He half-turned his face so that Jock might see the thin smile if he liked, but he appeared only to be listening to the men.

"It's a wonder they tackled it at all," said Dugald Sandison. He was a squat stout man with a reddish close-cut beard, and had joined the group only two minutes before. He worked a small croft above the seabrae, but had at one time been a "hired man" under Hugh's father.

At this a curious silence fell on each mind.

"You could see it was coming to something," con-

79

tinued Dugald, casting a look at the sky, for he felt the silence against him.

"Oh, well," said the Viking, evenly.

Though eighty years of age, the Viking was a great upstanding man, with a broad chest under a blue guernsey and no jacket. As skipper-owner of the *Viking*, he had been in his day one of the finest seamen on the coast. Too big a man for sarcasm, he was kindly and just. His uplifted head carried the seaman's look. The blue eyes gazed at you in the first moment; then they looked past you. Afterwards you would remember their colour, but be puzzled to describe its sea-tone.

"Ay," said Dugald, finished with the sky. "Yes, it looked bad," and he stamped unconcernedly, holding his own.

"They had their lines baited," observed the Viking, almost gently. "They wouldn't want to let the bait rot for the second time."

"Of course," said Dugald slowly; "there's that in it. Yes." His head remained fixed, his mouth half-open, while his mind gathered all the implications. Then he nodded to himself, and so became one with the others.

The Viking's grandson, Jimak, a youth of twenty who was learning to be a tailor, came round the corner.

"It's brightening," he said, his face pinched, his shoulders rounded. There was left, however, the blue in his eye.

"No sign?" asked Dugald.

"Not a sign."

"If they're not here any minute now . . . I don't know," said the Viking, and looked straight in front of him to a great distance. The look broke and he announced quietly, "We'd better be ready. Take the ropes." And he went round into the weather.

All the others followed him. The women went round their own corner. Soon along the crest of the beach were knots of people, huddled together. Most of the men were with the Viking, near to the sloping piles of the breakwater, which ran straight out into the sea.

The harbour entrance stretched between the outer end of the breakwater and the solid quay-wall beyond. The waves in making for the beach came smashing over the quay-point in great clouds, swinging across the harbour mouth, and racing in white smoke along the piles. To make the harbour in such weather was for normal seamanship impossible. To attempt it and get stove in on the breakwater was to invite disaster, though, with the inward rush of the sea, luck and daring might keep the boat bumping on the sloping slippery piles towards the beach. To head straight for the beach might be the short way out, when, with willing hands and ropes and any luck at all, at least life might be saved.

But there is also the life of a boat. There is always the pride of seamanship. Finally, with a smashed boat there is no fishing, nothing coming into the house. It is a complicated problem for the man at the tiller, who for hours has fought with death, slipping him by inches, smashing into him bow first, yawing and lifting, but never for an instant relaxing a tension that grows cold and implacable as the green sea water; that, in desperate moments of crisis, grows colder still. It is not easy to give in to the ancient enemy.

VIII

Even when the first boat was no more than an elusive dark nucleus of the murk, a great cry went along the watchers on the beach. Bodies drew taut and a shivering ran like cold fire over the skin.

"Here she comes!"

And after the throat had yelled it, the mind would cry it silently to itself, with sometimes the lips moving and the breath hissing the cry.

Hugh felt his body tremble to a dissolving weakness. His excitement became a great lump in his throat. All at once his strength seemed to go out of him. Jock went past, shouting in an excited happy voice, "Here they come!"

Hugh swallowed and kept his face to the sea. Then he moved towards Seabrae a few paces until he was on the far edge of the men. Feeling very uncertain of himself, he tried not to think of the boat. Closing his teeth, he blew in and out through them sharply. His eyes gathered a film. He stooped to pick up nothing. When he raised his head he saw Kirsty coming running towards him. There were tears in her eyes. He saw that she could hardly contain herself. His face grew cold and hostile. His eyelids narrowed. His lips tightened against his teeth.

"Oh, Hugh—there's one coming!" She caught his arm. "They can't make out who it is."

Her voice, however, was brave and thrilling. Bronze hair and blue eyes and whipped face. As an excuse for getting rid of her arm, he searched in his pockets.

She immediately stepped over to the men, who were arguing now as to the boat, their eyes glancing with excitement. In a minute more, no doubt remained: it was Kenny Macleod's boat. Those who had at first said it was Kenny Macleod were jubilant. They knew exactly the peak of sail, the cut of the bow, the way she rose to it, and other distinguishing features. Anyone who had suggested anything else didn't know what they were talking about.

Hugh found Kirsty beside him. In a choked voice, she said, "It's Kenny Macleod." Neither their brother's boat nor their father's. Her eyes pierced far into the sea. All at once Hugh felt his arm squeezed to the bone. But he knew why. And at that moment the shout went up:

"Here's another!"

The cry was like laughter. The excitement was magnificent. The boats were coming back! They had fought through everything, they had weathered it, and were coming home! A voice cried out: "That's the stuff for you, by God!" And because the voice throbbed with ardour, no one felt that God's name had been lightly spoken.

It was stupendous fun to see the two boats come tossing on—out of the nightmare from which they might so easily never have come. No one, except the Viking, could stand still, as though by moving a yard this way or that, a man could get a better view.

But as the boats came nearer a silence fell on everyone and bodies grew still. The first great relief was passing into the menace of the harbour bar. The storm leapt alive again, its thunder pounding on the beach, its drift stinging eyes that stared with unwinking fixity. The women had drawn a little nearer the knot of men by the breakwater, and their wide skirts flapped in the wind below faces hooded and peaked by tight-drawn shawls. They looked like a group caught in a grey dawn of history, or legend, their separateness from the men fateful and eternal.

It took Kenny Macleod's boat to show off the tumultuous action of the sea. That that small craft, with her slim bow and toy-blue gunnel, had fought out of so dark and stupendous a fury, seemed hardly credible. Yet one saw the purpose in her fighting shape, the pertinacity of that slender bow. She was never flung before the wave-top; rather she clung to the top of it, crushing it under her to a seething froth, racing with it, until, baffled, it outleapt her, thrusting her on end into the trough behind. But in a moment she was seen again, gathering herself, making way, preparing for the next. Every moment was a moment of poise, of balancing, at dizzying angles. The toy figures with head and breast above her gunnel must have been pegged in their places or surely they would have been spilled out. Yet out of this orgy of drunken movement, out of this supreme sport of chance, tossed aside, buried, staggering and wallowing . . . the slim bow rose again, quivering, indomitable. The thrill of its purpose was heroic.

The tension among the watchers grew as she drew near, and it was perceived that Kenny was putting her at the harbour mouth. The unmanageable element in the ground swell began to have its effect. The members of the crew became distinguishable. A great wave smashed over the quay-head and raced for the breakwater, leaving a wide, froth-strewn, swinging trough. The Viking's unwinking eyes measured and judged. His voice rose:

"She'll never do it!"

Hugh's mortal body was quivering like a leaf. Cold

shivers rayed over his skin, under his hair, made his teeth click. From a hot central spot inside him an impotent voice cried heroically through the thunder of the beach, shouted silently to brave men.

Kenny was sitting low in the stern, gripping the tiller, his body bending forward and unmoving as stone.

"He's putting her at it!"

She came round . . . almost broadside on. The same wave that smashed over the quay-head caught the frail craft like a dead plank and, having won its moment at last, lifted her into the air in order to hurl her upon the breakwater. Kenny threw himself back upon the tiller. She had just enough steering way to answer. Her head fell off, and instead of that slim bow smashing on the piles, or, worse, jamming between them, when death would have been certain, she mounted them in a glancing way, like a checked shying horse, showing a clean forefoot and a yard or two of keel.

At that moment the wave passed and the boat was left clinging to the piles, with the water sucked from under her. Instantly she heeled over to a desperate angle, two men on the port side being shot into the sea; fell with a bilge smash upon the water; hesitated sickeningly; then righted herself.

A groaning shout had gone from the men on the beach.

"Get out the rope!" roared the Viking.

But already his grandson had a loop of it round his body, and was making for the perilous passage of the pile-tops, his jacket buttoned tight, his cap down on his ears, his feet leaping nimbly as if they were winged. The pinched face, the rounded shoulders, the tailor's legs that were not quite straight—and the Viking blue of the eyes on fire, the blood singing.

85

All at once Hugh became aware of a strange and terrifying sound, as if the storm out of its heart had started keening. An answering echo rose high in his own heart, before he saw that it was the voices of the old women.

Dreadful! Dreadful! Who wanted them to cry like that? They were mad! He was ashamed of them! He caught sight of the white hands of the two men who had been pitched into the sea clinging to the gunnel, their black heads bobbing in a spouting jaggle of water. His brother's boat was at hand.

"He'll come on top of them!" shouted the Viking, throwing out an arm as if to ward off.

The moment became a fine-drawn tension of terror —that the wrong thing would be done, that one boat would be piled on another and the baffled sea yet contrive to make men cheat each other into death.

Kenny's boat was either making water fast or had half filled herself in the process of righting. The two men had been hauled aboard. The piles were round and sheathed in green slime. An oar-end slipped off them. Purchase could only be got with the iron-spiked boathook. When a wave came, a man, forward, lay full weight on the boathook, while the others, reached over towards the piles with both hands, except in the case of one man who levered with his left only, the right arm hanging limp. The wave lifted them. The man with the boathook seemed to lunge overboard as his leverage vanished. The wave outsped them, churning along the piles. The boat sagged back when the wave had broken on the beach, and the thunderous recession down the stones had started. White-flecked, like a great skin, the whole body of water could be seen swaying out to sea.

But clinging to the pile-tops, directly over the boat,

was Jimak, slipping the noose from his body. The noose fell amongst upthrust hands. He yelled something at them, his dark body hovering like a great bird, then he turned for the beach.

Duncan Bain, the skipper of Alan's boat, was a rather silent man with a slight stammer that helped a dry humour. He was a good man in a crisis, having no fear and a capacity for sound decisions. At the last possible moment, he deliberately put the nose of his boat at the beach. She had lost little of her seaway, and caught presently by the piling wavetop, rushed past Kenny's boat at a great speed, missing her by inches.

It was a nice bit of work on Duncan's part, and his boat should have been thrown clean. But somehow the wave lost grip of her and she slid down its back. Yet she was carried by her own impetus so far through the slack water that as the wave fully receded, she scraped noisily seaward.

The Viking had anticipated this, and was now on the slope where the waves broke, a coil of rope in his right hand.

"Look out!" he roared, and lifting the coil high over his shoulder, flung it at the boat.

Alan was on his knees in the bows, arms spread-eagled. The rope hissed out to a straight line. The distance was just too great, and the tail-end curled up in the wind a yard from Alan's face. He lunged for it, his body falling with a heavy splash on the white water and disappearing. The water, however, was almost slack, and in a moment he was seen clutching at the bows. Before a member of the crew could rush forward, Alan had kicked bottom and was climbing aboard.

He had the rope in his hand.

87

"Good boy, Alan!" shouted the Viking in a great voice. Then he retreated.

As a towering wave advances, the slack water in front is sucked back to meet it. The *Morning Star* grated along her keel. Life went out of her. The oncoming wave curled right over her, hardly even broke as it swamped and buried her. At the same time there was a bumping forward motion felt by the men on shore laying on the rope. This pull on the rope kept the boat from broaching and turning turtle. No wonder the Viking had shouted his praise of Alan's feat in a voice that had made Hugh's body remember itself by gulping a burning lump.

First the men's heads and shoulders, then the decks, came streaming up out of the flattening sea. Immersion could hardly have lasted more than five seconds. But the weight of the water had pounded them, and for a moment the crew, heads down, swayed blindly. Alan was the first to notice that Alastair Fraser was missing. He stood up, the sea already rushing back all round him, and pointed. Then he staggered aft and went clean in off the stern.

It was at that moment that Kirsty knew that Alan had to be drowned. Fate has its own way of dealing with a man for whom love trembles with too great an anxiety. Fate will take such a man through the great danger, through the crisis, in order to kill him in a final odd moment born out of pure chance. That was the knowledge that was in Kirsty's bones. She knew it as a foreboding. Alan's chance visit. Geordie Macleod's illness. Their mother's fear. Her face and eyes as she told her son not to go to sea. Alan's disobedience. Then the storm, which Alan had to live through because of the crew, followed by this snatching of him at the very last moment.

"Hugh!" The thin moaning cry half-choked in mortal agony. "He's gone! He's gone!" Tears streamed down her face. "Hugh!" She choked back her sobs. Yet never for a moment did her wide eyes leave the boat. A vivid transparent flush gave a purity of anguish extraordinarily moving. Hugh, glancing at her, saw her mouth closing on what would have been a high keening cry.

"Be quiet, Kirsty!" he muttered. Tears scalded his throat. "They'll hear you."

"Hugh!" All her body moved upon itself in a dreadful impotence, while the cry came in a queer choked sound through her nostrils. "Look! Look!" It was as if the oncoming wave were going finally to obliterate.

As it broke over the boat, however, it carried the bodies of old Alie and Alan well up the beach, and as it receded the bodies, interlocked, were seen turning and tumbling down again in the seething white water. The boathook was about the only unlashed gear still on board. Duncan Bain wrenched its hook out of a twist of rope, and thrusting it over the bodies, pulled firmly with the action of a man gaffing a fish. The point stuck in Alie's side, penetrating several layers of clothing, and Duncan hauled both bodies close in, when they were quickly lifted aboard. By this time, however, two or three young men, dashing after the receding wave, had reached the bows.

"Come back!" roared the Viking. There was an instant's confusion. "Back!" And they retreated just in time.

A quick-witted member of the crew had meantime hauled in the heaving line and double-hitched an end of stouter rope to the ring-bolt before the wave came again. This time the men ashore lay heavily on the rope, and when the boat grounded in the receding water, dashed for her, and gathering round the gunnels, gave the word to heave. All the crew, with the exception of the skipper, who was with the inter-locked bodies of Alastair and Alan, gave a hand to carry their craft the few yards to safety. Even then, the next comber soused them to the waist, for the boat was heavy and full of water. But the Viking had the women on the rope with him, and in a few seconds all the men were walking up over the crest of the beach carrying with them the still unseparated bodies, which they laid down on a patch of green grass.

The women came round about, and out of their mournful exclamations the voice of Morag suddenly rose shrill and stricken, She threw her dark apron over her head in a strange gesture and cried her husband's name. "He's gone! He's gone!"

The hands of her husband were knotted in Alan's jersey. It took a few seconds to prise the fingers open and draw the bodies apart. Immediately this was done, however, Alan's mouth slowly opened in a spewing yawn, the upper lip wrinkling from the teeth in a sickly way. The head fell over weakly, and the body gave a distinct spasmodic shudder. A trickle of sea-water came out between the lips. Exhausted by the effort, the body lay still, and blood from the cut on the forehead ran into the socket of a staring eye.

This sign of life from Alan had for a moment a paralysing effect on Kirsty. Her eyes widened, her lips came apart. It was the sight of the blood gather-ing in the socket that released her. Fumbling at her breast, she was through the men and on her knees by Alan's head before anyone could think of stopping her. Her voice was eager and tremulous; its undernote thrilled and happy. But when she had wiped the blood, the Viking lifted her gently aside.

"He's all right, lassie. We must get some of the water out of him first." The Viking then said smartly, "One of you run for the doctor," and to his grandson, "The whisky."

The Viking then doubled up a couple of jackets, and old Alie and Alan were put through the processes of artificial respiration on the spot.

"You go home, Morag, and get the bed ready, and put two hot bottles in it," said the Viking from Alie's back.

"Ow, do you think he's not dead?" cried her high sad voice that had hardly ceased in its woe.

Kirsty shivered with distaste. "Are you hearing her?" she whispered to Hugh.

"Yes." He hated that mournful sound. She ought to be ashamed of herself carrying on like that. It was a relief when she went; which, indeed, she did hurriedly in a ludicrous waddle.

"Look at her!" said Kirsty, wild laughter nearly breaking through her lips.

"Hssh!" Hugh clutched her clothes restrainingly.

"Oh, Hugh!" Kirsty wrung her hands, her lips pressing tight. She needed something to occupy her attention. She could not stare down like the men at the bodies of Alie and Alan being pressed and released rhythmically. She could hardly, in fact, look at Alan at all. The high hope singing at her heart was too impossible. Not that it was for herself; hardly even for Alan: it was for her mother.

But Alan was coming round. There was now and then an expiring groan with an edge to it of protest. Alastair, however, showed no sign of life whatsoever. And when the Viking at last turned him over, the face was clayey blue, the expression fixed, the grizzled chin upthrust. "We must get heat to him," the Viking decided. "Take Alan, too. Give's a hand, one of you."

So the procession started out for the Seabrae houses, the women who were standing apart crying sadly to each other, for the slow way the men moved had something about it of a funeral procession.

In the warmth of the Viking's house, Alan recovered rapidly. Two men undressed him in the parlour, whence in a little while Jimak came for socks. He was smiling, "The whisky is nearly making him vomit his inside out!"

They could hear the horrid retching. But Kirsty, flushed and trembling, smiled back. She had lost Hugh. She had forgotten even her father.

IX

But Hugh had not forgotten his father. For a while he had forgotten, it is true. But just as he was about to follow the procession, which included the crew of Kenny Macleod's boat, one of whom had broken his collar bone, the appalling memory came upon him. He had the sensation of his heart standing still in his breast, and drew breath with difficulty. Then his heart raced sickeningly.

The daylight was coming slowly. Well out the gloom was still thick, but now there were more wave-tops, so that the sea seemed to come pouring on out of infinity.

But far as his eye could reach, nothing lived in that tumbling waste.

He looked about him, and found men and women staring at the sea. There was a quietude about these people. A hush of awe crept over his body. All of them were figures left behind on the beach.

He turned to the sea.

The ceaseless onpouring of the wave-tops had a strange hypnotic effect. They came racing on and on toward the rhythmic thunder of the strand. His senses began to thin away on the wind that broke on his face and streamed past his ears, until there was nothing left in his mind but a vague surge, remote and out of time, that broke on the shores of sorrow. There was a curious quietening in this sorrow. Still and open-eyed, it gazed unendingly. And no red lance of memory touched its smooth pale body.

Hugh imperceptibly became one with it, knowing without allowing himself to know that he was taking refuge, yet out of his knowing raising a cry echo-thin of "Come! Come!" to his father's boat. Slowly the wave-tops drew nearer, began to pour down through his open eyes, so that his vision blurred and his body, losing weight, began to sway. Even if he wanted now to become himself, he could not. And he did not want . . . until a dazing pain came down like a shutter from his forehead and he staggered.

As he looked about him, men and women and breakwater and land and houses flowed in waves. Then a darkness whirled in wheels before his sight, blotting everything out. He shut his eyes tight, and by a sheer effort of will kept himself from falling. When he opened them again, a dark mist was clearing and things and persons were taking on their normal shapes. There were four women together, and one came towards him anxiously. He pretended not to see her and moved on towards a group of men, shaking himself and staggering slightly, as if it were all a game to get warm.

"Well, Hugh, you're cold!" Dave MacKenzie was a dark gaunt man with hunched shoulders. As he smiled, his unshaven face sank into blue hollows. Everybody looked at Hugh kindly, and, he felt, a little queerly. He had a suspicion that they had stopped their talk as he came up. Shyly, he turned his face from them. He was still light-headed and chilled to the bone. A few drops of thin water suddenly ran out of his nostrils. His face was ghost-pale. There was no food in his stomach. Yet he felt no great bodily discomfort, beyond the need of closing his eyes now and then to guard against the movement of the waters.

All at once he heard the voice of Tom Macrae, who was a youth of Alan's age, saying, "Keep looking there for a minute."

The voice was startlingly quiet. All eyes kept looking in the direction of Tom's pointing hand.

"See it?" said Tom suddenly on a sharper note, as if he were fixing a momentary glimpse for them. No one answered. Bodies braced and feet settled into the gravel. "Now, watch," said Tom. . . . "Look!"

One or two muttered uncertainly.

"Again!" And Tom's voice rose this time to an excited laugh. "There they are!" The pointing hand made an open gesture.

And it looked as if all the shore had seen the pointing hand of Tom Macrae, who had eyes that could contract like a cat's.

And men began to pick up something like a tiny black buoy that bobbed and disappeared far, far out. Soon all doubt vanished. It was a small boat making for the harbour.

"By God, that's them!" cried one man, and he hit another man on the back with a loud whack.

It was an incredible joke, the appearance of the boat. It was the greatest joke of all. Everybody laughed and stamped and shouted to everybody else. The wind whipped water out of their eyes.

Hugh wanted to race off for Kirsty. His body was light and buoyant. But he could not tear himself away from the sight of the tossing toy-boat. Even the four old women were smiling, with tears navigating the zigzag furrows of their faces. They were also catching each other impulsively by the arm in their sad enjoyment of God's mercy.

Possibly, after all, they were the greater realists, for they frankly saw the coming of the boat as "an Act of God", whereas the men made themselves believe that all along they had "felt sure" she would come of her own accord.

One man backed his "sureness" by adding, "And as I said—trust John MacBeth at the tiller!"

Hugh, staring seaward, glowed at this tribute to his father. Nothing that the man might have invented could have so exhilarated him. His pride could afford to become immoderate because he repressed it; had to repress it for pride's sake. But it was a strange and thrilling thing to have a father praised not merely for fine seamanship, but for the seamanship that conquers come what will. Even in this leisurely appearance of him out of the deep, when hope had at last faltered to the "sureness" that is desperation's make-believe, there was something characteristic and unique. The quickest mind of them all was in no hurry. No rush and tumble of disaster here. Bobbing up and down, surely, inevitably, having already fought the peak of the storm until it had burst, now in good

95

time and tide, making for the harbour mouth. By what subtle divination, by what inches or fractions of an inch, had so careless an appearance been achieved? And by what decisions, held to by what courage, by what instant reckonings? For, despite the lessening wind, the sea, working on itself, was bigger than it had been an hour back, the beach more thunderous, the wave-bursts on the pier-head more solid and engulfing. Yet that that oncoming little craft had conquered it, and now would ride it to a living end, was the only certain thing in the minds of the watchers on the beach.

And, as a joyous thing, it drew its full audience. Every person who was afoot came tumbling out of Seabrae; and here and there, down the ways, even an odd crofter straggled towards whatever drama might be showing at the local theatre where the furies and the fates played their parts in person, and man on his half-inch planking played back, the price of a missed cue being death.

Kirsty came with Alan. She had a firm hold of his arm, and he was laughing, sticking out his legs now and then to show off the ludicrous shortcomings of his borrowed rig-out. At the same time, faces that laughed back noticed how shaky he still was on his pins. So they laughed the more, waving an arm from a few yards' distance or, face to face, asking him if he was quite sober now. Kirsty's cheeks were flushed, her eyes glancing. It was a triumphal procession. No one would be crude enough to suggest that he had done a brave deed, but everyone thought it. And Kirsty knew that they would generously say what they thought, when her brother and she had passed.

To crown all, the man he had saved was still alive, suffering apparently not so much from sea-water as

96

from a crack on the back of the head. The doctor had just said that his condition was delicate, but that he should pull through. The doctor was busy working on him at the moment. Oh, he was all right! It would take a pretty hefty crack to split old Alie's brain-box! . . .

The crest of the beach ran with the utmost good humour. The thicknesses of heads were compared. Alan drew up alongside Tom Macrae, his special friend, and the merry talk continued. Kirsty left him and turned to Hugh, who had been too shy to greet his brother. At such a public moment there was nothing to be said between brothers.

"So there's father coming", Kirsty accosted him in a light laughing voice.

As though the coming was ordinary!

"Yes," Hugh answered, with polite reserve and without looking at her.

"Wasn't it wonderful of Alan?" said Kirsty in her story-teller's voice.

"Yes."

"Oh, Hugh, I thought—I was sure. . . . It was awful. That time when they went tumbling down the surf, with the stones—"

"Yes," interposed Hugh.

"If anything had happened, think of—mother; think of going home to—to . . . Oh, Hugh!" Her legendary voice trembled with happiness. She glanced over her shoulder at Alan, at those who were with him, as though she were anticipating the merriest of flung jests; then she glanced over the other shoulder at the women, and hid her amused expression by turning to the sea, but saying closely to Hugh, "Did you hear Morag? Wasn't yon awful?"

"You cried yourself," said Hugh.

"Cried? I did not!"

Hugh was silent.

"You don't mean I cried out like Morag?"

Hugh muttered indistinctly.

"Well, don't be silly, Hugh! . . . Poor boy, are you cold? You look pale."

"I'm all right."

Hugh gave himself a disengaging shake, stamped the ground and blew through his lips. "There's father coming," he added, and in his stamping backed close to the men.

" . . . won't I?" rose the heated voice of the Viking's grandson, Jimak. "And what's more, I'll lay you any money you like that he takes the harbour, and that though there's a bigger sea running now than ever."

"I hope so," said Duncan Bain, quietly, at his back.

Jimak half-swung round, stopped himself, flushed all over his face, and could plainly have bitten his tongue out.

Hugh looked away to sea, the confounded lump coming into his breast again and sending all sorts of weakening tremors throughout his flesh.

"Did you hear what he said, Hugh?" whispered Kirsty happily.

Hugh made no answer. He longed to get away to be somewhere by himself, where no one would see him.

"I do hope he manages to get in," went on Kirsty.

A great loud voice rose up in Hugh telling her to shut up, but he kept his teeth on it. He stamped the ground very hard; he fixed his eyes on the boat.

But the boat did not help him much. She came on so surely, with such a quiet but gallant air, that she might have drawn tears from stone eyes. There was such confidence in her, such restrained buoyancy, yet withal such a modest mien, unhurrying with speed, side-slipping with reluctant grace, creaming the wave-crest with so neat a forefoot, that any hope of finding relief in the violent vanished. This boat was going to do nothing to help Hugh. She was going to have his tears.

Kirsty saved him for the moment. The growing silence of those about her as they were caught in the spell of watching began to communicate its excitement. Her eyes winced before the bursts on the pier-head, from the seething gluttony of the breakwater.

"Oh, Hugh," she murmured, "he'll never do it."

"Of course, he'll never do it," said Hugh at once. "What do you expect?" His voice, guided to her ear, was impatient and intense. It relieved him mightily. What on earth did the woman expect?

But the boat would not let him off with it. And Jimak's voice escaped, high-pitched, "Boys, isn't she coming!"

She was coming with a deceptive speed. They could see that now. Naturally she could carry more sail than either of the others because the wind was not so strong; but there was somehow more to it than that, an incommunicable something extra. She rode so comfortably the blessed waves that they slid from her in a round dismay. Obviously she wasn't shipping a drop. Obviously no one aboard was in the least concerned. Only once did she make a slightly grandi-loquent gesture when nothing was seen of her but up-pointing bows and a glimpse of breast. The impression of rising sheer up out of the sea was for a moment rather terrifying; for a vessel in her throes has been observed thus to trouble dumb heaven before slipping stern first to her doom.

At that moment, too, heaven ran red, a stormy ribbed blood-red. The fierce colour was reflected on

99

the water, and watching eyes grew dazed, not so much by light as by instinctive fear. From cloud to cloud rolled this red thunder of daybreak.

No word was spoken now. A faint roseate hue touched the boat and grew warm in the faces of the crew. They were making straight on the pier-head where the great seas burst in solid splendour, throwing arched thin sheets of fluted loveliness whose green was momentary glass against the red horizon.

There was no way of making more straightly for their doom. Against the masonry the frail ribs and planking would smash like match-sticks.

Even the Viking, who knew the skipper's "tricks", thought he was adventuring too much, But his judgment was now against that of a seaman whom he might convict after the event, but dared not before. Divination and action became a single force, nice as a razor edge, in this man for whom in a crisis an inch was wide as a mile.

Nearer and nearer, until the Viking was driven to cry aloud:

"He'll never do it!" The whole thing was madness! Madness!

And to settle matters, at this mad moment the sail fluttered loose, just as the great wave, piling itself up, piled them up, clutching all along the keel for the final smashing onslaught. The boat went languid; her head fell off; with a weak sidelong gesture she disappeared down the wave's back. Shaking its vacant crest, the wave threw itself on the pier-head and rushed in tumultuous fury for the piles. In its wake, the boat was seen coming with sail taut and bows trim, nose on the quay-wall. She got caught in the swing of the water across the harbour mouth. And for a second the crowd had their thrill.

The solid landward heave of the water could be countered only by the boat's headway. She had manœuvred herself into a position where she could make use of the full distance between pier-head and breakwater. Thus she lived for her perilous moment in full view of the beach, the crew sitting quietly, each in his place, strangely unconcerned. Then one young man aboard raised a hand in greeting, and before it had time to fall the boat had skinned the piles and was lost to view in the safety of the harbour.

"He's managed it!" said Kirsty breathlessly to Hugh.

Managed it! Managed it!! He turned from the woman, his soul a flame. "Oh, Father!" sang the flame to generations of Norsemen and Gael.

He saw the Viking mutter huskily, "God, that's uncanny!" his blue eyes the colour of fluting green sea-water.

O ecstasy of the morning! The whole crowd swayed for the harbour. Hugh ran, Tears were streaming down his face. Rid Jock, who was in front, turned and saw, and as he ran sideways his mouth opened to cry something. But looking on that face, drawn instantly white and implacable, he thought better of it, and the mouth weakly dribbled out ambiguous sound.

But he would yet pay for merely having seen. There was nothing more certain than that! Nothing under the red sky! Nothing!

O red ecstasy of the dawn!

PART TWO

I

One fine March morning some two months later, Hugh sat down to his porridge in silence. His face had the polished look that comes from a half-hearted washing and a damp towel. Sleep was dark in his eyelids, but the eyes themselves shone feverishly. His brain was harrassed and anxious. He was in a bad humour. His sister Grace, who didn't take porridge, moved about, the intimacy of her slow charming manner upon her. He paid no attention to her, didn't see her. When his mother went to the back-kitchen carrying the iron porridge pot, Grace leaned on the table, and asked:

"What's wrong with you?"

"Nothing," he muttered, slapping the porridge with his spoon. Into the hole he made in the middle of the plateful he poured some milk from his blue-ringed bowl. That would make the stuff cool. He was in a hurry.

"Oh, all right," she said in a certain tone, withdrawing her hands lingeringly from the table.

He flushed. His expression grew dour and stormy. He recklessly thrust a spoonful of porridge into his mouth. It was scalding hot. He opened his mouth wide and blew out and in rapidly, while he grabbed the bowl of cold milk and put it to his lips. Half-choking, he had to cough. A lot of the mouthful came spluttering back onto the plate.

102

Grace made a disgusted sound. "Oh, you pig!" she said and laughed. Though he had not looked directly at her, he had seen her face wrinkle up and turn away. She turned back, however, to finish her soft laugh. His right fist gripped the spoon convulsively, and for a moment it looked as if the porridge were going to be slapped violently. His mouth closed tight. With the back of his hand, he wiped away the water that the hot porridge had brought to his eyes. Then he started eating deliberately.

Now when he ate before Grace he never made noises. This morning, however, he made slight but firm sounds. They were not exaggerated, but neither on the other hand were they over-subdued. To do this hurt all his finer feelings, but nevertheless he did it like a man. His father made sounds. Grace would see that he also could make sounds.

Sounds are made blandly. That his sister wasn't quite sure whether he knew that he was making them or not was the most interesting thing—for it probably would irritate her. But she at once "let him see" by drawing in her breath in a slobbering way. "You little pig!" she added.

He caught a drop on his nether lip with his teeth and windily sucked it in. This also was exaggeration. Yet he would not go the whole way and smile and admit the game. Clearly she was waiting for that, was waiting for an excuse to be kind and friendly. And to complicate matters, he could not forget that she was going away the following morning—together with Alan and Tom Macrae and David o' Sandy's.

It was this near departure that had made last night such a wonderful one. Alan had taken him with him, and admitted him to the late hours, the talk, the fun of grown-ups. He had not got home till well after

103

eleven, Alan having parted with him at the gable-end
of Geordie Macleod's. "Well, I'll go in and say good-
bye to them here—and you can slip home before me,"
Alan had said. "All right," Hugh had answered at
once. And on the way home he had thought of how
Alan might bid goodbye to them. Of course, anybody
could hear Geordie saying: "Ay, ay, Alan, so you're
for the long road." And so on, half-jokingly, quietly.
And Alan would be in good form, and probably say
once more, "I'll be back to see you before you know
where you are—and maybe you won't hear my footsteps for the jingle in my pocket." Cheerfully, the
embarrassment nearly covered over. Then Cathie
would be at the door with him—just outside the door,
perhaps, to keep the draught from her father in the
kitchen. . . .

Hugh's imagination clouded over. A curious shy
warmth made him happy and alert. Secretive and
knowledgeable, the emotion was without any picture
of what might or might not happen. True, for one
sliding vanishing instant, there was Alan about to
embrace Cathie. . . . The image sank in the high wind
which Hugh whistled so pithily through his teeth.
He would have fought anyone on the spot who would
have dared to imagine their privacy. The idea of such
a fight in such a cause exhilarated him. For he knew
there were minds that could think anything. But not
the brave fine minds that were secretive and strong
and kind. He raced a few paces and laughed to himself. Alan had been so good to him that night, taking
hardly any notice of him, speaking naturally and
companionably to him (when he had to) as to one of
the others. But always between them the silent something more, the blood secret of brotherhood.

But it had been a different story when he went in.

104

His mother wanted to know where he had been. "What about your lessons?" Yet not in a stern voice. If she had been stern and called him a rascal it would have been all right. He could have smiled to himself upstairs and not cared. But her voice had been quiet, almost without any emotion at all, so that he had carried away with him the horrid impression of having betrayed her. It had taken the pleasure out of the evening. He could not think over it, smiling to himself at this and that, at how Soorag of the round shoulders and big hands swore, not because he was foul-mouthed, but out of good nature. He could not help thinking afterwards of a swear. Only he never allowed it to come into his mind more than vaguely. It was the sort of terrible destroying thing that one did not see, and yet that was just round the corner of the eye. But in bed last night he had seen several of the swears distinctly, looking at them askance, it is true, but still at them, before turning the eyes away with a queer little smile. And Grace's championship had not helped in his mother's presence. Besides, she had been with Charlie Chisholm earlier on. He had seen her. And Kirsty . . . where had Kirsty been? . . .

But he would get up an hour earlier in the morning and go over his lessons. He had done it before. That would be all right. No need to worry. Memorizing the poetry was the worst. *The Lady of the Lake*. The picture in the book of the tall beautiful lady with the long white robe, in the foolish little boat. . . . Like Grace. Grace . . . and Kirsty. . . . They came before him all at once with a startling vividness, their faces alive with emotion; Kirsty's clear and challenging, red-haired and blue-eyed, stinging like the sea; Grace's less direct, palely dark, full of a smiling

105

secret knowledge. The emotion became dreadful, unbearable, and mixed up with horrid words that he had overheard a man say . . . when suddenly, but quietly, between the two and a little farther back, so that their faces faded out, was his mother's face—white, and not angry—looking steadily . . . knowing all. . . .

Thus was his first sleep troubled, and he did not wake an hour earlier. And now here he was just in time for school, with not a word prepared. What was he to do? It was terrible! Suddenly laying down his spoon in the half-consumed porridge, he drank the rest of the milk, got up, dived for his bag of books under the corner of the bed, grabbed his cap.

"Hugh—"

"I'm off. I'm late."

"Here, Hugh—"

"I can't wait." His voice rose impatiently. The front door rattled. He was gone.

She half-started for the door, bit her lip, poised and hesitating. Her dark eyes were full of fire. Then she climbed slowly to her bedroom, took out the letter from her pocket, smoothed it over and over between her fingers as she stared through the window. She might find another way of delivering the letter. For they mustn't meet to-night—not to-night. Not this last night. . . .

There came a singular, almost childlike, innocence upon Grace's face. The skin was pale and smooth about eyes that were troubled with pain, that was none the less acute for being indefinite. It was the face of a young woman who had all the instincts of beauty and yet was profoundly chaste, and who had inevitably reached the point of being afraid; not afraid of anything or anyone so much as of being scorched, of being burned, in her body.

106

The virginal fear was fascinating, not only to others, but to herself. All the exquisite gifts she had she could play with so superbly, without effort. Her body moved, her eyebrows arched, her smile came, her neck bent, her eyes spoke (and dared and invited and stayed) with such smooth ease.

But she was afraid of fire. A hot breath on her neck made her heart jump, her body start away. She was getting afraid of Charlie.

She had never really intended to take him from Kirsty. The game, the clandestine meetings, had never been arranged by her. Yet she knew in her heart that they had been tacitly accepted, that she loved their gaiety, their dangerous homage, their very secretiveness.

But she feared him. Like Hugh with his swear words, she never thought of it directly. And it was only because if she didn't put Charlie off this night that she would have to . . . might have to. . . . She moved restlessly—but still would not look. Pain was in her eyes. She hid from the fire by thinking of Kirsty. She owed something to Kirsty. To honest Kirsty, her own sister. She had behaved shamefully to Kirsty. Giving her presents, giving her—hope. Deceit and worse. Oh, bad! bad! She was becoming a bad woman.

But she knew so well that she wasn't a bad woman yet. And Charlie—he could be so gay, with his easy manners, and his daring laugh, and his almost shockingly intimate beginnings of nothings. . . . Then sitting beside her, his face would grow moody, his eyes veiled and tired, his voice faintly petulant and sarcastic; and all one had to do was to touch his face, to say in a certain voice, "Charlie" . . . until the desire became overwhelming and one did.

107

And his kisses had been such amusing hit-and-miss affairs—for a time.

Grace's body grew still; a feverish look came into her eyes as they stared unseeingly through the little window at Hugh going down the open land with a book in his hand.

He was trying feverishly to memorise:

> *And ne'er did Grecian chisel trace*
> *A Nymph, A Naiad, or a Grace*
> *Of finer form, or lovelier face!*
> *What though the sun, with ardent frown,*
> *Had slightly tinged her cheek with brown,—*
> *The sportive toil, which, short and light,*
> *Had dyed her glowing hue so bright,*
> *Served too in hastier swell to show*
> *Short glimpses of a breast of snow.*

He found that he had to take the first three lines together, and then, after that, two by two. He spoke the lines aloud to himself, saying them over and over rapidly. But they were difficult lines to remember. Very difficult—as things always are when you are in a hurry and anxious and time is short.

They had also to be parsed and analysed, but he was never frightened of that. *Ne'er did Grecian chisel trace a Nymph of finer form* or *ne'er did Grecian chisel trace a Naiad of finer form* or *ne'er did Grecian chisel trace a Grace of finer form* or—all over again with *of lovelier face. Chisel*, subject; *did trace*, predicate; *Nymph*, object; *of finer form*, enlargement of object; and the same with *Naiad* and *Grace*. That was clear. He rattled off the three lines once more without looking at the book.

But the next six lines were decidedly puzzling. *What though* as a part of speech was bad enough, but what did *sportive toil* mean? What did it MEAN? *The sportive toil short which had dyed her glowing hue so bright* and *the sportive toil light which had dyed her glowing hue so bright*—was that it? and that *this sportive toil served to show short glimpses of a breast of snow?* But, first, what was the *sportive toil* itself? Was it the result of the sun's ardent frown or work or toil?

Dash it! If only he had had more time to it! He began rattling off the lines in couples again. The last two were very easy. *Short glimpses of a breast of snow* was like suddenly coming on a curved snow wreath. You couldn't forget it. It stood out—even if *breast of snow* made one feel a bit shy. It meant the woman's breast that you could sort of see down her blouse. But anything like that always raised an uncomfortable feeling. It was not so bad when you had your lesson at your tongue-tip. No one would then know what you were thinking to yourself. But when you didn't know your lesson and were inclined to be flustered, then there was always that extra discomfort lurking about. You might make a mess of your analysis and then be called upon to parse THAT . . . at which moment Bill Keith would probably nudge you. *Breast,* a common noun, neuter gender . . . it must be neuter, of course. What? Of course! . . . His head was getting dizzy. But he had the hang of it. And the master, if he was in good form, might give the usual two lines to each. Starting with the girls . . . he would be landed with the two lines . . . beginning:

The sporting toil. . . .

That *sportive toil* would get him, sure as fate! His sensitive face grew worried. But he was wise enough now to know that his mind was too mixed-up to work it out. If only—

"Whoop!"

109

Two feet landed beside him *plonk!* from the back of a dyke, and a voice declaimed:

> *Served too in hastier swell to show*
> *Short glimpses of a breast of snow.*

Bill Keith, of course, with right hand upthrust and right toe, like a stiff grotesque. As a pursuer of Redskins, Bill, given the slightest suggestion of cover, always appeared with a whoop. Slightly thicker than Hugh, if not quite so tall, he was much more self-confident. His fair hair came down over his brows. His quick look had something at once sly and of the woods in it. Hugh regarded his smiling, uncaring face.

"Bill, did you do your lessons?"

Bill's eyes opened, their light blue knowingly measuring the extent of Hugh's dark discomfort. Then he laughed enigmatically, showing two big front teeth, "Oh, not much!" and kicked a stone.

"What's *sportive toil*?"

Bill paused.

"*Sportive toil? Sportive toil?* Why, it's just *sportive toil*—what else?"

"What do you mean?"

"Ho! ho! You don't know what *sportive* means?"

"I do."

"Do you mean you don't know what *toil* is?"

"Of course I do."

Bill's body ceased.

"Well, what's wrong with you?"

"I mean, what does it mean in poetry? How does it come in?"

They regarded each other.

"Come in!" breathed the mocking Bill, then laughed out loud and completed his balancing feat.

Hugh remained quite solemn, thinking with close

110

surprise: "So long as I can give the meaning of the words, why bother about the meaning in the poetry?"

He knew that this was a wangle. He knew also that Bill had never begun to see the ignorance of it. This was a curious revelation. He stuffed his poetry book in his bag, feeling a lot better.

"Come on!" shouted Bill, "or we'll be late," and he broke into a trot. By breaking into a trot he made Hugh follow him. To be a leader gave Bill a deep secret pleasure. Hugh called to him. Bill neighed over his shoulder and increased his speed.

II

For a mile from Hugh's home the path sloped gradually to the river, twisting round knolls, edging ploughed fields, running by greystone dykes, and skirting a birch wood. Croft houses were set here and there upon this broken upland, which some few hundred yards behind Hugh's house passed into heather and bleak moorland. From any cottage upon it, the sea could be seen.

Beyond the river the land rose again, at first abruptly, but then very slowly until it touched the skyline another mile away. There, too, were crofts.

The land was thus the usual cultivated coastal strip divided by its small river. As one followed up the river, houses disappeared and a wooded glen or strath became sharply defined, narrowing as it penetrated the moorland, and ultimately giving up its trees and its beauty to an austere barren hinterland.

At the place where the trees die and the glen is

111

smoothed out, there is a curious silence, as of things listening. Adventurous boys know this magic, and rise up from the last wooded slope to stare.

To reach school, Hugh had to cross the river. The school was a rectangular stone building at the tail-end of a little hamlet on the rise beyond.

From Grace's bedroom window the clustering scholars looked like bees about a hive; tiny black figures flying in and out the school gate, circling upon the roadway in front, and, in ones and twos, winging straight in on converging paths.

It was a clear spring morning with no trace of damp in the fine air. Here and there teams were ploughing slowly, each with its cloud of white gulls. A lamb was said to have appeared at the Home Farm, whose out-fields lay between Grace and the sea. From her gable window she could not see the farm house with its sheltering trees and long steading. But to her right, far up the glen where the skyline on the other side of the river dipped down to the moor, she could see the roof-tops of Barrostad House.

Out of a profound thoughtfulness she suddenly jumped to her feet, her face taking on an extra-ordinary wrinkled intensity, as if her body were being snared. She pushed out her arms, turned her head away, breathing heavily, and struggled free. Then half-dazed, she backed a pace or two, hating and fascinated.

Yet she had seen nothing clearly. The revulsion had been quite spasmodic and involuntary. It left her spent, with a hectic red in her pale cheeks. Slowly her dark eyes glowed with a strange half-smiling fire. Lingeringly. She made a tiny mouth at herself. Her eyes laughed, in a slanting reflective way. She became quite herself, acting a little before an unimagined audience. Her eyebrows arched. Suddenly she dropped to her knees before her trunk, her eyelids lowering. She hid her amusement behind the loud thought that she'd better get on with her packing, or her father and Alan would be home before she knew where she was.

They were just then at the dividing of the fish on a patch of green grass back from the harbour wall. The sea sparkled beyond the breakwater in the bright morning, Near at hand wheels of light soupled over the moving waters. Men strode leisurely. Up at the Seabrae cottages women went about their business, and occasionally a high voice could be heard calling to an adventurous child. . . "Ee-an!"—a double-winged "lost" cry, that made one man stop and scratch his beard as though he saw the little devil hiding behind a barrel.

Alan's father was driven to one of his quiet but searching jokes. The haddock for the market had been all boxed, and the remaining fish—whiting, codling, a coal fish, a great skate, three ling, and a small ugly dogfish (shoved into the basket as a joke)—were being divided by Sandy Sutherland into five lots.

In their long leather seaboots the men swayed about, smoking their pipes, wiping their hands with plucked grass, and talking lazily. The slow rhythm of the sea with its swaying lights swayed through them. It was a fruitful morning; a morning of blessing. Humour dwelt in small quirks about their faces. Their eyes were alive and ready to be puckish.

Straightening himself, Sandy Sutherland dug his knuckles into the small of his back:

"Well, boys, that's the best I can do for you."

It was admitted he had not done badly. Every eye slanted on the dogfish.

113

"Turn your back, skipper," said Magnus Sinclair all of a sudden. It was hardly his place to say that.

But Alan's father nodded in a perfectly natural way, and faced the sea.

Magnus gave a wink to the others, the strings of his neck tautening as his head jerked.

"Whose is that?"—and he pointed to a lot.

"Sandy's," replied MacBeth quietly.

"And that?"

"Willie Mackay's."

"And that?"

"Alick's."

There were now two lots left; in one was a fine cod: in the other the dogfish. Usually the skipper named everyone's lot but his own, which was thus the last. Magnus pointed to the lot containing the cod.

"And that?"

"Mine," said MacBeth, leaving the last lot with the dogfish to Magnus. As he turned round innocently, everyone laughed.

"Dammit," said Magnus, "you saw me!"

MacBeth smiled then.

"I did," he admitted, "but not with my eyes."

This verbal turn to the joke capped it. Magnus blustered. He swore. He kicked the dogfish over the green. Each attended to his lot with rich humour. Sandy winked to Alan. The morning was fulfilled.

"He'll make a good feed for the gulls anyway," blustered Magnus, trying to get out of it.

"Oh, grand," said Alick, "grand!" He was a stocky dark man with a squeaky voice in an innocent expression.

Everybody chuckled again. Gulls wheeled overhead, their anxiety sometimes getting the better of them and breaking into a hard rapid curlew-call.

114

"Never mind," said Willie Mackay consolingly, "listen to the gulls blessing you already!"

"That's more than they'll do you!" But Magnus could never contrive to say the neat thing.

Willie Mackay was the young man of the crew. His father, a bearded, straight-backed giant of great strength, had died in the autumn from the kick of a cow.

The smaller fish were put in the heel of the skoo and the big fish on a string.

"All the same," said Magnus, when they had given each other's skoo a heave to the shoulders and were preparing to set out, "I'll have my own back on you for that, skipper."

"I'm afraid," said the skipper, "you'll have to get up a bit earlier in the morning."

Now Magnus was always first at the boat and never failed to "take a rise" out of those who came last. But this morning he had happened to have been last himself and had "heard about it" in all sorts of ways, open and veiled.

"Go' bless me, but your father has the words on him to-day!" said Sandy to Alan, who was strapping his father's skoo to his back. Alan had not been to sea.

Before turning away, each man lingered a moment, saying, "We'll see you before you go, Alan, boy,"

Magnus, red but cheerful, called, "Be sure to look down and say good-bye." And they all knew he meant it sincerely.

"Ay, ay!" answered Alan.

His father walked beside him carrying the string of fish. Alan always felt a trifle shy when walking with his father, and as a rule little was said. To-day, however, he was excited. This was the last morning in the whole of time that ever he would walk home with a skoo on his back! The old familiar places had

115

a curious still look. He would remember them like this for ever. To be doing a thing for the last time! Amusing. His mouth twisted.

"You fairly had Magnus to-day!"

"Oh, well," said his father quietly.

Alan gave him a glance, then happening to look up saw a white apron being waved beyond the Home Farm fields.

"Kirsty is giving us a salute," he said.

"It looks like it," agreed his father.

Alan took off his cap and waved it round his head. Kirsty saw the action and her heart jumped with pleasure. "It's father and Alan," she said aloud to herself. Her eyes glowed with delight and colour flooded her cheeks. She gave a final whole-hearted wave and made back at a run for the dairy, feeling so intensely happy that she also felt sad.

Elsie turning towards her after a moment, saw tears in her eyes.

"What's wrong, Kirsty?"

"I don't know," said Kirsty. "I just can't help it."

All at once she sat down on a milking stool and bent her red head and wept.

"What is it, Kirsty?" Elsie came beside her. She was a slim fair girl with a child's face and the quiet eyes of a woman. She put her hand under Kirsty's arm. "Don't cry like that, Kirsty." She smoothed her hair. "Don't cry like that, Kirsty dear." Her own eyes grew damp. "Is it Alan—going away?"

"Y-yes," said Kirsty. "Yes. He's going away in the morning."

"I know. I know. But still—"She caught her trembling lip.

After a time Kirsty quietened.

"I know—it's foolish of me. But—" she wiped her

116

eyes with the end of her apron. She searched for her handkerchief. "You see, he's—he's going away to Australia." She blew her nose. "It's to Australia." She drew breath in little spasmodic gulps. "And there he was walking up the road just now." At this, tears threatened again. It was a strange sight to see him walking up the road just now from the harbour with his father's skoo on his back. It was—it was—queer.

"I know," said Elsie.

"Oh, Elsie, you know what it means? His father and his mother can never hope to see him again."

"Surely they can."

Kirsty shook her head with a sad smile.

"It is likely none of us will ever see him again. My mother's brother—who has paid his passage—he never came back; and now never will come back. Alan also will work out there, taking years and years to gather money to start a place of his own. Then he will settle down and marry. He will die out there, and this old dun land will know him no more. It's sad." Her lips pressed tight. She smiled, staring out through the open door that tears blurred.

But Elsie had gone quickly away and was busy.

Kirsty's head turned slowly, looking after her.

Elsie's bent shoulders moved in a queer way.

Kirsty's eyes grew round and wondering. She got up and went towards Elsie.

"What is it, Elsie?" she asked gently.

"Nothing," answered Elsie abruptly.

"Elsie, what's the matter?"

"Nothing. It was you—made me cry." Her voice was impatient and annoyed—and broken.

"Elsie—"

"Leave me alone!"

"Elsie dear—"

117

"Can't you—leave me alone?"

"Elsie—"

"No!" Elsie walked away.

A deep tenderness, lit with revelation, came upon Kirsty's face. Elsie—secretly in love with Alan . . . who would have thought? This quiet girl, with something so fine and true hidden in her heart that in reflective moments the wonder of it made you feel tender and generous. The sight of the slim figure overwhelmed Kirsty. She stole up behind her and put her arm round her shoulders.

Elsie struggled ineffectually, then she broke down, and Kirsty took her against her breast.

Out of her delicacy, Kirsty made no mention of Alan. And thus Elsie's secret passed over to her without a word.

As the father and son went on their way, Alan, for something to say, thought aloud:

"I suppose Kirsty will be at the churning to-day."

"Is it the day for it?" asked his father.

"Yes," replied Alan. But there was nothingmore in that for one's mind.

Lifting his head he saw their home, a blue-slated, stone-built house, with two windows looking from the roof to the sea. A thatched byre was just beyond it.

As they drew near the house, they could see Grace with one foot out on the doorstep looking for them. She waved her hand.

III

Alan did not take off his cap and swing it merrily round his head, as he had done a little while before to

Kirsty; rather he saluted gaily, with a curious pleased half-shy expression.

"There's Grace."

"Yes," said his father.

About his own home his father was the quiet head of a house. There wasn't the snap and verve shown now and then amongst other men. Except that one could see it glisten for a moment when he was provoked. But normally he was mild. And on Sundays this mildness became patriarchal, without, however, losing its humanness.

"Hallo!" called Grace, like a little boy, her body swaying.

"Hallo yourself!" returned Alan.

"Are you tired, Father?"

Alan felt himself grow warm with pleasure at the nearness of Grace.

They were now at the back door, which suddenly opened upon their mother.

"So you've got back?" Their mother's voice was sensible and welcoming, but her body immediately bustled actively.

"Put them in that tub," she said to her husband; who did so and thereupon released Alan from the skoo. Then she added:

"There's the hot water to wash yourselves. Your breakfast is ready, for Grace watched for you coming."

"I knew she would be busy," Alan agreed.

Grace laughed provokingly.

When the men were washed and seated at table, the mother dished them up boiled cod, with some rashers of bacon and a few drops of gravy from the frying-pan. They ate with slow rich relish, and when they looked up their faces shone.

"I like the bit of bacon with the cod, Mother."

119

"I knew that," said his mother.

"Have you plenty bacon, boy?" asked his father. "Take this: I have too much."

"No, I won't." Alan shoved his father's arm back. Grace winked to Alan and turned away.

"Oh, I say, tell me: was Hugh in time for school to-day?" Alan asked suddenly. Grace made him feel self-conscious.

"Only just," replied Grace.

"He didn't finish his porridge, the rascal," said his mother.

"He was in a bad temper," said Grace. "I wouldn't have believed it."

Alan nodded. "I know."

"Why?"

"Because he hadn't got up one word of his lessons. He'll catch it!"

"Will he?" said Grace with quick sympathy. "How he'll hate being shown up before the class!"

"Won't he just!" chuckled Alan. "I should have wakened him when I got up—only it was too early."

"What a shame!"

"It will be a lesson to him," said his mother.

"He'll be as good as any of the rest there if he never opens a book," said his father. The mother tried not to look pleased.

"Quite right," agreed Alan.

"Does that mean he'll get off with it?" asked Grace.

"No," said Alan. "It doesn't."

Hugh, however, was getting off with it pretty well.

In the reading lesson he scored a cunning triumph. It occurred during the "meanings".

"To mitigate?" asked the master.

Molly Macrae, right at Hugh's back, could not answer.

The master waited inexorably.

"To mitigate?"

"Please, sir, I—I forget."

"You forget! Ho-ho, you *forget*!"

"Yes, sir." Her voice shook.

The master was a strongly-built man of variable temper. Some days he cracked jokes with them. Other days, with blood threads in his eyeballs, the slightest trace of ignorance or stupidity made him intolerant and brutal. He would shout and thrash. This was one of his fairly bad days.

His eyes jumped from Molly Macrae to the girl beside her, Sarah Sinclair.

"You?"

Sarah was silent.

"To mitigate?"

"Please, sir—I forget."

"You forget, too, do you?"

"Y-yes, sir."

"You mean you didn't learn it?" His voice rose. "You mean you have come unprepared?"

"Please, sir—I—did learn it."

"How could you have learned it if you don't know it?" he thundered. Did the girl think he was a fool?

The class grew quiet and smooth. Ignorance and fear made their shoulders sleek. Not a muscle moved, not an eye turned.

The master perceived that this word was going to stump the lot of them. His nostrils worked. It was seldom that he stumped the lot of them.

"You?" he shot at Nancy Grant.

"Please, sir, I forget."

"You?"

But all the girls "forgot."

121

"You?" swinging to Rid Jock, the outermost in the front row of boys.

"Please, sir, I don't know."

"Honesty at last!" Then, louder than ever, "Why don't you know?"

"Please, sir, I—I forget."

"You fool!"

The only other variation was introduced by Bill Keith.

"Please, sir, I can't remember."

This stopped the master. He glared at Bill. "You can't remember," he said, almost under his breath.

He swung upon Hugh, the last, so that the matter be finished and adequate punishment meted out to the class as a body.

"To mitigate?"

"To modify," answered Hugh.

The master slowly straightened himself. He looked around his pupils. "This boy, the youngest of the lot of you, can put you to shame . . . if you *can* be put to shame." He eased his collar. Then he opened the book again. "'To mitigate: to modify, to—'" He stopped before adding "change", attracted by a surreptitious movement that Jock had made to scratch himself.

"You. To modify?"

Jock was silent.

"To modify?"

"Please, sir, I forget."

The master regarded him brutally. Bill Keith couldn't remember. The master swung to Molly Macrae.

"To modify?"

"To change," answered Molly at once.

Hugh' drew in a silent quivering breath. Having forgotten what followed "to modify", he had not known what "to modify" meant!

The arithmetic was child's play after that. The three questions that the master wrote on the blackboard were polished off by Hugh in no time. He "proved" two of them, and went over the third twice. Then leaning his head on his left hand, he drew forth *The Lady of the Lake*, spread it open, and appearing to be figuring on it with the blunt end of his pencil, memorized as hard as he could. He knew that no one would get off with two lines to-day. The master, down the room on his left, was examining a class in grammar.

Presently Hugh felt the gentle tap of a shoe on the end of his spine. The printed words tremored and ran before him. A strange excitement came swirling through his breast. He commanded his disordened breathing and swallowed. Then sticking the end of the pencil against his teeth, he raised his head thoughtfully and stared at the blackboard. No one was looking. His eyes fell to his paper, and the fingers of his right hand, from absently tapping the desk, slid down his right side slowly, thoughtlessly, till they touched the shoe, till they curled round the heel of the shoe, and held it.

His brain swam. A tremulous weakening beset his body. A delicious perilous warmth flowed about his heart. Yet all the time his senses were exquisitely alert to the sounds in the room, to invisible eyes and movements.

The toe tapped him twice.

He crushed the heel spasmodically.

The toe tapped the end of his spine a trifle impatiently.

Slowly he released the small foot and brought his hand up.

The toe became insistent.

Pretending that his pencil had dropped, he half-turned and stooped. In the process he glimpsed Molly Macrae's face. Within that momentary glimpse her eyes were so eloquent that they not only told him what they wanted, but also contrived to convey a personal message.

Straightening himself, he slowly pushed out to his right the paper on which he had "worked" the three questions, so that Molly Macrae, who was splendid at poetry but no use at the mathematical sciences, might see for herself how they were answered.

Yet for all her brown eyes and their pleading expression, Hugh felt the least little bit let down. He had made a fool of himself. Here he had been holding her foot—as though each had been feeling in the same way. Hanging on to her foot like an idiot—while all the time she had merely been wanting to crib his sums!

Yet no one knew that, and therefore it did not matter so much. No one but Molly. And there had been anxiety in her eyes and pleading and a strange melting light. He merely ought to have been quick enough himself to have understood that it was the sums she was wanting. Catch him doing it again! She might tap away. He would merely shove over his exercise book.

Besides, the risk he ran was appalling. Supposing Bill, who sat on his left, saw the—the thing! Hugh's skin crept. Supposing Rid Jock saw him at it! Hugh's skin curdled. Supposing Jock accused him in the playground? Ah, he would kill Jock then. He would throttle him to within an inch of his life until he crushed him stone dead.

But—*supposing the master saw him!*

O God of our fathers!

Hugh cowered, though at the same time it wasn't a swear. It was Soorag who said, "O God of our

124

fathers!" when something astonished him uncommonly. If you said it without being funny or laughing, and with your mind feeling in the queer way it felt when you said "rock of ages" on Sunday . . . like a great cleft rock in a glen . . . and if your mind went on to make it up like a hymn and to hum it, then God would never notice but that you had meant to hum it from the beginning.

With this slant of quite wordless vision, Hugh shut out his emotion, drowning the sound of it by hissing in and out through his teeth the first few bars of "Rock of Ages cleft for me".

The tune calmed him; the hissing through his teeth made his gums cold, his mind keen.

> *And ne'er did Grecian chisel trace*
> *A Nymph, a Naiad, or a Grace—*

He said the words over slowly, chiselling each on his memory. He felt ruthless towards the lines, felt a fierce mastery over them.

> *The sportive toil, which, short and light,*
> *Had dyed her glowing hue so bright,*
> *Served too in hastier swell to show*
> *Short glimpses of a breast of snow.*

Gently as a finger-tip the tap landed.

The lines tremored. Three seconds passed. His right hand began sliding of its own accord. He should stop it . . . only this time there was no doubt . . . the foot was wanting nothing . . . the hand kept sliding . . . he shouldn't! . . . sliding right down. . . .

The foot was gone!

A hot prickling went over his body. The fool that he was!

Only once before had he held her foot. For the

whole past week the memory of it had bothered him at the oddest moments, so that he had had to run away from it, humming on the wind.

He drew back his exercise book. It was bitterly humiliating to know that, of course, the toe merely signified that the copying was over. He would never hold a girl's foot again. Never! No matter though—

Tap!

Oh, tap away! tap away! *The sportive toil that* tum-ti-tum—he had lost the lines again. This was maddening. He concentrated on the print. He went over the lines at a gallop, completely vaulting some of the words. This was no use. Down the room, the master bellowed. Ah, that would make her draw back her toe! It wasn't there now; that was certain!

(Wasn't it?)

Now take *sportive toil* to see exactly. . . . (Sitting back an inch he thought he felt a slight pressure—or was it merely the pull of trousers on seat?)

The real meaning of *sportive toil* evaded him more than ever. It became a thing of toils like the coils of a rope, in which he was caught, or the toils of a serpent. Entwined and exasperated and excited. His hand slid down his right side, tapped the seat a moment, then— went into his pocket. With a noble indifference he brought his hand back to the desk. But this time the pencil slipped through his defeated fingers and rattled on the floor. After waiting a moment, he stooped to the floor and on coming up caught Molly's expression. There was a look in her eyes that increased the blood flow to his face. She was laughing at him. She was smiling to him. . . . He did not know which. Except that there was *something*. . . .

Oh, what a fool he was! He would never do the like again! Never! Holding her foot! He squirmed. But he would show her how it made no difference to him. As if it did! As if it did!!

The master returned.

Molly and Hugh had all three sums correct. After half an hour's general heart-burning, the master threw a glance at the clock. Only quarter of an hour left. This was what came of dealing with dunces. He picked up *The Lady*.

"You," to Molly Macrae.

From the first word to the last Molly never hesitated. She had brown eyes; her skin was clear; her hair was dusky without being black. But her voice when she spoke poetry had the curious intimate quality that Kirsty's had when Kirsty was telling a story to move the heart. Into the rather high-pitched sing-song delivery she imported something pure and memoried. She did not dramatize the lines, she certainly did not "speak" them, and no word was stressed.

The master regarded her a moment. The smoothness of her performance annoyed him. For the better part of a year he had been drumming into them the need for "speaking" poetry. Their high-pitched iambic gallop he had mimicked to everything but death.

Between the red threads in his eyeballs came an arid light suggesting a smile. His clean-shaven face was full, and all morning had been reddish. His breath was quite audible in his nostrils. But it was an intolerant rather than an ironic face, a clever rather than a cruel one. He might thrash harshly, but could not torture subtly. In his worst moods the boys were mortally afraid of him, but it did not occur to them to hate him. In the end he gave Molly up and looked at Sarah.

127

Sarah could not remember a word. She remained absolutely dumb and obviously in great distress. The master continued to look at her.

"Well?" he asked.

"Please, sir, I—"

"Well?"

"I—I can't remember how it starts." Her voice was a burst on the verge of tears.

He lifted the book. *"And ne'er did Grecian—"*

Sarah took the words from his mouth and at breakneck speed, with but one gulp midway for breath, rushed hectically to make up time. An astounding performance, word perfect.

Hugh lifted an eyelid at the clock, while the master was recovering. With any luck at all, the lesson might not reach him. Usually he was the first after the girls, but to-day he felt sure that the master would continue to take things the wrong way round.

But the master jumped from Sarah to Rid Jock, who was so taken aback that he started:

> *What though the sun with ardent frown*
> *A Nymph, a N-nahyad, or a Grace*
> *Of lovelier form and finer face*
> *The sportive toil which—which—*

He hesitated, then took the final desperate plunge:

> *Which*, something and, *dyed her glowing breast*
> *of snow.*

"*Something and,*" roared the master. He leapt for the three-fingered strap. "*Something and!* I'll give you *something and!* Stand up!"

Jock stood up and held his hand out six inches. The master caught the fingers and jerked the arm to its full length. Hugh, trying silently to remember the

128

lines, knew he was lost. A reckless desire came over him to pull out the book a few inches from its ledge under the desk and have a look. But Jock saved him from such desperation by drawing back his hand at the instant it ought to have met the strap. The hard leather fingers bit into the master's knee.

Jock, aware of his own superb folly, began to make sounds like a gull with a bone in its throat. But this primitive form of supplication merely infuriated the gods. Jock goaded himself to take three straight. Three was the usual. Before the fourth—he drew back. His whine gathered body. Horrid anticipation played on the bone. Four, five, six. A boy could no more. He drew back—again. The master held his hand at the wrist. Seven, eight, nine.

Doubled up in his seat, Jock nursed his hand.

"That will teach you *something and*," roared the master, working his neck in his collar and giving a hunch to his shoulders to set his jacket straight.

Bill got the length of *sportive toil*—and then, by a curious nemesis, stuck.

"Yes?" waited the master. The clock struck one. No foot moved the whole length of the room.

"*The sportive toil*—" fumbled Bill.

"I'll show you the meaning of *sportive toil*," said the master. "Stand up!"

Bill took his three, eyes opening before each stroke and blinking after it.

"The lesson will be continued in the afternoon."

School was dismissed.

Outside the boys crushed in their rush for the gate. Released animal spirits soared to reckless heights. In the midst of his exuberance Hugh saw Molly's face coming up behind. Quite wantonly he charged into a boy.

"Stop it!" yelled the boy. It was Rid Jock.

Hugh knocked off his cap, laughing grotesquely. He was intensely excited.

Jock being in an ugly mood retrieved his cap with a challenge; indeed he offered to knock Hugh's bloody teeth down his gullet.

Hugh mockingly made sounds like a gull with a bone in its throat.

"Come on!" roared Jock infuriated.

Molly was close behind. Her presence could be felt.

Several boys stopped, scenting a fight.

Hugh's mortal honour was at stake. He was in magnificent fighting trim. But if he turned he must meet her face to face. He wavered, broke, and took to his heels, trying to laugh derisively.

IV

That evening Hugh was late getting home from school. Alan was waiting for him near the birch wood.

"Where were you?"

"I was kept in."

"Because you didn't know your lessons?"

"Yes."

Alan laughed in the friendliest way.

"I knew that. Did you get whacked?"

"No. He asked me whether I'd like to be thrashed or kept in for half an hour."

"Oh." Alan looked at him closely.

"I asked to be thrashed," said Hugh.

Alan laughed again. "So he kept you in instead? That was a dirty one!"

Hugh understood exactly what had passed in Alan's mind. He suddenly felt happy.

"Oh, he was in an awful rage to-day. Rid Jock fairly got it! Nine in the morning—and three in the afternoon."

"No!"

"Yes. I had forgotten something in the geography, so he asked me what I'd have. So I said the thrashing. Jock didn't know either, so then he asked him what he would have. And Jock said: 'Please, sir, the thrashing.' And he gave it to him!"

"Ho! ho! Jock thought he would be kept in also!"

"Likely."

"Did Jock cry?"

"Yes. But he got a proper dose in the morning." Hugh imitated Jock's hand popping in and out, and described how the master got it on the knee.

The whole thing was very funny now. The master was a terrible fellow! Oh, great! If you could stand up to him, there was nothing much wrong with you! Only sometimes he gave you a "dirty one". But that was because he was cute and could see your game. Afterwards you laughed and perhaps swaggered. But not at the time. At the time you were in terror. The old people discussed the master also. Some boys "told" at home. The master occasionally thrashed the big girls, too—but only when he was beside himself. The old people would shake their heads. There was no doubt the master went sometimes "clean beyond the bounds". It hardly did, as you might say. No, it was just going beyond what was natural. But there was always this at the end: he was a clever man. Oh, he was clever, there was no doubt of that. And he could speak seven languages. Seven. Ay, ay. The old men nodded their heads. Learning was a great thing.

131

They looked far beyond one another. A great thing, learning. A far and wonderful thing. There was no denying that. It was a strange thing, too. Its strangeness excited them a little, and its wonder. Love of learning was in their marrow. Their eyes for a moment became fixed and dreamy. They spat contemplatively.

"But I didn't mind afterwards," said Hugh, "because in the half hour the master paid no attention to us, and instead of learning the geography, I learned my poetry for to-morrow."

"It's just as well," nodded Alan. He looked cautiously around. All along Hugh had known there was something in the wind.

"Why?"

"Because—ah, well, we were thinking of going somewhere to-night."

"Where?" Hugh became excited at the off-hand secretive manner.

"Don't say a word on your life. Tom Macrae and Davie and myself thought of having a night on the river. It's the last night."

Hugh thrilled. Alan's eyes glanced. Hugh watched Alan, who suddenly said, "Would you like to come?"

"Oh, yes!"

"All right." Alan nodded as if he didn't see his young brother's excitement. "There may be some difficulty with mother. But we won't tell her till nearly the time."

Alan kept talking as they walked homeward. His every word was romance. The way they had got the net, where it lay now, how the others were to bring it to Hector the Roadman's cottage, and the pools they would tackle.

Each pool had its own name. Strange evocative names, half of them Gaelic. They went back into

Hugh's earliest childhood. . . . One day when I am big I will go to these pools. When I have done that, I will be a man and know the boundaries of the world. . . . The only other far places that had an echo in his mind were places in the Bible. Canaan and Bethlehem and the River Jordan. One day long ago in school the master had told them a story about an old wifie who had said, "No, no, you needn't tell me that Jerusalem is on this earth!" The master had laughed, his eyes looking back over his shoulder as he had walked down the room. Hugh had smiled— but an odd uncertainty had kept him thinking about the wifie for days. If he had met her, he wouldn't have looked at her while she was looking at him. She would be wrinkled like a witch and would go in at a little door.

His brother talked in the friendliest way. The world was sweet to Hugh. It was splendid and light and bounding. He loved this brother, who was too kind to him. Often he had run after Alan and wouldn't go back, and Alan had hit him a clout on the head; a hard sore clout that had made him run home crying as hard as he could, half in spite. That was because he was a child and not grown up. . . . If they were caught? And in the dark? He would stick to Alan and run like a hare. Yon day last summer he had run a whole mile without stopping. . . .

"Can you see him?" asked Alan.

Hugh heard the song, but couldn't all at once spot the lark.

"You're blind, man!" scoffed Alan.

"I'm seeing him now."

The blue was high and frail, born of sun rather than frost, yet with something invigorating in its airy light that made the blood dance; clean and shivering-sweet, with the lark-song ascending; summer memories afloat in spring skies. The heart moved in a new birth; the body caught the foreshadowing ecstasy, eyes entranced. Then the song ceased, and close-winged as a hawk, the lark stooped. But not all the way. Its prey was not on earth, but in heaven; and reluctantly it gave up the heavenly chase, catching itself back every now and then on fluttering wings to ease a heart grown troublesome. Finally it swooped to earth, shaking, as it landed, the last bubbles of melody from its wings.

"Neat, uh?" suggested Alan.

"Wasn't it!"

For a moment there was a delicate, faintly self-conscious wonder between them, as they faced the grass in the field where the lark had disappeared.

"They'll be nesting there again," said Alan.

"Yes, but it's too early yet."

They leapt the stone dyke and found the spot.

"It's making! Look how the grasses are twisted round!"

Alan was doubtful. "Come away," he said; "they'll see us."

"Would that put them off it?"

As they walked away, talking, they instinctively looked about them.

Teams were still ploughing, each with its cloud of gulls. To each cloud of gulls, one or two rooks. Away on the other side, Totaig whistled his dogs, a shrill whistle produced by putting four fingers in his mouth at once. They saw him, his black collie, and the rushing white sheep—all so many agitated specks. This amused them. They knew Totaig. They smiled, saying, "Listen!" and picked up his raucous yells. Alan told Hugh that Totaig should never have to yell at all, and went through the hand and body pantomime of the men at the sheep-dog trials. Hugh himself was full of speech, too, and thought that Totaig was the greatest fool, so that some of the things you would be hearing about him would make you die laughing. But Alan also had heard things that were better than Hugh's, and he told them in a few words with a dry sparkle. The superior art of this made Hugh say "No?" in a wondering delighted way. Plucking a dry grass he would catch it between his teeth and with a sharp snick break it off short. Spitting out the bit in his mouth, he would pluck another one and do the same again. All the time they floated upon what was going to happen that night.

"There's the baiting, of course," said Alan, "— and the bait."

Hugh drew up short.

"The bait!"

"Of course," said Alan. "What did you think?"

"I thought—" He could not hide his dismay. "I thought Father wouldn't be going to the sea in the morning."

"Why?"

"Well. . . ."

"Nonsense! What difference does that make? The whole crew couldn't stay ashore because one or two happen to be going away."

"N-no," muttered Hugh, cutting quarter-inches from a grey grass with his thumb nail. His voice lifted earnest and pleading: "You'll wait for me? I'll run all the way to the ebb."

"Oh, I think so." Alan was doubtful. "Then there's the baiting. Uhm. We'll certainly have to get a move on."

"Well, I—I'll run." There was a catch in Hugh's voice. His anxiety glistened.

"It's hardly worth running now," said Alan, looking up at the house.

"But—I'll get the bag." And Hugh shot off.

"What are you running for?" asked Grace, who was by the gable-end and saw his face.

"Nothing!" he muttered, with an even greater petulance than when he had left her in the morning, and dashed in at the back door.

Grace, about to follow, decided to wait for Alan. For Hugh would stumble on their father sitting in the back-kitchen, more than half-way through with the baiting. Which was what happened.

"Go' bless me, boy!"

Hugh stood stock still.

"What is it?" continued his father, looking closely at the boy's face.

"Nothing," said Hugh, drawing breath. "Alan told me—you needed bait."

"And after taking the best part of two baitings from the ebb himself!"

Tricked!

"How did you do with your lessons to-day?"

"Fine."

"You didn't get a thrashing?"

"No."

His father was in his kindliest mood. Hugh, smiling awkwardly, twisted himself out of the door and closed it behind him. Then he walked slowly, with a cunning expression. Just as he reached the gable corner, two faces shot out at him, so that he was startled.

From open mouths came great guffaws. With their hands against their stomachs, Grace and Alan rolled drunkenly away.

"Oh, ha! ha! ha!" mocked Hugh.

They laughed louder than ever.

"You fairly got a sook!" cried Grace in the broadest tones.

Hugh denied that he had been taken in.

Alan became convulsed.

Grace made a bucolic mouth:

"Boy, Alan, did he no' get a fair sook?"

Alan waved a helpless arm.

Hugh's denial was sharp and hot.

Grace put the question to a local worthy, and replied for him with an "Oh, clean!" at the same time wiping her nose with thumb and forefinger, "Imphm! ay!" and spat.

But the way she spat was entirely feminine, and a small bead of saliva dropped on her breast. "Pf-f-f!" She made a face of comic disgust as she cleaned off the bead with a forefinger, which she wiped on the grass.

"You think you can spit!" said Hugh ironically.

"Man, I'll spit in your eye and chok' you!" quoted Grace.

Alan rocked afresh.

"I see nothing to laugh at in that," muttered Hugh, twisting a sarcastic mouth.

"No, because you had a sook," agreed Grace, her large dark eyes upon him, smiling in a taking-off way.

Both her brothers were excited by her. She played up to them perfectly. Everything was slightly exaggerated, with a curious air of unreal tension. Hugh strove to right his discomfort, but all he could think of was:

"You're very smart."

The ineptness of this was doubly amusing. Alan guffawed wide-mouthed.

"Watch your mouth will not swallow you," said Hugh, twisting round—and disappearing.

"Ho! ho! ho!" Alan laughed after him.

"Poor boy!" murmured Grace, making a face of sweet pity.

"Oh, never mind," smiled Alan.

"What happened to him at school to-day?"

Alan was glad of the chance of speaking at length. It was not often one had much to say to such a charming sister. Here was a funny story to relieve the embarrassment. In the middle of it, Grace tip-toed to the corner and disclosed Hugh.

"He was listening!" she mocked.

"I was not!" said Hugh hotly, flushing.

"Who would have believed it?" Alan shook his head.

"I tell you I was not!" cried Hugh. His voice rose dangerously. He suddenly turned and walked away, dropping the handful of peat dross that he had been stealing up to shower upon them.

Half an hour later Alan found him in the byre.

"What are you doing here?"

"Nothing." Hugh's face looked pale and cold in the half-dark. He drew the back of his hand slowly across his nose. But he did not look at Alan, who studied him a moment silently.

"Come on up. Tea is ready. Didn't you hear Grace calling?"

Hugh did not answer.

"Come on!" Alan turned away and Hugh followed.

"Where were you?" asked his mother as they went in. He often had this impression of *meeting* his mother's face.

"Nowhere."

"How could you be nowhere?" And Grace pouted amusingly.

"Sit in," said his father.

Thereupon they all delicately ignored him.

His mother was in good form this night. Her kindness lapped all round them. Her heart was overflowing with kindness. Her gestures were warmly inviting. She had a great tea for them. Liver and bacon and gravy. Plenty of butter, abernethy biscuits, scones, jam, a crusty loaf. "Be eating, now. Make a good tea, bairns."

"You've given me a great helping here, woman," said her husband, pausing.

"We'll see what's left," said his wife.

Grace and Alan exchanged glances. But Hugh did not smile. Their father looked from plate to plate. He stared at Hugh's, and a whimsical astonishment came into his eyes.

"Bless me, boy—will you manage all that?"

Hugh, colouring slightly, did not answer.

"What!" whispered his father, trying to see his downcast face.

"There's nothing there, Father," said Grace.

"I can hardly see it," agreed Alan.

"You leave him alone," said his mother.

"I cannot even see his plate," added Grace.

"Were any of them at you to-day, boy?" asked his father.

"No," said Hugh quietly.

Alan coughed. But Grace was silent, as her dark lashes lifted on Hugh's pale face with its clear-cut almost fragile features, capable of such sensitive restraint. He might be the son of. . . . Her mind drifted into rich societies, calling up scenes and speech and surroundings so very different from these.

Hugh suddenly lifting his eyes met hers, and she turned away with a slight confusion which she covered by an odd half-inviting half-amused smile.

139

There was an instinct in the boy that made her all in a moment queerly proud. She would give him a bigger present of money in the morning than she had meant to, and would kiss this half-angry dark intolerance until it shyly broke. . . .

She helped her mother in the gaiety of the feast. By an extraordinary intuition she made her father laugh. It was a rare thing for her father to laugh. Usually his eyes lit up, and you could see him looking at the point of a story with an inner glimmering, or with an air of wonder, "Are you telling me that?" or, moved by a fine delight, tilting his chair back and blowing smoke to the ceiling.

They drew near to one another. Hugh felt the kindness, and though he could not thaw all at once, yet his belly warmed him wonderfully and tiny spouts of pleasure flooded up in his mind, so that he had to put a careful restraint on his tongue.

Alan was in excellent form, with a slight swagger in his gutturals and an occasional hunch on his shoulders. He and Grace might easily have overdone it, moved by that very excitement which sprang out of an apprehension of the meaning of this last night.

For this was more than a normal tea; more even than the evidence of a mother's kindness. She broke oatcakes for them and cut bread. She filled their cups. She watched each one, and helped him to the elements on the table. She smiled. Her heart was full of love and broke itself amongst them. That which she loved she was about to lose. "You will have another cup of tea, Alan?" "I can't, Mother." "Just give me your cup." "Thut!-thut!" inhaled Hugh obscurely. Grace's voice snuggled. "Be quiet, bairns," said their mother. Alan passed over his cup with a large gesture, saying, "Little boys should not be heard." When

140

their mother's face turned to the glowing fire, the eyes were glowing bright. "It's a good drop of tea," said her husband. "Pass your cup," said his wife. The paraffin lamp shed down its soft light upon them. Their mother's body swayed in its chair, and her hands moved among the cups and poured the tea and offered to each one. Her brow was wide and calm, and her dark straight hair was combed from the middle to either side.

Near the end of the meal there fell upon them a sudden silence out of their mother's mind. She said:

"I wish Kirsty had been here, too."

At that the silence steepened. Alan put a crust into the last of his gravy and concentrated upon wiping in big circles. Hugh's eyes remained on his plate, an uncomfortable quickening in his brows. Grace pinched a small piece of bread over and over, her colour deepening in an odd smile.

"Well, well," said their father, as in gentle benediction.

Alan could not find a word. The crust was difficult to swallow, because not having been chewed enough it was dry.

As the meal finished, their mother forgot herself and sat staring blankly into the fire, as she often did when she was alone. She came to herself with a slight start and a smile.

"Are you sure you'll have nothing more, Alan?"

"No, Mother, thanks."

"Then—that's all."

It was the end of their last supper.

Grace got up all of a sudden.

"I'll run over to Ina Manson's," she announced. "I promised I'd say good-bye."

She did not look at her mother nor at any one. Her

141

voice was hurriedly cheerful. Because of what she was about to do, guilt was at her heart.

Her mother lifted her head. The face was still serene. It was a beautiful face. Alan and Hugh got up.

"Don't be late," said her mother. "Kirsty would like to see you."

"No, I won't be late. You can tell Kirsty to wait— if she likes."

"Why did I add 'if she likes'?" Grace thought, going towards the stairs without showing her face to them again.

The mother's look rested on Alan. He turned away towards the door. Hugh followed him.

V

An hour later, Alan and Hugh left their home under a half moon. It was a calm night with a touch of chill. Alan did not speak to Hugh, who now and then looked sideways at the uplifted face against the sky. The darkness of that face was like the discomfort in their minds.

For their mother had offered no objection to their going. They had somehow thought that father or mother would have objected strongly to Hugh's being included in such a dangerous expedition. The father had merely turned away, as if it were no affair of his. And all the mother had said was:

"Are you really going, Alan?"

It wasn't an appeal. Oh, it was nothing. It was only her face, which had looked at him for a moment with its white light. The tone had been quiet. He had

142

turned away saying that Tom Macrae and David o'
Sandy's were going too, and that it was all arranged.
His voice had somehow begun to mutter harshly and
trail off.

Spending his last night away from the old home,
leaving his father and mother alone, with folk dropping in to say good-bye—and him not there! It was
partly to avoid the embarrassment of leave-takings
that in a moment of exuberance they had arranged
the outing.

But Alan saw now exactly what it meant, and his
heart was heavy in him and tormented, and his mind
was dark. Hugh understood this. They walked all the
way to the birch wood in silence, their steps thudding
on the empty night.

"If I hadn't promised to meet the boys in Hector
the Roadman's, we might have hung about for another
hour or two," said Alan.

"Yes," said Hugh.

They went on as before.

"Dash it, I'm vexed about it!" Alan's voice was
thick.

Hugh said nothing. Alan's head seemed lifted
higher than ever against the night.

Suddenly he broke into a torrent of talk. What was
the good of hanging about the house? Nothing to do,
nothing to say. Old Alexina coming in to mourn over
his departure. What was the use of that? Damn the
thing. Honestly, it would make a fellow swear. So it
would. Honestly. His voice grew angry and harsh and
sarcastic, and suddenly ceased.

They went on again in silence until they approached
the county road, where they avoided two lots of
people by slipping over a bank.

Soon they were on the footpath that ran into the

glen. They went carefully, treading the grassy verge and keeping eyes and ears open. Where a side path went up on the right to Hector the Roadman's cottage, Alan paused.

"Look here," he whispered, "if there's any way of getting out of this, we'll go back home. What do you say?"

"Yes."

"You see—it's hardly right. I mean—"

"I know," helped Hugh. Suddenly he touched Alan on the arm.

They both listened.

"That will be Tom and Davie. Let us squat and give them a fright!" whispered Alan out of his tormented mood.

The moon was rising at their backs. They would see at once who it was when the footsteps came round the bend a score of yards away. They did. It was Grace and Charlie.

Alan's fingers closed on Hugh's arm, compressing it, forcing it down, till Hugh could have cried.

Grace and Charlie came on. They were a little bit apart, and Grace gave the unusual impression of walking hurriedly. Once her foot hit a stone and stumbled. A small sound came from her throat as she caught herself up quickly. In the moonlight her face, thrown up, looked strangely pale and excited. Yet the sound in her throat had not been a real laugh. It was the affected sound of one who would be at ease, who did not care. But it was not at ease, and it cared.

Charlie walked on evenly. There was a dull rhythm in his movement. He was like a man who could walk like this to the crack of doom. Nothing could defeat a mood of this sort. Silence has only to wait. Nature, grown over-sensitive, will break to bits on it. Every moment the sensitiveness increases, the silence grows more intolerable. Yet nothing can be said, for the cause is known, and hidden in it is the end—the end towards which they were walking. So that even a man's mood can become sombre in its frightening certainty, and his mouth smile secretly to himself and almost sadly. He had conquered when he had got her to come. All the talking had been done then. Light talk and persuasive laughter, but with the throat constricting in its excitement, and the voice dropping to a husky whisper. "Just a little walk—for the last night." What harm was in that? The spindrift from the dark wave. She made herself believe in its lightness. She clung to the spindrift. But she had to go quickly to leave the wave behind. No wonder she caught herself up with a jerk when she stumbled.

For her first reluctance to come had shown the fear at its heart. A certain fear. And now she had come.

Her two brothers, crouching to the earth, caught the trembling from the ground, so nervous her step, so taut her body; and as she passed there came upon their nostrils the delicate scent she used when she was dressed up.

It had a strange unlawful effect upon them, this scent. Books of martyrs and whores of Babylon. Its invitation was a betrayal. It was bodily and fatal. They feared and mistrusted it. There was no use in it, no grey truth, no firmness, no iron. It drifted past their nostrils, wanton and exquisite.

Grace's footsteps clicked on. Charlie's stride was steady. No word of talk came from them. They disappeared.

Alan rose slowly. He stared along the path where they had gone for a long time. At first his arm had swept Hugh back as if he were going to start after

145

them himself. But he had not taken a step, had not moved a foot.

Slowly he turned round and began to go up the little path towards Hector the Roadman's cottage. He never spoke to Hugh. His body moved with a reluctance which Hugh felt.

This reluctance had a disturbing effect on Hugh, who, like all boys of his age at the school, knew the meaning of sex. The ways of domestic animals, of cocks and hens, of a cow going a-bulling, of the per-ambulating entire, were all subject to boyish laughter, laughter the more secretive and rich for being taboo before grown-ups. For it was all mostly a matter of manner, and a boy could answer his mother by saying that he saw so-and-so, but he was taking his cow to the bull, without any self-consciousness so long as he said it frankly. It was secretiveness and lewd laughter that the grown-ups objected to in boys, not necessary mention of the natural. The boys knew this, and so won to a healthy balance between good taste and their own spirts of dark fun.

Accordingly Hugh could not normally brood over any conceivable relationship between Charlie and Grace. His mind out of sheer instinctive loyalty could not penetrate to the only way in which it understood such things, namely, in pictures. It was not so much frightened to penetrate as unable; it was not a question of sacrilege, but of healthy instinct.

So Alan's reluctance had a disturbing effect, brought darting tongues of doubt and tongues of shadow, contorted the simple and made unimaginable the night. Hugh's mind got beset by dark premoni-tions of disaster. Ribald things he had overheard pressed for entry. Fear entered into him, and the beginnings of a hot strangling shame.

146

Birch trees laced the narrow path, shutting out the moon. Alan's body in front could be felt rather than seen; indeed, its bulk seemed to increase before him, as though swollen by a brooding wrath.

They emerged upon a sloping pasture beneath a wide sky and a half moon. Beyond the pasture shone the solitary light of Hector's cottage.

Alan went on now more slowly than ever. Hugh could feel the travail of his indecision. Once he stopped for a minute and gazed towards the dark hollow of the glen, muttering a word or two. But when they came to a stone's throw from Hector's cottage, Alan pulled up decisively.

"Look here, will you bolt off home?"

"Yes," said Hugh at once.

"You can tell them that I—you can say—"

"Look!" whispered Hugh.

Two figures came out from a wall on their left.

Alan's clenched fist came up to his breast.

"They've seen us! Curse!" he hissed.

"We spotted you coming over the field," said Tom Macrae, as he and Davie came up.

His voice was low and laughingly confidential. "We've just slipped the net into the stable. Everything ready. What a night for it!"

Alan nodded. "Yes."

"So you're here, Hugh? Not frightened, are you?"

"No."

"Of course not! Breaking you in to the true ways of the tribe. Seen anyone in the glen coming up?"

"Not a soul," said Alan.

"Everything will be as right's the mail. What a night! Come on."

And through the silence and plash of the moonlight, they went over and into Hector the Roadman's cottage.

147

VI

Hector rose from the wooden armchair by the right of the low peat fire as the inner door opened and the boys came in. His face was wrinkled up, smiling in welcome. He was tall and thin, and didn't quite straighten himself. His voice could be gentle as a woman's, and beneath twinkling eyes would often probe about for a laugh. He was about sixty years of age and a great piper.

The lads greeted him with a shout. Clearly it was the happy place to come into. Alan's eyes glittered brilliantly.

In the middle of receiving them, Hector saw Hugh. His gaze widened; an odd astonishment made his voice quieter. "Hugh, is it yourself, boy?" He peered. "Well, well, God bless me, doesn't life ripen like the ear in the barley? Come over here beside me." And he placed a chair for him.

Smiling shyly, Hugh went and sat down. He had nothing to say for himself. But his brother made up for that. Full of reckless fun, Alan didn't keep still or silent for a moment. There was a flash of colour in his cheeks, an extra vivacity in his movements. He demanded the pipes.

But Hector couldn't get over Hugh.

"When he came in on the door there, sure as death I thought it was his brother Duncan—only Duncan was a year or two older . . . at the time."

Alan's body twisted on its chair. His mouth twisted and he winked at Davie. Yet he could not too brutally break in on Hector, whose mind was glimmering as if this was the beginning of a ceilidh.

And, indeed, in no time Hector was well away with the tragic story of the *Fateful* and of *The Scots Rose.* It was his personal epic.

" . . . Old Hendrison offered to stand by your father, Alan, when going north-about. By your father! by *The Scots Rose!* Well, well; Hendrison meant it and, to give him his due, there was something in it, too; for the weather was dirty enough. Oh, dirty. Great snow squalls, blotting out everything for three or four minutes at a time. Oh, wild. Fierce. Your father was at the tiller with two twists of a rope round him. Everything battened down. Not that it was blowing a real gale. When the snow-squall passed it wasn't so bad. The squall just came, completely flattening everything. The water boiled, hissing as if it was in a pot. It got quite dark. Oh, dirty. Fierce. Well, now, there we were holding at it, the big *Fateful* standing off a little from us, and by way of looking after us. A cold bitter afternoon it was in late April, but very bright between the squalls. There's the two of us going along like that. Then a real snorer comes down from the nor'ard. The worst yet. Oh, wicked. The snow is blinding. Your father lets out a mighty shout. We hold on by instinct. The boat half swings round—rises—water rushes down the decks—she lands with a crash—shivering in every plank like a beast . . .

"There's no doubt your father is a fine seaman. Yet we all knew that he had to a certain extent been taking a risk. What I mean by that is this: he was crowding on a fair bit of sail when he could. Of course—well—"

"What you mean," said Tom, "is that he was
149

damned if he would let old Hendrison outsail him, big boat or not'!'

"Well, well, it's not for me to say. Perhaps old Hendrison knew how much he himself could carry, with safety, and I'm not saying that the *Fateful* could have shaken off *The Scots Rose*, even if she wanted. That's all foolish talk and young men's nonsense."

"And your eye glistening there!" probed Davie.

"Hush, be quiet, Davie boy," said Hector; and after a moment went on: "The squall passed. It passed as if someone was drawing it away like a trailing white curtain, and there was the face of the sea glittering and swinging, and, far as the eye could reach, utterly empty. Of the *Fateful* there wasn't a trace, not a spar, not a plank, nothing. She had sailed right under."

The lads got the thrill again from the old story. Hugh shivered a little hearing it from Hector's lips. Duncan had been his mother's first-born child. At the time of the disaster Hugh himself had not been born.

"Well, what I was coming to is this. Everyone knows how your mother dislikes the sea. She has great cause, and that's true. You see, she would rather lose you to Australia, where you will live, even though she should never see you again—rather than that you should follow your father.

"Now that's a strange thing. You won't understand it yet. You think you may, but you don't. I'm telling you it's the queer thing. But it's the way life gets a person in the end."

Alan gave Davie a slow wink. Hugh saw him and felt very uncomfortable. There was something so fine in old Hector, so full of quiet humour and understanding. Hadn't he been spying out the gamekeepers for them that day when working away up on

150

the hill road? Hadn't he entered into their ploy? Wasn't this the house of the young men's ceilidh? of any man who hadn't lost his youth? What gay nights had there not been here? And ever, to top all, the piping. Couldn't Alan feel for what was in old Hector's mind?

"That's your mother, Alan. But now look at it from your father's side. The sea took Duncan, it's true. And no one knows what your father may have had in his heart. Duncan went with Hendrison. It's maybe always better like that. But isn't it certain your father would have preferred Duncan to be with himself? And if only he had been! . . . However, that had not to be."

"I know. That was where the *Fateful* came in," remarked Alan.

"Yes," nodded Hector, profoundly.

Alan slipped his wink again. Davie, a good-looking, dark, honest lad, awkwardly responded. Tom's narrow eyes were on Hector's face.

"But from your father's side it's different. You see, a man likes someone to come after him. It's a queer thing that. And no man understands it until he has passed his prime. Then it begins to gnaw at him. A man founds himself, and his race. It's not a bad old race. It's all we've known. You see what I mean? And then in our old age, there's no one left—no one of our very own. . . . Yes, maybe it's nonsense. For what is there here for a young fellow of spirit now? Not much. And your father sees that, Alan. Only now and then—when he has a dram or two in him, let us say—he forgets the cold work and the poverty. He would out-point the devil himself. Oh, he's royal then. He is the sea-rover. And when all is said and done, you and I know there are moments when the

151

ways of the sea are the ways of brave men. Don't you forget that, boys. It's a good thing to have behind you." He paused a moment, then leaning forward a little, smiling: "Never give in to the thing when it's coming at you. And at the worst—at the worst—"

Alan leapt to his feet with a laugh.

"At the worst, battened down and with sails set— sail her right under!"

"Good for you, Alan!" said Hector the piper, who had used all these cunning words to cover his blessing.

Alan swayed, stretching his legs. He looked in royal form. "And now out with the pipes!"

And when Hector asked what it was going to be, Alan cried, "Nothing but the big music to-night! To the devil with marches and strathspeys and rubbish of that sort! What do you say, boys? Let's watch Hector—sailing them right under!" And he laughed in great style.

"I'll give you the *Tinker's Lament*," said Hector. "Isn't it all as poor as tinkers we are?" An odd darkness came to his face like a flush.

Hugh heard no more of the talk for watching Hector, whose body seemed to unfold itself and grow tall, as the drones fell over his shoulder and the bag filled. A quick pressure of an elbow set the reeds humming, but it took a little time for the tuning to suit Hector's nice ear.

Hugh knew the theme of the *Lament for Katherine*, and its first statement, as Hector took the floor, went prickling all over his skin. His throat made little dry swallowing motions. His body grew rigid and a strange lightness came to his half-turned head. Every note was clear and distinct. The grace notes were like tiny golden sparks. The drones sent a waving flame ascending among the rafters; it grew solid, a beaten wave,

152

reverberating, near and far, insistent; against it, the theme, slowly, so slow that every note became freighted unbearably, every phrase a piece of sorrow set in eternity, so that no time could conquer it, so that it must hang there on the nail that man has driven through eternity's heart.

The variations came as a relief. One could listen to the fingering, the clever neat work. The fingering became more intricate. The ear grew more anxious; but as every turn, every difficulty, was flawlessly overcome, the eyes glistened. Delicate work! The *Crunnluath Doubling* was an astonishment and a joy. Hector stood still for the final variation. The eyes of his listeners interchanged shining glances. The technical excellence thrilled them. Had there been one effect of slurring, one blurred flaw, in that very difficult feat of fingering, not a mind there but would have shivered in on itself, and more out of pain for Hector than for itself.

Then as it finished, out of it stepped once more the opening theme. But now heightened by contrast. When all had been said, when the ways of art had been demonstrated and man's conscious ingenuity in expression had been satisfied, there came, purified and lovely, the pale figure of sorrow's self.

"They're going well to-night," said Alan, in a tone still cheerful, but with most of the bluster knocked out of it.

"Not bad." Hector sat down. "Did you like that one, Hugh?"

"Yes," answered Hugh.

"I never heard you play it better," said Tom quietly. "Never." He had a narrowing, half-wistful face.

Alan stretched out his legs with a laugh. "It was

good, right enough, But I think we're due something more cheerful."

He was recovering. He felt the seductive mood of the music against him. He would kill it. He would slay anything. Why not?

Hugh's dark eyes shot him a glance. They had not faced each other since they came in.

"Come on, Hector! *The Cock-fight!*" demanded Alan.

The Desperate Battle of the Birds was considered a humorous piece. With forefingers strutting in time to the music, Alan imitated a cock on its own midden. There was a comic dignity in the slow challenging action. Alan pecked with his head. Davie accepted the challenge. The first variation was brilliant. Both of them grew hectic.

"Good Hector!" roared Alan.

There was a variation they called "the bubbly-jock." They all chuckled, their eyes dancing with admiration and excitement. When Hector finished, Alan shouted "Hooray!" and was answered by voices from without. The door burst open and several men entered, shouting greetings and laughing.

VII

Two hours later Alan withdrew his forces by stealth. "Quick!" They slid round to the stable, got the net, and in no time were in the shadow of a dyke. "We couldn't say good-bye to Hector. He understood all right."

The pipes rose on the night air. Involuntarily they

all drew up. The theme was: *Cha till mi tuille* ("I shall never more return").

"That's his farewell!" Alan laughed. "Come on out of this," he said harshly, shouldering his way. The music followed them, growing more haunting as it grew fainter. None of them could find a word. I shall return no more. Never more. Their ears stretched for the last echoes. They stopped involuntarily to make sure of the silence.

Then they went through woods, clambered up slopes, down gullies, following little bypaths and sheepways, and finally took to the trackless moor.

The going was difficult and fast. The night was lovely and serene. Hugh felt lean and tireless. His body slipped round and on. The silence of the night swathed them about. The *thud thud* of footsteps and the bobbing of heads. The nearness of four bodies breathing, in single file, winding without a word across the dark moor. It was exciting, and Hugh had been excited enough that night already. Continually he was holding his breath and listening. Then the strange realization of what they were upon would come over him afresh. Sometimes his glance would sweep around and run along horizons. Always he was intensely watchful. Anything might start out of the heather; anything might come over a sky-line. The sudden flurring of a cock grouse brought his heart to his mouth. Alan hissed, "Damn!" The old cock shouted, "Go-back, go-back!" in a voice that could be heard a mile away. Hugh hit an outcrop of rock, and the sudden click shattered the world.

Gradually a new mood was born out of this overbearing anxiety. It thrust out here and there crushed tongues of delight. A secret exaltation spirting out of fear. A bowed head, slightly hunched shoulders,

155

slipping within the secrecy of the night. An imaginary head turned over a shoulder, laughing silently back. Once his face quickened and he found himself smiling secretively, hither and thither, watchfully, while his hot body ran over cold with exultation.

Silence and remoteness and peril. The vast night world of the moor. The high dark sky. Threading it to the river and the poaching of salmon. The half moon, wanly tilted over and sinking. Every sense in the boy grew so alert that shapes and instincts crept out of his blood. An occult ecstasy rimmed the dark hollow of his fear with white fire. He was being born to the earth, to the mother that is behind all mothers, as the sea, the father, is behind all fathers.

But deeper the earth and darker, more mysterious and fertile, secretive and vivid, red under the dark, instinct under reason, eternity under time. There is a movement on the surface of the waters, but there is a pulse at the heart of the earth.

Before cresting the last low rise to the river, they all slid to the heather, and for a few moments lay dead still, listening and peering. Then they drew deep breaths and whispered, their teeth bruising the heather-tips. They all agreed it was "safe as a church", and listened again and peered.

The head-keeper's house, which they had widely out-flanked, was now a mile below them. "Come on," said Alan; "no good wasting time."

But down the river a peewit swung upon a startled night. Lips fell apart. The urgent twofold cry curved away and died. They could hear the rumble of their hearts.

"It's nothing," whispered Alan. Then they all listened, breathing noiselessly through open mouths. Minutes passed. "Follow me."

They crept over the ridge, and slid down through a brae-face of stunted trees to a moon-grey pool.

At first the water had a quiet rumbling song, going on monotonously, yet with a far quality, strangely haunting. But as they crouched to the grassy bank for a final listening, Hugh detected hidden sounds of an odd wayward menace. Thus once he turned his head quickly to the throat of the pool where he could have sworn he had heard the *clack* of stones trodden by swift feet. As he watched for its recurrence there came into the gurgle where the tail of the pool slid over stones a distinct tinkle as of a metal rod struck in water. Even as his eyes turned, he caught this again, but now faintly as a coin in a glass. When he really concentrated. however, he heard nothing but a spinning gurgle. But all at once, farther down, there were sounds as clear as footsteps. And away below these, a splash. Or was it a gush? While he held his breath, the sounds beyond the top of the pool stole forth in bodies of their own.

Alan's whisper came among them:

"Not a soul about. Did you see the rabbits as we came down?"

"Yes. No one's been here: that's certain," murmured Tom, his cat's eyes penetrating the face of trees and slowly sweeping the narrow river-flat.

"Davie—down a bit. Hugh—up there. And remember—keep an eye on the ridge behind. Tom will take the line across and draw over the net. I'll haul in here. Right, then!" And Alan went into action.

Hugh was only a score of yards away from his brother, but he felt completely cut off from him into an inimical world for which he was alone responsible. As his body stood fixed, space crept all round it. His senses drew to a tension that was painful. What before had been shadows, now became shapes; what before

157

had been motionless, now moved. There was no longer silence, but an infinity of creeping stealthy sounds. A second was drawn out to such exquisite divisions that time all but vanished. He had never experienced anything like this before, except in nightmare. Adventure got crushed down and upon its cold skin rayed crepitations of fear. The rays touched the sides of his mind and crept up, like fingers, like tentacles. Farther up. They became a horror. He could not trust his senses. If anything rushed from there—or there—or up there—suddenly—at full speed—a grown man—a dog—a gun—he would choke—his legs would give in. His heart boiled in his ears. When his eyes blinked in spite of him, they opened on everything afresh, and in the opening, things in the corner, things just out of focus, swayed treacherously.

But he had only to watch for just another minute or so and then it would be all over. They would be finished with the pool. . . . *Clack! clack!* Stepping from boulder to boulder just below the pool . . . Davie . . . going to the other side. They had not yet started! . . .

He tried to argue with himself.

If it came to capture . . . no one could *prove* anything so long as you weren't doing anything. But when you *were*, they *had* you. Everything depended on the person who was watching. If he failed. . . .

But his anxiety persisted in growing to a trembling agony as the horrible mistrust of himself increased. In the moonlight, on the rabbit-cropped grass, he saw his isolated body grow taller and taller, a dark pillar visible from any distance. No one could mistake it or fail to spot it. He saw eyes looking at it, through the heather, from under the trees at the up corner. Cunning faces: "Ha, there he is! . . . hsh! this way! . . ." on hands and knees, nearer, nearer. . . .

158

It came just at the culminating moment of his terror, a heave and splash from mid-pool, a voice, a hurtling darkness where Alan invisibly crouched, followed by violent head-and-tail slappings on a rock-face.

The sounds of these slappings shattered the night. Now, now, they would rush in, the eyes, the creeping men. This was the desperate moment that would convict. This was what they had been waiting for. Look out! now! . . .

In the clutching silence that followed, Hugh found himself low to the grass, a cold sweat on his forehead, a desire in his throat to be sick.

But he wasn't sick. Alan had killed the first salmon. The swaying world was settling down. Here on hands and knees he was in the hollow of it. In a moment he could spring up and be off. Reality touched him with a forefinger. No one was coming. He looked to see if he could spot Davie. He couldn't. As his eyes swept back, his own corner of the world became more familiar. He was breathing as quickly as if he had run a race. He could run a race like the wind. Slowly, yard by yard, he backed nearer Alan. An overpowering hunger came on him to speak to Alan. He could say he wanted to see the salmon. . . . He stopped himself, but could not stand up. He realized that with his first breath of confidence he was treacherously allowing his terror to have its way. Not though he died—must he give in to that. . . . Something striding at his back—tall, a man. . . . A warm blindness went over Hugh's eyes, his supporting arm knuckled under.

Alan's voice stooped: "A beauty! Thirteen pounds and clean as silver!" He strode past, his husky throat full of confidence, his body alive and virile. He got lost in the shadows at the neck of the pool, then reappeared on the bank. His body lunged and immediately there was the loud splash of a heavy stone. Again. Then silence . . . followed by a whistle from the other side. Alan rushed back past Hugh: "He's in it!"

Hugh got to his feet. What a fright Alan had given him! He tried to think lightly of it. For abject fear is unclean.

He strolled deliberately to the edge of the bank above Alan, and saw the salmon heave into the air and fall with a full-length splash on the glimmering-dark surface, and disappear.

Alan called loudly, "He's gone!" as if it did not matter who heard him. His voice was fierce with disappointment. When Hugh turned round to have another look, Alan was still leaning back doing nothing.

Then slowly he crouched to the water again, called "Right!" and began to pay out the net, holding every now and then to unravel a knot and sometimes standing upright, stretching the net between him and the sky, to make sure that its body fell straight from the back line of corks. He muttered aloud that the fish had escaped for the same old reason—mesh too small—as he sank back on his heels and waited for the nig-nig on the line that betokened a strike.

But every fish in the place had now gone to earth. He called to Hugh: "Throw in some stones."

From the throat of the pool, Hugh dug out two big stones, and clasping them to his stomach got on the bank again. Like an athlete putting the shot, he landed each in turn far out, then swiftly peered around him. Each stone had a double-barrelled report, which someone was simply bound to hear.

He hoped he wouldn't be asked to throw in any more.

He wasn't. After they all met and had a look at the salmon, it was decided to try the next pool lower down. Alan, who had the net already folded, was still lamenting the loss of the second fish. Each voice spoke in husky whispers, in a sort of devil-may-care excitement. Davie chuckled. Tom breathed, "What a night!' Alan said, "We must get four anyway."They were silent for several seconds after that, listening and peering.

In single file they passed down the river bank, and at the first bend had to stoop under trees, where it would have been the simplest thing in the world for a hand to come out and land on a shoulder, for a voice to say, "Well, boys, so this is your game?"

Hugh's eyes were alive and darting as he followed Alan; an undersurge of lawless confidence was spouting up through the dark fear in his heart.

Alan suddenly halted. They all stopped, thinking he had heard something. He said: "I don't believe there's a single soul on the watch. We'll have a royal night!"

He was emphatic in an amusing dramatic way. They all chuckled huskily. This was daring the fates with a vengeance! Every soul felt keen and dangerous and swift. Alan added, "It may be for years and it may be for ever!" and with a laugh moved on. Without conquering it, Hugh got the better of his fear, and entered into this land of memorable youth.

VIII

Three hours later, carrying their net and four salmon, they passed down the roadway that ran by the keeper's house as bold as brass. Their hearts were gay, their heads up. Alan as ringleader was irresistible.

"What would MacAulay say if he saw us now? 'You wass after the saamons you puggers!'" He exaggerated. He told them MacAulay's latest story, which concerned a pair of boots that Alan had inveigled him into buying—a local brand of "heathercutters". MacAulay had hesitated for a time, but then had got them. They were very hard. "Pegod," he complained to Alan, "I had to wear them three weeks before I could put them on."

They got into the liveliest humour.

"Don't you think we should get off the road a bit when passing the house?" suggested Tom.

"No," said Alan. "Why bother? It's our last night."

Their footsteps rang on the hard surface.

"The dogs'll hear us," muttered Davie.

"Let them!" said Alan.

They all kept their eyes on the white gable of the house, which wasn't a hundred yards from the road.

Excitement began to get hold of Hugh again. It would be so easy to step on to the heather. This was asking for it, and they were so near home after the most wonderful night he had ever known. He had been allowed on to the net for the fourth fish.

Rid Jock and Bill Keith and the boys in his class were but little children, sound asleep hours ago. They would have been running in from the dark and then going to bed—last night. This was to-morrow morning. What bairns they were, crying after their mothers for food!

Within his mounting excitement the figures of his companions gathered a sort of secondary vividness. He smiled, his eyes upon the keeper's house. He could hear Jock's voice, peeved and querulous, "Give me my tea, Mother! Give me my tea!" Jock had challenged him that day. Jock! . . . Before *her!*

162

They were now so near the keeper's house that he must not think more about them. Yet his mind stretched itself desperately, trying to hold on to them. She had thought that he was giving in and running away. She believed that he was frightened! Let her! . . . She would yet see. . . . And then in the middle of the fight, when he had knocked Jock down, and Jock was bawling and wouldn't get up, she would suddenly come on them. He would not say a word, would not see her, would merely smile in a certain manner at Jock and walk quietly away, shouldering through the boys, Bill at his elbow. . . .

His mind had rushed the scene in order to finish it, and now he breathed sharply with a cunning exhilaration as they came opposite the green gate that gave on the path to the keeper's house. All were silent.

In the first of the night the moonlight had been alive and quickening; but now the moon was low down, and a veil of strange darkness was falling upon the sinking earth. Out of this deadness the keeper's house rose with a secret menace. It was like a house seen in a fairy story, it was so very still and yet liable to motion. And its peaked roof windows might well be eyes.

But the very devil was in Alan. He had no sooner got them breathlessly past the gate than he hauled them into a small quarry where Hector the Roadman broke stones. His low voice danced.

"What are you saying?" hushed Tom.

" . . . cut off a couple of tails and tie them to the knob of MacAulay's door. . . ."

They agreed it was a very funny idea, oh, very; they all, in fact, choked with silent mirth; but . . . it was so dashed late.

"Late be hanged!" Alan took out his knife.

163

When he had tied the two tails together, he motioned the others on. "Wait for me at the foot of the path," and he disappeared on his toes.

They hesitated, listening, able to follow him as far as the gate.

But the sudden furious barking of a dozen dogs made them take to their heels. Alan had wakened the kennels. They left the moor road and slipped down through the face of trees, net and salmon bumping on their backs.

They were beginning to get anxious when a rush of feet started them off again. Alan caught the net from Hugh's back. "On you go!"

They had only gone a few yards when the night was splintered by a gun-shot. A shower of pellets pattered among the trees. They doubled like hares. After a little, Alan swung to the front. "Up here!" On the crest of the tree-slope they scouted and then rested, listening.

"It's all right now," Alan whispered. "He couldn't have had his clothes on."

But Tom stopped him. "I thought I heard something down there."

"Couldn't," breathed Alan. But they all started off again, nor did they slacken pace until they had come among the stunted bushes within hail of the pastures whereon Hector's cottage stood. There they lay back and wiped their faces.

"A perfect finish," said Davie. "I'm dying for a smoke."

But Alan was into his story.

" . . . I stopped when I heard the dogs. Dash it, I didn't know but someone might be at the kennels. They were to wind'ard. How could they have smelt me? I watched. But I had to do it now. I crept up

164

to the door. And just as I put my hand on the knob—the knob turned in my hand!'"

Alan lay back with husky laughter.

"I hung on to the knob. There were the greatest wrenches. Oh, fierce! as Hector would say. Oh, wild! I got my heel against the step. The door opened in. He would heave it a foot or so, and then I would jerk it back. 'Let go there, you puggers!'" Alan kicked his heels. "He slipped and cursed, And then he gave one terrific pull—and I let go! He went clean by the backside, heels over head, in among all the pots and pans in creation. What a row!" Alan doubled up.

His helpless laughter rocked them. They pushed one another's shoulders. They became weak and groaned. They repeated MacAulay's oaths in squeaky breathless voices. Alan nursed his stomach. They lay over, begging for mercy. And even when they had straightened themselves and wiped their eyes, a word threatened to set them off again.

There followed a delicious exhaustion, when they sat staring before them, their faces sealed in a smile, a deep peace at their hearts, a profound reflectiveness. The stillness of the darkening world was breathed upon by a sighing air. The dark spidery twigs of the birches stirred as in a dream of a far sea-surge. Their reflectiveness became conscious. They listened. They heard and saw, eyes open. This was their world. This was the old place, old, far back, far-r-r. . . .

Alan suddenly shivered. "Pegod, it's cold!" And he jumped to his feet. They followed.

But Hugh knew he had not lost himself so completely as the others. Never at any time, perhaps, during the whole night. Always a little anxious, over-stretched. But how vivid each moment, how steep each fear! And even sitting back there in the birches in that final mood, he had known not only the silence of the world, but the silence in their hearts. It was as though he had looked round under his eyelids on them and on himself. With them, but not quite of them, because he was not grown up. Yet deep in his boyish loneliness he guarded a secret thrill.

Silently they filed towards Hector's stable. As Alan opened the door, the old horse stood over with a clacking of iron shoes on the cobbles. After he had halved a fish on a wisp of hay, Alan fixed the under-jaw to the inside latch, then backed out, carefully closing the door behind him.

They stood uncertainly for a moment.

"Come on!" They all started off together. After a time Alan added, "There would be no sense in wakening him up."

Hugh was left with the feeling that they would probably have wakened him up any other night.

Presently Alan gave a chuckle.

"Did you hear him to-night talking about a man being left alone and all that?"

"Yes," said Tom. "He's left alone anyway."

"All the same—think of it. His two sons in Canada. His wife dead. His daughter married to a butler and living in London. Well, dash it, he's alone all right, when you look at it like that," said Davie, honestly.

"Go on!" said Alan, with dry humour.

"A fine chap, young Hector," Tom said reflectively, admiration in his voice for the piper's oldest son. "He could play the chanter for quarter of an hour without taking a breath." Tom loved cunning tunes, and was a musician himself.

"Wasn't his fingering sweet?" Alan remembered.

"The sweetest ever I heard. It was like honey. Do you know what his drones always reminded me of?
166

The hum of a hive of bees." Tom's voice was faintly excited.

"There was no one that ever I heard in my life could whistle like him," remarked Davie. "But wasn't it a queer thing that he would never whistle before anybody?"

"Yes, when you think of it," Alan agreed. They all went on thinking of this.

"When old Hector's gone, there won't be a piper left in the place," said Tom.

Alan chuckled. "What about Donald Angus?"

"Or Peter Crock?" Davie added.

This sarcasm gave them the relief of a laughing humour.

"They should be forbidden by law," Tom declared, "so they should. Hector is the last of the great pipers."

"Oh, but they think they're fully as good as Hector!"

"Do you remember the time . . . "

And so they came to where the roads met.

"So long. See you in the morning. . . . Good night, Hugh. You're the great poacher and no mistake. So long. So long." Quiet voices, parting.

Alan and Hugh went on alone.

"Are you tired?" asked Alan.

"No," said Hugh, "not a bit."

They felt lighter without the company of the others and curiously sensitive, as though a dark covering had slid from them. They did not speak again until they came to the birch wood, when Alan asked:

"Sure you're not tired?"

"No. I'll carry the salmon a bit, if you like."

"No, no. A nice fish. About twelve, I should say."

"Yes, and clean as silver."

"Yes."

167

They didn't speak again until they came near the house.

"We'll go in quietly."

Hugh nodded. He saw Alan looking at the house. Then he looked at it himself. It was dark and still, known and strange; it was almost sad, so that one smiled. There was the old place. That was it, that house there. . . .

As they approached the back door, Hugh whispered: "Father will soon be getting up, surely?"

Alan paused.

"No. They'll go without him. Sandy was coming across last night for the skoo."

His whisper was familiar and friendly. His warm breath struck Hugh's cheek. This was a titbit of information that had at one time been meant no doubt to surprise Hugh. Alan cautioned with his hand, "Shh!" and carefully lifted the latch. The door swung open—as they expected; only the front door would have been locked. He nodded with a knowing smile, an expectant air. Without being able to see, Hugh knew that he winked as he breathed, "Now for it!" His head beckoned, and they went into the back-kitchen.

Alan struck a match, and the first things his eyes rested on were—a candle in a candlestick, a towel, a basin of water, a slice of soap, all in a row. They both gazed at this unusual display on the clean-swept table until the match burned Alan's fingers and he dropped it hurriedly.

As Alan lit the candle, Hugh saw the odd twist of a smile on his lips. His eyes were faintly self-conscious and there was warmth in his cheeks. He looked at Hugh and nodded inwards in mocking pantomime.

"I wonder who did this?" he whispered, amused.

"Grace, likely," said Hugh.

Alan paused in his stride, but Hugh could not see his face. Then his nostrils made a dry sarcastic sound and Hugh regarded his bent back.

Alan laid the salmon bare. They both gazed at it in adoration.

"A bonny fish?"

"A beauty," murmured Hugh.

Alan put his head to one side, his eyes critical of proportion. "I bet you he's heavier than you think."

"Yes. Look at his girth."

"Thirteen, I should say, what?"

"At least," whispered Hugh.

"That's what I call a perfect fish. They're coarse when they get bigger than that." He turned the salmon over. "Not a mark on him." He studied him a moment, then in a little rush, "He is a beauty, isn't he?"

Hugh nodded. "Perfect."

"The only thing . . . maybe . . . is that I like the small head of the hen fish. You know, the neat little head, curving in like that."

"I know. But still . . . "

"Yes. I know." A final lingering look, and Alan covered up the body.

They washed and dried their hands together.

"A good night, wasn't it?"

"Great," breathed Hugh.

"And now—ssh!" Alan opened the door into the kitchen.

But the lamp, turned down, still burned on the dresser. He winked to Hugh, making a cautioning motion with his mouth. On tiptoe they were both slipping round the great bed when their mother's voice came from its curtained depth:

"What time of night is this to come home?"

Alan's mouth opened in an embarrassed silent laugh to Hugh, who tiptoed more quickly, Alan following.

No further word was said. The stairs creaked so loudly despite their care that they hissed at it. In their bedroom, they shut the door.

The warmth in Alan's face had increased. Self-consciousness burned in his eyes. He went and sat on his bed; stuck out his legs and put his hands in his trousers' pockets. "Mother wouldn't have slept a wink all night!" It was amusing. The warmth in his cheeks grew to a dull red.

Hugh threw him a glance, then turned to the window. Slowly he began taking off his clothes.

"'What time of night is this to come home?'" muttered Alan with a husky laugh. It was amusing. He had known it was coming. Certain!

He stretched his arms above his head.

"That's the last time I'll hear that, boy."

He half-yawned a lazy chuckle, then let his hands drop between his knees and stared before him, his shoulders hunched up, the twist on his mouth gradually smoothing out.

Hugh, in his shirt, skipped into bed. When he got the chance, Alan always gave him a smack on the bottom. This time, however, Alan did not move, and Hugh covered himself up unctuously, all the time taking side glances at his brother. He made happy laughing noises in his throat. Bed was the greatest place! "Oh, special!" he breathed. "Oh, extra!" he tempted.

Alan made the dry sarcastic sound in his nose, but did not stir.

Hugh heard a strange surge coming over his mind

when he lay flat out, like the air coming over the birches. He had been too excited, in the end too pleasantly weary, to feel sleepy on that night of adventure. And now with Alan sitting there like that, sitting so long . . . like that . . . mother down below . . . like that. . . .

Alan should let him go to sleep. It wasn't fair. His whole body rebelled querulously. He tried to shake Alan's hand off his shoulder. "Leave me to sleep!" he cried, maddened by sleep's fumes.

"All right, Hugh boy; good-bye!"

Something in the tone, lingering and gentle, penetrated to Hugh's consciousness. He struggled desperately out of the mists; half-open blinking eyes grew steady under lowering brows that smoothed. Something had gone wrong. Alan was dressed in his best clothes. A strange fear caught Hugh so that he stared unwinking, his eyes glittering in the near candle-flame. The room, besides, had a queer light in it, coming in through the window. The candle was wavering in a twilight, a grey unearthly light. Alan's face was shadowed.

"Good-bye, Hugh," Alan said again. "I'm off."

His mouth open, Hugh looked about him.

Alan smiled.

"It's the morning. You've been asleep, man. We're just to have our breakfast, and then we're off. We'll need our time. You needn't get up." His hand came out.

Hugh turned the clothes back slowly and slid to his feet. Alan smacked his bottom.

"Stop it!" said Hugh automatically, and picked up his trousers from the floor. He staggered a little when trying to stand on one leg. His confused mind was warmed by a vague apprehension. This warmth

171

was also in his breast. It made him weak. His fatigue was overpowering. His hands fumbled.

His mother's voice was heard calling Alan.

"Coming, Mother," cried Alan. Gripping the open door, he hesitated a moment, looking at the slim slow figure pulling a shoulder strap, moodily tucking in a shirt. Then he went.

So this was the morning, and Alan was going away. The time had come at last. This was it now. Hugh stared at the window, at the grey light, a light of leave-taking.

When he had got all his clothes on, he stood by the window a full minute. He wanted to flatten his face against it and do no more. Reluctantly he pulled himself from it. He must go downstairs. The end was at hand.

As he reached the stairhead, Grace's door opened and she came out hurriedly.

"Hallo, Hugh!"

She had on her coat with the fur collar. It was unbuttoned. Gloves flicked in a hand. Her voice was friendly, her face smiling, and there was the faint scent in her clothes. She put her arm round him and pressed him against her side.

"Are you coming to see us off?"

"Yes," he muttered.

"Good for you!" And she was gone, leaving him in the swirl of last night's scent.

As he entered the kitchen, his mother turned round:

"What are you getting up for, boy?"

One glimpse of her eyes, and he looked away.

"Mother," demanded Kirsty, "will you leave our brother Hugh alone?"

His mother's mock tone remembered last night. It was intimate and tonic, and had little to do with the strange look in her eyes. The lamp was burning

172

on the dresser and made the kitchen unreal. Each
one, too, was doing something as if there wasn't a
minute to spare. Alan beckoned Hugh secretly to the
back-kitchen. Stooping through the half-light, they
held a private view.

"Bonny, isn't he?"

"Yes," murmured Hugh.

Life came back to him as he looked at the salmon,
the strange world of last night, the dark, the pools,
the fear, the secrecy, the thrills.

Alan covered the fish with the canvas bag, and they
went in to breakfast.

"You're not giving Hugh an egg, Mother, are you?"
demanded Kirsty in mock astonishment.

"I can't say that he deserves it. Be eating, Alan."

On Alan's plate of bacon were three eggs. He nudged
Hugh with his elbow.

"Fit for a Lewsach!" nodded Grace.

Her face was pale and pure, her eyes dark and
challenging. Alan did not retaliate; indeed, he did not
look at her.

Kirsty now and then cast sidelong glances at her
mother. Her father ate in an abstracted way, and
made slower noises than usual in drinking his tea.
Kirsty's fairness was faintly flushed all over, and her
bracken-bronze hair held loose ends and strands. Her
voice had an odd excitement in it and she spoke
quickly and readily, though her eyes had a way of
lingering on Alan not so much affectionately as
remotely. It was as though some delicate appraisement or wonder passed of its own volition in front of
her mind.

Grace was more charmingly practical. She tackled
her bacon and eggs, taking small choice pieces on her
fork. She was excited with the rush of going away.

The following morning she would be back in London.

By the time they were half-way through the meal it was difficult to find anything to say. The clock was questioned twice. Kirsty's unconscious appraisement or wonder lingered now sometimes on her mother, on the symmetric face, the unfurrowed forehead, with the dark hair combed flat and smooth to either side behind the ears. She appeared to be eating a piece of dry oatcake. "Now, Alan, make a good breakfast," she said to her son. There was no sadness in her voice, no resignation. It was cheerful and sensible. Like the flicker of a flame, light passed over Kirsty's face, gleamed in admiration in her eyes. A proud admiration for the greatness of her mother. Her expression shone as it always did at the culminating point in a story; then she glanced across at Alan, finishing up with eyes thoughtfully on her own cup which she turned round and round, and from which she sometimes drank lingeringly.

Hugh kept to himself. He felt the strain of the meal and hardly lifted his eyes. In an odd way, too, he divined that nothing would be said about last night. His eyelids looked sleepily heavy with the secrecy of his thought. Had it been any other morning, then they would have been slyly digging at him. Kirsty would have asked the most cunningly simple question, such as, "Weren't you frightened in the dark, Hugh?" Alan would have grossly exaggerated, even invented; and it would all have been carried on in an indirect way so that their parents need not appear to understand.

But this morning nothing would be said. One was sensible and cheerful, but not airy and normal. Behind all wisdom was the quietude, the sanctity, of the inevitable. The breakfast had hardly the benediction of a true meal at all. It was merely to give strength for a journey, and hurry and preparation broke it up. It was not like their supper last night. Already the journey had begun. The father pushed his chair back, casting a glance at the clock. "It's getting on. You'd better hurry, bairns."

The table was rattled back into its window-niche. Everyone searched about for this or that. No one paused for a moment or stood idly. They spoke or shouted. Grace was off upstairs again. Alan followed, three steps at a time. As quickly they returned.

"I'm ready now," said Grace at last, quite out of breath.

They were all ready. The moment had come.

Grace said, "Good-bye, Mother dear," very tenderly. She took her mother's hand and kissed her. "Good-bye, lassie," said her mother kindly. Grace turned away, a quick flush of emotion in her face.

Then Alan swaggered up, "Well, Mother!" his voice cheerful and laughing, his hand out.

His mother's face was pale and quiet and very sweet. She took his hand. Alan shook it up and down, laughing, his face glowing red, his eyes flashing here and there.

Kirsty and Grace and Hugh watched them, their looks constrained, heads lowered as if they would turn away but could not.

"Good-bye, Mother," said Alan, "good-bye."

"Good-bye, Alan," said his mother.

"Good-bye," laughed Alan, "good-bye; good-bye, Mother." He could not let go his mother's hand, he shook it so, up and down. Then before he quite knew what he was about, he strongly put his left hand round her shoulders, drew her to him, and kissed the first part of her head that met his mouth.

At that all her serene courage completely left her. In a moment from being calm and self-possessed, she was sobbing in a way that shook all her body. Her face was hidden, her shoulders heaved, her sobs were harsh racking sounds.

Alan stared straight over her head through the window, his stung eyelids blinking upon his fixed laugh, while he patted her shoulders. The others turned away. He had no memory of having ever kissed his mother before or of having been kissed by her. When she drew back and looked at him, her eyes were clairvoyant and terrible through their glistening tears. He followed the others, still murmuring, "Never mind, Mother!"

None of them looked at him. They kept in front.

As they came to the corner of the house they saw their father before them trundling the large wheelbarrow containing Alan's American trunk and Grace's leather case.

Grace almost stopped, then nudged Kirsty:

"Look at Father!"

In their excitement they all smiled at this. It was somehow extraordinary that their father should be there wheeling their cases in the barrow. It was something for their clamped hearts to laugh at. Their father—look at him!

Yet he went easily about the task, with a quiet efficiency, staggering sometimes to the side to counteract the jerk of the wheel on the uneven surface.

The sight of their father got the better of them. "Look at him!" said Grace. But they did not meet each other's eyes. Nor did they turn round when, behind them, they heard Alan's footsteps.

Their father went on strongly, his stamping legs holding to it. Grace repressed her mirth, and wiped

her cheeks, not caring who saw her. Hugh wanted to
wait for Alan, but dared not. He let his sisters get a
pace in front and drew his sleeve over his face quickly.
He tried to make a cold blank of his mind by hissing
in and out through his teeth notes of no tune. He
dropped a little farther behind, and presently Alan
caught him up.

"Well, boy," cried Alan, "Father's got a load
there!"

Grace turned at the sound of his voice, her chin up-
tilted, charming and sad, and gave them a humorous
smile.

Alan acknowledged wryly, his eyes sweeping an
uncomfortable flash.

"Come on! We'd better give Father a turn!" he
cried to Hugh.

As they came up, Kirsty cast a look at the house.

They all saw her involuntary pause, and knew that
their mother was watching.

No one spoke, but Alan forgot to catch up his father.
After a moment Grace, however, turned round and
waved her handkerchief. Immediately she did this
Alan went forward muttering cheerfully that he must
give a hand.

But his father wouldn't give in to him. They strode
along arguing about it.

"I'll give it to you," said his father, "when we
come to the corner."

They came to the corner, the last point from which
the house could be seen. There his father set the
barrow on its legs, and straightened himself slowly.
The others came up. They all turned towards the
house.

Their mother was on the doorstep, standing quite
still in her dark dress.

"Poor Mother!" said Kirsty in a tone to break a man's heart.

They saw their mother's arm go up. Alan's arm went up. They heard him draw in a great breath through his nostrils. He waved his hand once or twice then turned abruptly, the breath coming back through his choked throat in a tearing sob. He walked straight on, head up, teeth clenched, mouth pinched and drawn tight. But the sobs came through so that they could see his shoulders jerk.

Hugh followed him, tears streaming down his face. Grace was crying huskily, her head down. Kirsty walked by her side, biting lips which sometimes sucked the salty bitterness to a swallowing throat. Her face was open and her eyes on Alan. When they had all moved on, their father quietly got in between the stilts of the barrow once more.

After a time Alan stopped, and waited for them to come up without turning round.

"I'll have a go at that now," he said briskly.

"All right," nodded his father.

"Look!" cried Kirsty suddenly. "There's Elsie waving to you!"

They all saw the fluttering white beyond the stone dyke across the field on their left.

Alan took off his cap and swept it in great circles round his head. "Good old Elsie!" he cried in the friendliest way.

Kirsty looked at him. His eyelids were red, but his face was full of rising exuberant spirits. He got hold of the barrow and trundled it along firmly. Kirsty saw Elsie's apron flutter down and out.

Above the field larks were weaving their song of ecstasy. Kirsty could not help feeling for what would be in Elsie's heart as she slid down in a heap behind

the wall, hearing nothing but that outpouring of
Spring's love and hope. Her lips quivered. She loved
Elsie, her quiet loyalty, her deep woman's heart. Poor
Elsie. For a little she couldn't get the sight of her out
of her mind crouching there behind the wall, her face
hidden.

IX

They could now see folk coming in twos and threes
here and there towards the meeting place at the
bridge. The whole district would be speaking of
nothing else to-day. Everybody liked the lads. Tom
might be quiet, but he was a grand hand at the melo-
deon, and how were they to manage without him for
the dancing? Oh, great on the music, especially the
pipe tunes. Davie, again, was knacky with his hands
and very obliging. Many's the good turn the lad had
done. Nothing special as you might say about him,
but, who knows? all the more dependable on that
account! Alan was a strong, daring fellow, with somewhere in him a flame of laughter. "Here's Alan," a
man would say to himself or to his friend, and as they
waited for him their eyes brightened. The place would
miss them. There was not a doubt of that. "Ach,
damn it, man," said Soorag to the two men walking
with him from the Barrostad crofts, "there'll soon
be nothing left but old scrogs." "Like yourself!"
"It's a fact—sure as God's alive." His eyes blazed.
"If you could tear ten years off me, I'd be away too.
So I would, curse me!" As referee of all football
matches, he added, "What the team will do without

them God alone knows. They can take down the posts." He made a sweeping gesture, and on the point of spitting, paused. "There's Alan coming down there, boys; look, with his sisters and the old man. By God," he added abruptly, "it must be a sore wrench!" In his thin ginger-fair scrubby face, his eyes grew bright. He brought the back of a big hand across his nose and then he spat. But the blue eye remained alight and watchful, troubled with the torment of an imagination which no swearing at could ever quite subdue.

As Alan trundled the barrow round the bend to the bridge-corner, young voices called, "Here's Alan!" and quite involuntarily cheered.

Alan, letting down the barrow, straightened himself, and with an affected bow acknowledged the plaudits. "Isn't that Alan!" voices chuckled, delighted. A crowd had collected, men and boys, and not a few women and girls. The older folk came and spoke to Alan. "Ay, Alan, you'll be leaving a few sore hearts behind you this day!" Bearded men, smiling. Round-shouldered crofters. Straight-backed men of the sea. Here was the Viking. "Well, Alan, boy, you're for off!" "Oh, we'll give it a trial," smiled Alan. "You'll do all that," said the Viking. It was the quality of his tone that made the tribute so delicate. Alan coloured in the momentary silence.

Hugh's emotions threatened him. Listening greedily for everything that was said to Alan, he yet kept a few yards from him for safety's sake. He would rather die than bubble here. To weep when one was proud and excited! How childish, how maddening! He looked around on the crowd. All the football team. Of those at sea, he would have liked most to have seen Sandy. Alan must have said good-bye to them when he was down for the baiting. And Geordie Macleod . . . over there was Cathie, fair and pleasant, laughing excitedly with two other girls. And Rid Jock showing off. . . . . If he, Hugh, disgraced himself, that would mean a certain and terrible fight with Jock. He would make his nose run like a pump! . . .

He was beginning to get his emotions under control, when suddenly, down a gap between moving men, he saw Tom Macrae's young sister, Molly, and at the same instant Molly saw him. Hugh flashed his face away, and for a time heard no more what Alan said. Then his eyes were arrested by Soorag's arid expression as he looked at "Polished Jack" from "the Shoppie", a decent enough fellow, "but a man of no damn sense whatever . . . and a bloody rascal, too, if you ask me."

"I suppose it's good-bye, Alan," said Jack, with a half-solemn, half-friendly smile, befitting the occasion. He wore a felt hat, a clean creased lounge suit, and a fresh soft collar. He looked Alan straight in the eye. It was his habit.

"Oh, I suppose so!"

Jack's voice lowered to a confidential, sympathetic note.

"How's your mother taking it?"

Soorag's lips pursed to a small round hole through which he actually shot a spittle.

"Oh, all right! all right!" Alan swayed from foot to foot, laughing.

Men's eyelids drooped in an odd reserve. Sea-faces and land-faces; the faces of men and girls. Not hearing and yet hearing, laughing and joking, but tuned to the hidden sanctities.

All at once the shout was raised:

"Here she comes!"

Heads turned; excitement leapt up. The time had arrived. Hand-shaking started. Alan worked his way

181

back to where his father and sisters were with the trunks. "Here she comes!" he said, his face flushed with strong life, his eyes glowing.

Hugh was now trembling a little, as with cold. Still he kept a yard or two away. His father and Alan were ready to heave a trunk, their eyes on the slowing bus.

Grace turned to Kirsty. Her face was open and full of an affection so intense that it looked like pain. She seemed to feel the parting more than Kirsty. It was also as though she could not say what was in her heart. This was clear to Hugh. He loved Grace at that vivid instant; loved her quite irrationally; was secretly proud of her, thrilled by her, so that he could have wept for the something that struggled towards impossible expression in her face.

For it was a strangely chaste face. It might have erred, but not irretrievably, not beyond the bourne, or how could it have been so anxious to communicate rather than cunningly to hide? There are certain things a heart can tell even if with pain and sorrow, with bitterest regret, with humiliation, because it has not the ultimate thing to tell. Here a last wild generosity is fired by a last hope, not for itself.

Grace kissed Kirsty, and as she did so the coat collar slipped from her white neck, whereon Hugh saw a thin red scar the length of a bite. Grace burst into tears. Kirsty's face came away from the embrace, her lips quivering sweetly, her blue eyes brimming. But her look was steady, the faintly flushed skin almost transparent, the eyes all light. Perhaps Kirsty the red understood what was in dark Grace's heart.

Hugh turned hurriedly away, moving all his muscles with explosive energy. "Hup!" he cried with the others as the trunks were heaved aloft. Everybody who could reach added a hand. "Up with it! Heave-ho,

182

my hearties!" They cracked jokes. "Hector, where's your pipes, man?" And for the first time Hugh saw the Roadman, who, smiling, answered that indeed he had been in two minds about it.

Merry laughter chased good wishes. Grace swept upon Hugh, kissed him, thrust two half-crowns into his pocket. The delicate scent embraced him. "Be a good boy!" Her voice was husky and tender. She turned to her father.

"Good-bye, Dad."

"Good-bye, Grace."

For a fraction of a second her eyes opened wide on his quietly smiling face as though something hidden in it smote her.

Alan shook Hugh's hand up and down, and looked as if he might give him a wallop for luck. He kissed Kirsty in excellent style. Then he faced his father.

"Good-bye, Father."

"Good-bye, Alan."

Just as the friendly hand-shake was breaking, nervous fingers gripped and fell apart. But nothing of the iron showed on their faces.

A tremendous burst of cheering set the bus off. Everyone waved and shouted. Tom and Davie and Alan cheered and waved in response. Grace's white handkerchief fluttered. Every face remained on the bus until, turning a corner, it disappeared from sight.

Then a great slackness came upon the people. They stood in groups, moved listlessly, drifted away, talking all the time in easy tones. "Oh, they'll get on all right, the same lads!" They smiled. "Trust them for that!" But their smiles were weary, as though there was a final element in them of defeat. The grass had grown greyer, the trees barer. Virtue had been drawn out of the place, out of themselves. Some turned to the sea, some to the crofts. Only in the very young did excitement linger. Some day they, too, might be going away like that. A wistful, half-fearful, secret excitement. Hugh's father was standing with the Viking and one or two others, all talking in a friendly hopeful way. His father was smiling.

Hugh drifted away from that smile. Besides, he assured himself, it was time he went home for his books. The school would soon go in. And Kirsty might have come back with him part of the road if he had waited another minute. She would have spoken in that remembering way that brought a lump to your throat. "Poor Alan!" That way. He took a little run to himself to stave off the threatening image.

The road back was completely deserted. Sometimes Hugh pulled a dry grass and, biting it, smiled to himself, before lifting his eyes hither and thither in an odd alert way. He seemed to be playing a game with what had happened, dodging it, halting before it, giving it the slip, smiling queerly at it; but every now and again there were long pauses when he walked straight on, his mind hazed into vacancy. From the suddenness with which he awoke from this vacancy, the clenching of the hands, the start forward, one might have imagined that he had been invisibly pierced.

He stood looking at his home a long time as if he had not the energy to go in, almost as if he could not be bothered. Amongst the whin bushes he twisted from one foot to the other uncertainly, biting at an acrid twig. He did not want to go in. He had no desire to do anything or go anywhere. He was tired. He was awfully tired. He was nearly sick with being tired. They should leave him alone. He walked quietly into the house.

His mother, sitting in her chair by the peat fire, looked round at him. Her face dazed his eyes. It was so calm and pale, its expression was frightening. He was conscious, as he avoided her look, of his heart stopping to listen. As he came erect with his bag of books, he stood trapped, glancing out of the window, twisting the leather strap, unable to go out.

"So they're away," she said quietly.

"Yes." He gulped. He could not look at her again. He swung his bag over his back. "I'll be going."

"Very well." Her voice was wise and gentle. He could not leave it; he could not leave it alone. He felt her face turning on him again, and immediately he started for the door, stumbling against a chair and hitting the door jamb with the swing of his bag.

Outside, he felt full of explosive energy. He bit the acrid twig that was still in his hand savagely. He wrenched and tore it. Then suddenly a great quietness came on him, came dazing down upon him from the sky, upon his forehead, smoothing it taut, and under this quietness he walked seeing his mother's face.

Tears came into his eyes. A profound understanding of his mother moved him warmly. He loved her face for its quietness, for its stoicism, for the strength that it had about those eyes which knew all, suffered all, and in the fires of suffering burned themselves clear. No other woman had a face like his mother's, with its kindness, its hidden suffering, its wise acceptance, its brave cheerfulness, its kindness, its kindness. He dared not imagine what she was thinking to herself sitting there by the fire, her back to the window. Not, indeed, that the idea of human sacrifice would have occurred to him. Only the poignant idea of persons parting.

As he walked on he saw his father coming towards

him, wheeling the empty barrow. Immediately his mind lightened and grew active. He would get into *The Lady of the Lake*.

The rattle of the iron-shod wheel came against him.

Hugh raised his head. His father set down the barrow.

"Well, Hugh, are you for the school?"

"Yes."

His father's voice was unusually mild and gentle, but in no way obtrusive. He put his pipe in his waistcoat pocket, leisurely looking far in front of him with his seaman's eyes.

"Have you got your lessons?"

"Yes," muttered Hugh, through an uncomfortable smile. He had not got them much!

"That's right," nodded his father. His eyes dropped to the handles of the barrow. After gazing at them a moment abstractedly, he stooped and caught them. "Well, well," he said, and went on.

After a few nervous paces, Hugh turned his head on his father trundling the empty barrow. He stood still looking back at him, fascinated. His father went on with the same quiet step, mild and terrible, alone against the upland.

The flood loosened in Hugh. It came up over him in a blind surge. He staggered in amongst the small birch trees, bruising their branches, tearing their whips from his face. A great cry was swelling in him, was thrusting up into his throat. He threw himself on the ground, crushing his mouth into a bed of thin blaeberry. At first he rocked on his breast, tearing and clawing, choking his sobs, gulping and frenzied. But after a little he lay still, letting sobs come as they liked, beyond caring.

When the storm passed he remained a long time

186

quite silent, as if he had gone to sleep. Then slowly he turned over and sat up, blinking about him shamefacedly, flushed, but clearly prepared to be defiant in a moment. Nobody, however, was watching; nobody had seen. He carefully wiped his face with the inside of his cap and looked himself over. After a careful listening, he got to his feet and silently worked his way back to the path. There was no one on it. He stepped out.

A quick relief, an elfish self-conscious smile. It was the face of one who had secretly won through—what no one would find out. For the luck of it, he could meet the world with double assurance. And even if he did not know his lessons, what matter? He would take three straight—six—and not turn a hair.

Alan would like that. A flush of happiness bathed his heart. His head turned quick as a hawk's. He started running.

PART THREE

I

Charlie Chisholm stood looking down on Hugh's
sleeping body. The smile was more in his eyes than
on his face. There was the least suspicion of a lift of
the sensitive lip, of a measuring flick of the eyelid.
Plainly the toe might advance to stir the curled body
—to see what would happen; but delicately as if it
were a curled adder. There was that grace in the man,
and slender bodily responsiveness. His face was fair;
in the July sun his hair had the yellow glint of a gay
humour. A wanton knowledge sat in his expression,
as though to provide him with the fine pleasure of
holding it in check. And the blue eyes had the veiled
attractive brightness of disillusion.

Hugh's bare legs and feet were stained and
weathered. His eyelashes lay long and dark on his
cheeks. His face was not tanned so much as sun-
darkened, the rich effect seeming to come from within, from his blood, leaving an outer glow still delicate
and pale. His lips were just parted; listening intently,
Charlie could catch the faint thresh of each exhalation.

The sun-darkness, as of something eastern, attracted
Charlie. The contrast was so effective to his own sun-
gold. And the family resemblance was there—to
Grace. Grace! Both lips curled and the nostrils flexed.
Amusement sparkled the more brightly for the
sudden hardening of the blue eyes. His expression
grew intense and mocking, poised and uncaring.

Upon its reckless glitter, Hugh's eyes opened wide.

There was something very disconcerting in this momentless passing from sleep to wakefulness. And the eyes, as if they carried a hidden unhuman quality out of sleep, stared at Charlie with a full unwinking regard. The very body, indeed, seemed to grow stiller, crouching. Then the moment passed, the face flushed dark with self-consciousness, and Hugh got slowly to his feet.

Charlie gave an odd laugh.

"Sound asleep, eh?"

"Yes," muttered Hugh, not looking at him, beginning to edge away, stooping to pluck a grey grass. In a moment he was walking on towards the Broch, conscious of Charlie's slanting eyes in his back. He got out of sight through the breach in the circular wall, crossed the court, and, stooping through a little doorway, entered a small stone house shaped like a beehive. Then he turned round and listened.

No sound touched him. In this little round dwelling, he always found quietness intensified. It was cunningly built, great flat stones overreaching each other to meet in a central stone. Amid the general ruin of wall chambers and passages it was perfectly intact.

And it had its effect on him, even while he listened for footsteps or noises beyond the outer wall. The first time he had entered it, Alan and Davie had run away from him and hid. What a panic he had got into! He had almost gone out of his senses, trying to escape from not only what was in the walls, but what was in the earth beneath. He kept the terror at bay by screaming and running here and there trying to find Alan or Davie. They had poked their heads round a corner at last and laughed and laughed . . . and had kept it up on him for long enough. It was an old trick, if he had but known. After all, he had only been six.

189

But years passed before he had dared enter it alone. And then his heart had been in his mouth, and standing in the little house holding his breath the earlier panic had touched him, and he had run out of the place on tiptoe, so that nothing would hear him.

Outside everything was warm and familiar and quite different. Inside was quietness in a shadow that was cold.

He felt that shadow now in the little house, but its effect upon him was to make him intensely wary rather than afraid. It was, indeed, extraordinary that he should have instinctively escaped from the embarrassing encounter with Charlie Chisholm into the small house, as though anywhere else he could be observed and spied upon. A person was alone here, was cut off from the living world. Yet this ancient world was anything but dead. Even the stones were too quiet for that, too knowing. And the unknown passages and rooms under the ruins were—well, they were there. *There.* Everything round one's body, under one's feet, was *there.* You looked at a stone— *there.* You observed everything on that stone, the least little crick and notch and colour, while listening to every other stone. Your mouth opened so that you wouldn't have to hear your own breathing. In this way your mouth got very dry as you found when you swallowed. And when you swallowed you moved— until you stood silent again.

And when you could do all this alone you got a certain secret power. It remained hidden in you, a live strength . . . a swift blow. A man's blow. No one knew about it! But when you left the place you could run and laugh to yourself, and give lightning thrusts, even inside your pockets, as if your energy in remaining silent so long had hardened and curled up like steel . . .

And if, deep, deep down, you were running away from the place itself, well, you had done your vigil and come into the sunny joyance of the world. Race is long, and its true knighthood not easily gained.

Hugh came out of the beehive chamber, stood before the door looking all round, listening. Then he tiptoed warily to the break in the outer wall and peered through a cranny.

There was no sign of Charlie Chisholm going down the glen path. Could he be still somewhere near? Why hadn't Bill come? Waiting for Bill, he had fallen asleep.

Suddenly he threw a look back over his shoulder at the door of the small house; then, his lips forming to whistle unconcernedly, his eyes veiling, he stepped across the wall. Charlie Chisholm had gone.

Nor was there a sign of Bill. Hugh moved quietly across to a grassy brink and looked down upon a slope of hazel trees, beyond which the path ran by the river. All at once, at a short distance from him, a man's face turned in a clearing. It was Charlie's face, the body invisible.

"Dash it! he has seen me again," Hugh hissed to himself as he turned instantly away. His face flushed and he walked on round the Broch. Dash it! He smiled to himself in an odd shy way, and after a little paused and tore at a tuft of grass with his toes, not thinking of what he was doing. Then looking up quickly and all around him, he started off in earnest, hissing through his teeth.

After a little he calmed down and thought of his mother, who was ill. But she would, of course, get better. She was bound to get better. He looked thoughtfully before him and up at the sky. If Bill had come they could have tried for the grilse more surely. Though it

191

would be fine to bring home the grilse whole, his own. It would be a delicacy to bring to his mother, so that she would look out from her bed at it and say something. The peats were done. There wasn't so much in the house.

It was the first year that his father hadn't stayed at home for the summer herring fishing. That was because the place as a fishing station was "going back". The curers had left—all except old Jacob Manson, who wore at home the round figured smoking cap with the hanging tassel. Once he had overheard Hector the piper saying, "The place is dying." Dying . . . like an old person. . . . His mother was. . . .What a thing to. . . . As if she might be! That's because he hadn't had plenty of sleep last night through sitting up after Kirsty had gone. But after an hour or two his mother had sent him to bed. "I think I'll go to sleep," she said, quite calmly. She must have felt the sleep coming on her. He had answered, "Good night, then, Mother," and stepped quietly away. But he had not gone to sleep for a long time after that, keeping his mind from thinking of death, and listening every now and then for his mother.

But if he got this fish now and Bill and himself set rabbit-snares to-night, it might be something. A great desire came upon him to provide for the house. To hunt and kill, to bring food home, and fire. His eyes glistened, but in their light there was also something of awe. Life could hold nothing more supreme than that. To be the provider, the giver. The importance of it made him quiver. He saw in a flash deep into man's estate. The glory, the power, and the self-restraint that smiles thanks shyly away. To be able to do that . . . and then for his father to come home, to learn about it, and—to look at him for a moment with his quiet man's look. Nothing on earth could beat that.

The light transfigured his face, drew to an avid concentration in his eyes.

He glanced about him as if his inmost thought might have escaped, then went on more briskly, dismissing such dreams (but secretly sinking them deep amongst the black roots of being that came alive in the Broch).

To get away from the urge of these preoccupations, from their piercing delights, he wantonly slipped from the path and came up against a drystone dyke that enclosed the cottage where Navook, the pigkiller, lived with his silly daughter.

There was a certain habit in this, too, for many a time boys crept up to the wall and stared over it to see what foolish thing Margat would be at. They did this fearfully, and when running away would laugh to each other boisterously, and some would shout "Foolish Margat!" at the top of their voices.

When Hugh's eyes lit on her she was sitting by the doorstep playing a girl's game with five little stones. She threw one in the air, then grabbed another from the ground in time to catch the falling one. Hugh heard the click as they met in her palm. Then she threw one up and grabbed two. In the final click she had all five in her palm. To this pastime she sang a little song. Hugh knew it, for the girls often sang it in their playground at school.

She was a woman of about fifty, but her face was smooth as a girl's and her hair the exact colour of Kirsty's.

It was the first time that Hugh had watched her all by himself, and a strange insecurity possessed him. It was almost as if something terrible and edged might fly out of her towards him if he was seen. Her actions, her expressions, were so like a little child's that their smoothness was awful and frightening.

193

Slowly he withdrew, and on tiptoe ran away, stooping so that his head would not show over the coping.

Boys shouted because they were really afraid. No boy would shout if he was alone. It was awful to see a woman who was out of her mind because long, long ago she had killed her bairn and they had put her in prison.

They said she was harmless. His mother must have felt sorry for her, because once she had made no answer when Mrs. Graham from the Pheasant Wood said it was the Lord's judgement that she should now be a child herself. A quiet sad light had come into his mother's eyes.

Her hair was the exact colour of Kirsty's.

Few spoke of her, of course, and no one would ever use her as an example even under terrible provocation. It would be much better to swear. But no woman may swear, and who else could use the name Margat Navook except a mother to her daughter?

These implications, and more, Hugh had gathered one way or another. But presently, when the path left the shelter of whin and scrub and the moor let him see and be seen, he forgot Margat Navook, whose real name was Margaret Mackay, and her game of pebbles. He walked at a steady pace, and no one would guess from a little distance the natural dodges he resorted to in order to command the world around him.

Presently he came to the tip of a tongue of trees that reached up to the road, and he smoothly faded out of sight.

Among the trees he became all alert, poised and listening. He had half-hoped to see Hector the Roadman, but could not go on past the keeper's house. A keeper knows that no youth goes a long walk for fun. There had been no sight of Hector or the keeper. Hector might be away towards the high ground. Or he might not be out at all. If Hugh had been certain where

194

old MacAulay was, he might have risked things on his own. The only way now was to stalk his house. The grilse lay in a pool that he could run to in less than five minutes.

Though his slim nervous body went stepping noiselessly, he would undoubtedly have walked right into MacAulay had not a natural accident saved him. Behind a bank in the wood near his house, MacAulay was making himself comfortable. A humble bee, investigating this sylvan innocence, was briskly warned off. The bee, for its own reasons, persisted. MacAulay hit at it with his cap. Finally he stood up as he was, thrusting at it viciously, and swearing in throaty guttural. But the entrance to the wild hive itself must have been thereabouts, for clearly more than one bee joined in a stinging pursuit that presently sent MacAulay tripping over a nether garment, which, grabbed at precariously in the press of the moment, had slipped.

Hugh faded again. He glided down among the trees, his mind in a wild amaze, rapidly on feet winged with silent laughter. The whole performance was too amazing to be funny all at once. And he had escaped being caught scouting by a bee's breadth!

What luck! What a joke to have to tell! He ran like the wind on the grassy verge of the path, thrillingly exhilarated. Nothing more rollicking, more apt could have happened to a man like MacAulay. The fun of it was wild, oh, fierce!

Yet the humour of it did not really touch Hugh at the moment. He was so rapidly nearing the pool that his mind was getting sick with apprehension. He overshot the pool by a hundred yards, scouted, and then raced back. Stealing to the grey boulder, he peered down. The grilse was there.

His body strung taut, he hesitated. Then he shot for a clump of hazel, took out his knife, sliced and tugged at a straight wand that ran to a working point no thicker than his finger, severed and dressed it. A large shining barbed cod-hook, in a fistful of string, he brought from his pocket. In less than a minute the hook was fixed to the slender point, the rest of the string twisting up the yard-long hazel to his right-hand grip.

Thus armed, and on bare feet, he stealthily got down to the pool.

It was not a very big pool, and in no place much more than a yard deep. Not a pool that anyone would have expected to find a fish in. But in his ranging last night with Bill, Hugh had leant over the grey boulder and peered down. They had had, however, no hook. And in any case, some scouting system would have to be worked out. But Bill not having turned up at the appointed time at the Broch, Hugh had every right to tackle the quarry alone. For right lies with him who first sees, even if ownership is inexorably vested in him who kills.

The river was fairly low. The fish had presumably come up on the tail-end of the last spate and not risked going all the way to the high pools.

It was a sunny afternoon in late July, and the soft water came over the stony shallows and swirling into the pool's narrow neck in a warm gurgle. Its brown tinge was scarcely perceptible, and already the sleepy stones were gathering a hint of green at the pool-edge. The trees on both sides of the narrow glen were heavily leaved and hung in a drowsy silence.

No inimical sound came to Hugh's ears. Nor had he time to dwell on hidden eyes. What he had to do had to be done quickly.

The fish lay on the bottom at a depth of some four feet, and was visible from tip to tail. Crouching over the water, Hugh saw its delicately shaped head, its lithe form, its desirable beauty. He saw them too clearly, so clearly that obviously the fish saw him. It was watching him. He stared at it, then slowly inch by inch he brought the hook to the water, sank it, inch by inch, slowly, down, down, more slowly, his breast hurting him from the pain of his beating heart. The fish would never wait. It was watching him. He could see its eyes. It was the maddest thing in the world to expect that fish to wait. It was going to bolt, now, at this instant, now, to dart off like a streak. Anxiety wrung his breast. He stopped breathing altogether. But the hook went down slowly, inch by inch, without a tremor, and well out over the fish's back.

His anxiety became unbearable. A whelming desire prompted to thrust and snatch. The water was deeper than he thought. His hand went out of sight. How deep? . . . With the water licking the knuckle of his elbow the hook grounded.

His nose was now immersed. His lungs were like to burst. But more slowly than it had yet moved the hook crept through six inches, inward and towards the head, till its point slid from view under the dark shoulder.

One balancing second, and Hugh struck straight up. The water boiled, and grilse and gaff went hurtling through the air, hitting a gaping rock-face behind and setting up an infernal slapping on smooth ledges.

But as Hugh threw he leapt. His fingers found the gills and silence. For a moment he crouched beside his capture, looking around him, as if in wary expectation of a blow. The fish writhed. He wedged its head, rapped it smartly with a stone; broke the hook from the gaff and stuck it in his pocket; shoved the inert fish under his blue jersey; scrambled up the steep bank; crossed the path; and disappeared in the wood.

A neat hunter, clearly born to the job. For a few

seconds he had brought to the river an intense eddy
of life. But the gurgle at the throat grew warm and
sleepy again. The quivering eddy faded out. And
presently nothing was left to show that Hugh had
passed that way but a splash of water drying in the
sun beneath a signature of glistening silver scales.

Hugh ran far through the woods, dodging, side-
stepping, gripping and swinging with one arm, as
though he were being pursued; but conscious that he
was not being pursued, that he was escaping from the
tell-tale spot to an exquisite freedom, that he was a
hunter swift and successful, that in the midst of an
encompassing fearfulness his heart sang. All great
joy is a little incredible. It has that novelty, that air
of a thrilling gaiety. In spite of everything, lo! here
it is, its white beauty shining like fairy silver, bathing
the eyes, drenching the body, and salting the blood.
Only when the first rapture has passed and belief becomes
absolute does the fierce hunger for possession burn.

But the silver sheen was still on his fish when Hugh,
slipping into a thicket of young hazel, brought it to
the light, his hands bearing it like an offering as he
slid to his knees and laid it, with fastidious care, on
unsoiled grass.

So on his knees he gazed at it, noting curve and
shape and sheen. That it should be here in this silence
of the wood, held an air of magic. He touched the
dorsal fin, smoothing it. Still and beautiful, but real.
And, above all things, clean, It was not spent or dis-
coloured. It was shapely and clean. Form and silver.

His ears were sensitively alert. Every now and then
he cast oblique glances between the young withies
at the old lichened trunks beyond. They, too, were
still, standing near each other and yet apart, each with
an odd shape of its own, a twist here, a leaning there.

How strange and exciting! His eyes grew full of laughter—and returned to the silver tribute at his knees, astonishingly there and so lovely.

The laughter spilt in glimmering silence over his face. His head jerked hither and thither from listening pauses. Overhead, the serenity of three small white clouds made the blue sky tall and remote. Down below, the tree-slope gave on a narrow glade, a secret pathway closed in by trees from the river-flat. The laughter came to his throat and he let it out huskily, softly, his shoulders doubling up. His face, wrinkling, took on a cunning look, full of gleeful triumph, that yet intensified its open innocence. At once a boy and something older; as if the wood had entered into him, the shape of the trees, the smell of the earth, the capture, the silence. He could have danced and slashed and danced.

His senses grew abnormally acute. The salmon of knowledge under the nuts of the hazel of wisdom. But deeper than that, deeper than conscious thought or myth. Sheering right through to the vivid and unconditional, where are born the pagan deities, who are lovely until conscious thought degrades them.

All in a moment, or a wood of moments, like a wood of trees. Listening intently, so intently that the trees listened and the grass, to a sound far away like a soft beat, a faint *thud thud* of feet, coming near, nearer . . . up through intolerable prescience to the final terrifying reality of a voice.

II

But not a harsh voice. Not a gruff, destroying, damning sound. On the contrary, something uncertain and nervous and feminine. A whole world of its own, going far back beyond Hugh's instincts and pagan glee.

With a slow stealth he shoved the grilse out of sight amid a tangle of tender shoots, and crouched close. No one on earth could spot him here from below. He was safe.

But fear had not left him, and though the sound came from below it was also as if arrested bodies crouched waiting all along the wood. Indeed, for one sickening moment he could have sworn he caught the treachery of a climbing foot somewhere above him and to the right. But listen as he would, nothing definite came of it, and just as he let his pent-up breath escape there entered upon his vision, walking up the narrow glade, side by side, his sister Kirsty and Charlie Chisholm.

All the world faded away from the presence of these two. Kirsty's face was flushed and constrained. Her emotion came and stuck in Hugh's throat. The awkwardness and the dreadful burden of her moving body, that yet moved so fairly, held an intolerable excitement. This was his sister Kirsty as he had never seen her, at the mercy of a power that held dominion not only over her mind, but over every cell in her body.

For to Hugh, Kirsty was the fighter. Nothing had ever frightened her to defeat; no midnight storm, no foreclosing of debt, no stress of danger, no poverty, no fear of the mind. Where Grace would blow away,

Kirsty could only blow into a flame. Against any force threatening her home, she would fight passionately, through tears, through darkness, with a harrying will to a final conclusion. A fierce turbulent spirit showing in a final resort no respect for any external authority or law. She had been known in a gay moment to laugh at the king, even to question the authority of the laird. Gaily, a gay spirit—because she had kings and queens of her own household.

And now here she was, all gone to pieces before the fight began. Like a little girl that might suddenly sit down and cry. With the face still up and trying to smile bravely. The mocking echo of herself—Poor Kirsty!

They halted directly beneath Hugh, as if their little play were being staged specially for him in this, the deepest part of the wood.

Hugh now knew for whom Charlie had been waiting at the Broch. An appointment—and here its meaning and its moment.

Charlie, golden and friendly, was going to make short work of it. After all, there was only one meaning, and it needed no words. With an intimate little laugh, he caught Kirsty in his arms.

Instantly the intolerable burden fell from her, and with an explosive energy she shoved him back. She was fighting! Hugh knew the face. Her eyes flamed above her flaming cheeks.

"No!" she said, her voice controlled but thin. In her violence, a pulse at her throat, she was enchanting. Charlie's face drew thinner, his eyes gleaming as he veiled them.

"Why not?" he asked, carelessly, toying with the phrase.

She had nothing to hang on to, no mainstay but her pride.

"Why not?"

He was fine enough to see the insulting, the degrading inflexion, but with fineness goes a fine cruelty. He added to it by waiting.

"Because—because it is not for me you care." Wrung out of her, so that her breast heaved, so much air the poisoning turbulence of her blood needed.

"Oh? What makes you think that?"

Yet there was something masterful about him. He knew his power. And she knew it. He could come down upon her with that power. He could crush her with it. And she knew it. Therefore his toying words, his waiting, were more than insulting, they were like a snare cast about her. In her final being, indeed, she was not insulted at all: she was exposed and shamed.

"What makes you think that?" he repeated.

"You know why."

"Do I? I don't see. . . . "

"You do! You do! And you know you do!"

"Well . . . and what if I do?"

"What then are you—wanting me for?"

"It's difficult . . . isn't it?"

"No! It's not!"

"Isn't it?"

"No! It's not!"

"What's not?"

Her face was now quite pale, straining. He was torturing her. Her fingers could not keep still. She was trembling.

What a fight she would have made of it—if he had fought! But she had nothing to fight against—and she could not run away.

Nor could she mention Grace—not point blank. Not to that half-smiling face, with its evasive yet penetrating eyes. Her look broke this way and that.

202

"You know," she said, utterly distressed. "You know you—you—"

"What?"

Her body grew slowly still and straight.

"Nothing," she said, and her mouth closed.

"Well, then, Kirsty, what's all the trouble about?"

"There's no trouble."

"Isn't there?"

"No. I'll be going back now. My mother is very ill."

She shouldn't have mentioned her mother. Her lips had to grip tight.

"I'm sorry—again," he murmured.

"Well, I'll be off."

"Good-bye," he said gently.

She hesitated a moment, as if the irrevocable thing had not been said—and must. She was not going to go through this again.

He took a step towards her.

"Good-bye, Kirsty, you little fool!"

Her eyes blazed.

"Well, aren't you?" He came quite close to her, smiling, his voice a caress. The words stood for nothing but a darkening power.

"I'm not. You—you don't care for me." It was an attempt at a statement of fact.

He suddenly laughed.

"And *I*—detest you," she finished.

"So we cancel out! What more could we wish for?"

All at once her body quivered, as if its warmth had been clenched in ice. "Oh!" she cried as her breath came shivering in through her teeth. She stumbled away, but he stopped her.

"Not yet," he said. "You haven't mentioned Grace, you know."

And then for the first time she really faced him. In

this release she lost a little of her enchantment and grew harsh. "I know you were playing with me. Perhaps you were playing with Grace. I don't know. I don't care. I detest you—and I'm glad of it. I'm glad to be free of you. I hate you." The harsh ugly primitive elements strove for utterance in a raucous voice. She was not magnificent: she was laid bare.

But the final basis is human, is flesh. The body speaks. It cries. It is urgent and without grace. But in the same measure it is potent and terrible.

She steadied him, and his eyes, never leaving her, gleamed. His mouth shut, his face paled a trifle, the smile fading. With unwavering look, he caught her. She struggled. She cried in an ugly voice, "Let me go!" He crushed her, his mouth twisting in an ugly strength. "Damn you, I'll crush you to death," he muttered.

"Let me go! Let me go! Oh, let me go!"

"Kirsty, my own!"

"No, no, it's not true. I'm not! I'm not!" She battered his chest with her forehead. Her voice broke. She began to sob.

"Kirsty, dear Kirsty."

"No, no!"

She sobbed as if her heart were broken. She struggled no more. She was done. She lay against him, sobbing.

He lifted her in his arms and carried her in amongst the trees.

"Oh, no, no!" she cried as he laid her down. She turned over on her face, and her brown felt hat rolled from her head.

Hugh saw that her hair was exactly the colour of Margat Navook's.

Charlie, on his elbow beside her, smoothed the hair. He looked at it and his face grew tender. His mouth

204

stooped to her ear. "Kirsty, my own!" His voice was gentle and so low that it broke huskily.

A mutter of protest came from her crushed mouth.

"Kirsty!" He put an arm over and tried to pull her round. She resisted passionately. But he pulled her slowly, firmly. She was ashamed to show her face. It flashed up and over. She hid it.

But he searched for it and laid it bare, crushed down through her protesting hands to her mouth. They were no more than fifteen feet from Hugh, who saw her eyes close, her mouth cling.

It was the first kiss of the kind that Hugh had seen. He lay breathless watching their long breathless silence. Kirsty's lost face and her falling hair, red gold, her face falling and clinging, utterly lost and blind. And Charlie's hungry mouth crushing down, but Charlie himself blind, too, and lost.

A thin fire crept over Hugh. The impulse to fight for Kirsty, that could have heaved a smashing stone at Charlie, that had hated the degradation of his sister, that had quivered with futile wrath, feeling weak and impotent, was now licked up by this warmth, this trickling, tingling fire.

A strange and terrifying curiosity beset him, grew in him. The glittering pagan look came back into his eyes. Secrecy drew her smooth ecstatic veil about him. His lips came adrift, his breath panting a little. Within this veil he was unseen and could see. No one in the world would know what he would see. And no one in the world would see but himself.

Their lips fell apart, and Charlie caught Kirsty up, against his breast. She lay there quite still, her face hidden. Charlie gazed over her hair, and as he gazed an odd half-sad expression dawned in his eyes; touched his nostrils, his lips. There was no triumph in it, hardly even defeat—as if the end inevitable had come upon him, upon them both.

He bowed over her head, smiled at the hair appraisingly, lovely hair, and kissed her ear. Passion had passed out of him. By a profound intuition Hugh was affected to compassion for his sister. At that moment Charlie and his mood came within the understanding of Hugh's instinct. Charlie and the mood were not enough. But—they were fated.

Fate was in Charlie's face grown whimsical and gentle, a trifle sad. A fine face, debonair and mannerly. Not desiring enough earnestly enough. Capable of a thin brutal cruelty through an excess of penetration; almost a feminine cruelty, yet wholly masculine.

Kirsty stirred. She sat up. Charlie retrieved her hat, but refused to give it to her. "You have lovely hair."

She did not look at him. "You are laughing at me." She tried to laugh herself, but failed.

"No, Kirsty," he said gently; "I'm not. I'll never laugh at you, God knows."

All her body could be seen to burgeon under this sweet rain. She regarded her left hand fingering dead leaves on the ground.

"Sometimes you do."

"Ah, but that is different," he said. No man could have more understanding, could have helped her more.

"I don't know," she murmured.

"We'll have to get it out, Kirsty, I suppose?"

"No. I don't want to hear."

He considered for a little. There was perfect silence.

"Have you ever thought what sort of girl your sister Grace is?"

"How—how do you mean?" She stirred restlessly.

"She is a good girl. There is far less passion in her

than there is in yourself. But she is, in some way, fatal. Do you understand that?"

"Yes."

He conquered the cruel desire to leave it at that, and went on:

"Occasionally a woman is like that, very occasionally. They attract. They are charming. Grace has it. It's an odd thing. I could tell you a lot about it. Somehow . . . I cannot help feeling these things just as occasionally I cannot help getting drunk. A woman like Grace is a challenge. The challenge comes over a man. But I know exactly what it's worth. That, you see, is the desperate temptation. Why does a man drink? For any clear reason? I doubt it. After a steady run of days and weeks he simply says to himself, 'Oh, to hell!' and goes and drinks. Grace is like drink."

Kirsty's eyes grew clear and honesty shone in them.

"No," she said in a small voice.

Charlie looked at her and smiled.

"You are simply taking a woman's way of getting at the root. You mean that I loved Grace."

"Didn't you?"

"Tell me this. Do you think—Grace loved me?"

So much was the question unexpected, that Kirsty suddenly looked in his face. Then looked away.

"You see—it never really occurred to you—not that side of it. Odd, isn't it?"

"But she would—if you did."

"Would she?" He laughed softly. "Yet if she had loved me—think—wouldn't you have known it? Wouldn't you? Yet that side of it never dawned on you. You thought: he will love Grace; he is bound to love Grace."

"Yes," she murmured.

207

He watched her eyes as they looked straight in front of her, heavy with light.

"And what do you think now?" he asked.

"It was natural that you should love her. I'm not blaming you."

"You really think I did?"

"Don't you?" She looked at him.

"And because I still love her, but can't get her . . . I'll take you—as next best? Is that it?"

"Isn't it, then?" She looked away.

The "then" had a curious inflexion. In it was all her question, all her suppressed hope.

"How do I know, Kirsty? What does a man honestly know about himself?"

Her head drooped.

"It is in your bones—that you cannot take the place of Grace. That's what's wrong with you."

She did not answer. Her fingers crushed the dead leaves.

"What are you thinking of?" he asked, watching her curiously.

She did not speak.

"Why don't you answer?"

He stooped to see her eyes; caught her chin and turned her face to him.

Her eyes looked at him frankly; they were brimming. Her expression was very still.

"Oh, God, Kirsty!" he cried, crushing the face against his breast, because he could not look at it longer. His mouth shut tight, and his eyes narrowed as if he were crushing his emotion flat as a blade. Then his voice came brutally definite:

"I'll tell you what it is, Kirsty. It's like this. If I was after Grace and another man was after her too, I would fight him, I would do him down in every damned way I could. But, Kirsty, if a man was after you—listen, Kirsty—if a man touched you—if a man laid hands on you—do you hear, Kirsty?—" his lips met her hair—" I would murder him, I would murder the—"

The intensely muttered oath made Hugh shiver. Yet his sister could not have minded it, because she never stirred. Something utterly unlawful in this touched Hugh fearfully. His sister, lying within the circle of a man's unholy oath, and not caring. It gave her a new significance, a scarlet power.

And having said his say, Charlie crushed his mouth into her hair. But that seemed to give him no satisfaction. His arms moved restlessly over her body. His expression was tempestuous and driving beyond all trifling. He broke upon her mouth. Full length, face to face, he kissed and crushed her. His arms moved restlessly. . . .

Hugh's being drew through excitement to utter suspense. From his choking throat, his body melted into warm vanishing waves of sensation. Soon even his throat thawed, leaving only his eyes round and, in their intense clear focus, mirroring the whole secret life of the body.

Hardly even the wood itself could hold suspense and apprehension in such fiery poise, and its satyr curiosity overbalancing itself, a freighted branch snapped and came crashing to earth . . . up above Hugh and a little to the right.

Hugh cowered, as if he'd been missed by that crash and no more, turning not even an eye. He saw Charlie's head rise slowly with an expression of wrath whipped to murder. For one brain-darkening instant Hugh grovelled in the desire that he would not be seen. To be seen by Charlie would be such a humiliation that he would rather die. All his flesh ran into abject abasement. His pride was a strangling rope.

But Charlie did not even look his way. He was now on his feet, staring towards the spot where the branch had crashed. Hugh had heard a scramble of some living body, but now there was silence. The wood was thick. Anyone could disappear in a moment.

Kirsty was sitting, her back to the brae-face, drawing on her hat. She had been dreadfully startled, even to a choked scream. Her shoulders were drawn, her head bent, her whole attitude was one of hiding. When she got to her feet she clearly wanted to be off without waiting.

But Charlie was in no hurry. He conquered the maddening upset with a rather fine carelessness.

"There's no hurry, Kirsty," he said, smiling. His slow voice was intimate and friendly. He caught her arm. "You don't mind?" He stooped and kissed her on the forehead in a courtly way. Hugh saw Kirsty's head go up. She was looking at Charlie. Something in her eyes, perhaps of admiration for his exquisite understanding, for his knightly covering, as a light in something still more profound, made it embarrassing even for Charlie, whose face flushed a trifle, but in a shy way.

Hugh's heart thrilled to the man at that moment, to his cavalier's spirit.

The shy flush broke in a little laugh, and Charlie offered Kirsty his arm.

Kirsty took it, as she would have done in a ball-room, and they threaded the few steps to the path. Her head was down, and Hugh knew there were tears in her eyes. Possibly in a single span life cannot repeat very often such exquisite moments. They turned up the secret glade.

III

Moving up from the thicket of hazel, Hugh heard no sound, and before going over the crest of the slope he stood listening into the wood. Whoever had broken the branch over there must have gone. In the dead silence only his heart was beating—until the silence leapt alive with a terrific—

"Whoop!"

And Hugh staggered back, staring at Bill grinning before him.

Hugh put out a hand against a tree and drew breath painfully. His knees were turned to water.

"What a fright you got! Ho! ho! ho!" laughed Bill, actively delighted. He doubled up. "Ho! ho! ho!" Hugh's fright would make a cat laugh!

Bill's love of mystery-working, of possessing grown-up knowledge, in short, of leadership, led him to say, before the effect of his dramatic appearance could pass:

"If your Kirsty is not careful, she'll have a bairn."

The effect was certainly all that he could have desired.

Hugh, drawing thin as a wire, lashed out:

"Shut up!"

Bill pivoted on his heel knowingly.

"Oh, I saw. Ha! ha!"

Hugh found that he could not add a word, could not move.

Bill took a step or two away. There was no need to show too flattering an interest in Hugh's state of mind. Besides, he had seen the bulge under Hugh's jersey all along. It could only mean that Hugh had

211

gaffed the grilse himself. And Hugh wasn't going to "blow" over that—now! It was enough for Bill to have missed the gaffing—which he would have done himself while he got Hugh to watch. He would have made a whole important conspiracy of the thing.

He half-turned with a sarcastic laugh:

"I suppose I couldn't be out on the branch of a tree if I liked?"

"You were spying!"

"Oh, and you have never done any spying?"

Now spying was a game, called "tracking" or "shadowing" according to the latest work in heroic letters. "Scouting" was a different thing, and of no male virtue at all unless it represented the work of advance parties for main or superior bodies, who were presently to clash to the accompaniment of whoops and swords. Ancestry is everywhere.

Bill began to realize how hardly he had smote Hugh, who looked as if at any moment he might fight—in earnest. They had never fought. It was a delicate position all in a minute, and not without its suppressed excitement.

"And, anyway," said Bill, "it wasn't their tree."

Hugh could not answer this. The prisoning tension, however, was easing. He was breathing; a dry scorn came into his eyes.

Bill observed these signs.

"And a fellow can crawl out on a branch if he likes. And if he wants to crawl farther—for the fun of it—or just to *see* anything—who's to stop him? Are you?"

"If I found you—at that, I would."

"Oh, you would, would you?"

"Yes."

"I would like to see you try it."

"I would." Hugh gulped.

"Because it was your sister, Kirsty. Huh!"

"If you say Kirsty again I'll hit you."

"Oh? You're good with your tongue."

Hugh's mouth shut tight. Bill did not invoke Kirsty. He saw how excited Hugh was, saw that he could not speak many words at once. If Hugh lost his head he would fight like a fiend.

"So you would stop a fellow from crawling out on a branch!" It was a good joke. Bill laughed affectedly.

"Well, then!" said Hugh.

"To see what he could see!" It was a capital joke.

"You mind yourself."

Bill turned on him.

"And what were you doing? Weren't you spying yourself?" His look penetrated slyly.

"I was not!"

"Weren't you?"

"I was not!"

"Spying on your own sister. I wouldn't spy—"

Hugh leapt for him. Bill wavered one desperate moment—then broke. After all, he was not roused to the same fighting pitch as Hugh, who even forgot the grilse. It bumped on his knees, was kicked by his feet, and so tripped him. He fell full length. As he grabbed the fish and thrust it under his jersey, he found himself all trembling and on the verge of tears, he was so blind with rage.

From a little distance Bill laughed.

Gripping his bulging front with one hand, Hugh was after him.

Normally Hugh approached a fight with trepidation, even though he knew he was going to win. For the most part in their joint expeditions, Bill led him. Bill had more self-assertion and less imagination. But every now and then a point had come where Hugh

213

would not be led. Bill's way was wrong. When the matter was too clear to dispute, Bill would begin expounding Hugh's own plan to him, showing exactly what Hugh had to do, while he himself did the other thing. Hugh would accept that, for he hated discord.

What had happened now was an entirely different thing. He would wipe all the Bills out of creation. He would smash them into the grass. For Bill's sly penetration had been poisoned. All Hugh's body flamed with the poison. This horrible poison—of having spied on his own sister.

Hugh was swifter than Bill, and at last cornered him where a grey dyke ran into the foot of a knoll.

"Keep off!" shouted Bill. There was no laugh on his face now.

Hugh carried straight into him, his left hand still gripping the rolled fish. A fatal preoccupation, and before he could blink Bill had swung his right fist with full force fair between his eyes.

Hugh staggered back, and for a moment stared in a dumbfounded way at what had happened. Then something came into his face. Looking secretively about him, he ignored Bill. He got on his knees by the dyke, laid the grilse hard against it, and hid it by tilting against the dyke a long flat stone. Then he stood up, pulled his jersey smooth, looked at Bill, and came towards him, not in a hurry but slowly.

Bill broke again, clambering up the grassy side of the knoll for all he was worth. There was fear in his face, a panting terror. He had often been in a fight. It wasn't that. But here—all alone. . . . Hugh had not the look of one merely going into a fight. He outsped Hugh to the top, where he grabbed two stones from a cairn and shouted, "Stop! Stop!" his right

214

hand behind his shoulder threatening violently to throw. Lifting his left arm, Hugh came straight on.

Bill backed away. He had not the courage to throw; he dared not; he might kill him. He backed round the cairn, Hugh following him. "If you come nearer, I'll let fly!" Bill's voice rose to a shriek. Hugh's eyes were glittering and watchful.

Never in his life before had Hugh felt like this. He had always been too anxious, too nervous, too fiery, lashing out in a high-strung frenzy. This was a luxury of cold self-forgetfulness. He had Bill now. Everything was swallowed up in this certainty. It was a marvellous feeling, so deadly, so exultantly clear.

"I've got you now!" he said through his teeth.

Bill hit a stone with his heels and fell flat on his back with a harsh squawk. He had only time to turn over on his face when Hugh was upon him, a knee in his spine, a hand at his neck.

"Drop the stones! Drop them! Go on! Drop them!"

The feel of Bill's body was having its effect on him. His voice was growing excited, was shouting a little. Bill, in dropping the stones, half-turned and grabbed recklessly at Hugh. They got interlocked. Hugh's frenzy of strength came over him. He had Bill by the throat when a voice above them said:

"What's this, boys? What's this?"

It was Hector the Roadman.

Reluctantly Hugh let go. Awkwardly he got up, face flushing darkly. He did not look at Hector.

Bill stared a moment, mouth open, at his deliverer, and then got to his feet.

"What were you trying to do to each other? Eh? Not having a bit of a fight, were you?" Hector's questions held a friendly smile.

But Hugh began to move off.

215

"Wait you, Hugh. Don't be in such a hurry. Here!"
Hugh hesitated.

"Come here, now, both of you, till I show you.
Don't you be shy. Here, now. You see, when two friends
have a boxing match, do you know what they always do
at the end of it? They shake hands. Come away, then."

But Hugh would not turn round.

"Now, I know the both of you. I know what you're
up to sometimes. Oh, fine that! I'll have been seeing
you! God bless me, aren't you growing up to be taking
the place of your brother Alan and the other brave
lads who are gone? They wouldn't be fighting amongst
themselves. They would be joining their forces—
against the enemy. What!" He chuckled knowingly.
By this time he had got hold of Hugh's hand and was
pulling it, rather forcibly, towards Bill. He joined
their hands. "Now, shake!" and he started them up
and down.

With great confusion they shook hands. It was the
first time they had ever done so. Blushing, they looked
anywhere but at each other. The whole proceeding
was mad! They felt so foolish that queer grins formed
on their faces and wriggling sounds came out of their
throats. Their hands slipped and flew apart.

"Now, that's better," nodded Hector. "But tell me
this—you weren't quarrelling over the fish down there?"

"No," muttered Hugh.

"Ah, that's all right then. I knew you wouldn't do
that. I was round the bend when I saw you put it by
the wall. Then I climbed up here after you. No one
else saw you. It's all right. Where did you get it?"

"In the Grey Boulder."

"Did you, though? I wouldn't have thought there
would have been anything there. Did you know
MacAulay was at home to-day?"

"Yes," replied Hugh. He smiled in an odd way. "I saw him before I went down to the pool."

Hector looked closely at his expression.

"Where did you see him?"

Hugh remained silent and obviously embarrassed. To Hector's promptings he added no more than that he saw him in the wood. He would not say what he was doing.

"Very well, then. Don't tell me if you would rather not. You're friends again, aren't you?"

"Yes," muttered Bill. Hugh nodded.

"I may be able to tell you both something—next week." With a secret smile to himself, Hector walked away.

"Do you think he will?" inquired Bill, of the high pools.

"Yes," said Hugh.

They did not know what to do with their arms as they looked at the farthest objects they could see. Their self-consciousness gripped them painfully. They sat down.

"What was MacAulay doing?" asked Bill.

Hugh began to laugh. Bill began to laugh too.

Hugh explained in an abrupt sentence, and Bill doubled up.

They laughed until tears came into their eyes.

"But that's nothing," said Hugh.

"Oh, oh!" cried Bill, trying to stop himself.

"I would have walked right into him—if I hadn't seen a hand hitting out—hitting out—like that."

"At what?"

"A bee!" cried Hugh.

"A bee!" rose Bill's voice once more. He rolled over. "A bee!" He lay spread-eagled under heaven. "Oh, oh!" he gasped, waggling his head. Then, "Bee-hee!" he wheezed, and was off again.

Hugh rocked helpless.

"It—attacked him!" he spluttered.

Bill beat the ground with his feet. "Stop it!"

"He—stood up!"

"No, no!" yelled Bill, pedalling a frenzied bicycle on the air.

"Bees—whole hive—"

"Oh-h!" grovelled Bill.

"—attacked him!"

"Gug-gug. . . ."

"He ran!"

"No! No!"

"Trousers slipt!"

They collided. They sprawled, hands on stomach.

"'eript!"

"Wha'?"

"He tripped!"

Bill beat the earth with his fists and kicked the sky.

"An' d' they sting?" he screamed.

"Yes!" yelled Hugh.

They rolled over drunkenly. They became helpless. Soon they were moaning over the pains in their bellies. Long quivering sighs broke from them. There was a prayer in their eyes that neither would start again. But the first mutual glance was enough. They cried, "Oh, oh!" afresh, and gave in; and not until they were properly and healthily exhausted did Hugh remember his grilse.

And it immediately assumed a splendid importance. They searched the landscape round with stealthy eyes. They slipped down the slope like Redskins. Hugh turned back the stone and Bill got down on his knees.

"Boy, he's a nice fellow," he said.

"Not bad."

"Fat, in grand condition. You got him here— just in the right place. Out of sight with him—in case."

Hugh whipped the grilse under his jersey. They both looked around.

"Come on!" commanded Bill, and they started for the wood below Hector's cottage.

On the way Bill asked Hugh how he had gone about the capture. Hugh went into detail, stressing how the fish lay and with what slow care he had stalked it.

"You couldn't have done it better," nodded Bill.

"I don't think so," agreed Hugh, pleased. "But you can imagine how I took to my heels once I'd got him in my jersey. Right up into the wood and along until I was tired. Then I sat down in a bushy place to take my breath and have a look at him. It was when I was sitting there that I heard voices coming, so you bet I clapt pretty close!"

"Yes, rather!" nodded Bill emphatically. "I was out on a branch trying to get a view of the glen road myself, looking for you, when I heard the voices too."

If it was a lie, it was a good one.

Hugh nodded. "Yes."

They walked on for a pace or two, their hearts beating.

"Why weren't you at the Broch in time?" inquired Hugh.

Because of this delicate avoidance by Hugh of the danger point, Bill's bearing gathered some of its old assurance.

"Oh, because I had to go to Badrea to see why the fool of a man hadn't come with the peats. Boy, he's the born ass yon!"

"He is."

"Do you know what he said?"

"No?"

And so they went on talking about Badrea and his horse that had "gotten into the clover and come out

219

of it with a twist in his guts", and what Jemima, Badrea's wife, had done and said about it.

They hardly laughed at all, so interested were they measuring Badrea's idiosyncrasies. They talked thoughtfully, like grown men.

"I would have waited for you," said Hugh, as they at last rested in Hector's wood for a little before parting, "if it wasn't that people were moving about the Broch. I thought it might look suspicious, as there wasn't a sign of you to be seen. So I started off as if I wasn't going near the river at all."

"Up by Navook's?"

"Yes." Hugh hesitated. "Yes. I went up past Navook's."

Bill glanced at him.

"Did you look over the wall?"

"Yes, I did. I saw Margat."

"What was she doing?"

"She was playing at five-stones, like a little girl."

"No!"

"Yes."

"Isn't she clean off her head?"

"It was queer to see her."

"Playing at five-stones!"

"Yes. And singing a little song to herself."

"It's not canny. If it was anywhere else she would be taken up."

"But they say she's quite harmless."

"That makes no difference to the law."

"Doesn't it?" asked Hugh.

"No. It shouldn't be allowed. Who knows what she might do?"

"What could she do?" Hugh's eyes stared past Bill.

"Who knows? Didn't she murder her own bairn?"

"Murder," breathed Hugh.

"Well, it's fact as death. She smothered it. She had it in the barn at night."

"Yes."

"And then she went and put it in a hole."

"I know." Hugh's eyes were bright with horror, so he looked at the ground. "But they say that she maybe did not know what she was doing."

"How couldn't she know?"

"If she was beside herself."

"She didn't want anyone to find out. That's why. She wanted to hide it. She was frightened."

"But no one can be certain how it happened, seeing no one was there."

"She was tried and found guilty, wasn't she? How could they find her guilty if she hadn't done it?"

"She said she didn't do it, didn't want to do it. She cried out in the court that she wanted her—her baby. I heard that once."

"I heard that too—often. But that was afterwards."

"How afterwards?"

"After she'd done it. If you were in court, wouldn't you tell a lie to get off?"

"I don't know."

"Oh, wouldn't you? I bet you would."

"Would you?"

"Wouldn't I just!"

Bill smiled from a superior knowledge. He knew a daring thing or two. "You think you mightn't, but you would," he nodded. "Take it from me."

"I don't know," said Hugh.

"Ho! ho! Have you never told a lie?"

Hugh remembered his recent hot denial of having spied on Charlie and Kirsty.

"Perhaps I have," he said, a trifle coldly.

"Everybody who has ever lived has told a lie."

"How do you know?"

"Because I know. That's how."

"It's easy to say that. Just as easy as it is to say that Margat Navook smothered her bairn. Anyone can *say* a thing."

"Why did she put it in a hole, then?"

"Because it was dead."

"Of course!"

"But if it got dead, then it was no use. That's why."

"What sense is in that?"

"There's plenty of sense."

Bill did not let his sceptical smile become too obvious. The restraint annoyed Hugh.

"Anyway, any girl who's going to have a bairn is frightened of being found out."

"Everyone knows that," said Hugh.

"I wouldn't like to be a girl who was going to have a bairn. That's certain."

"No one's asking you."

"Ho! ho! As if they could!"

"Well, then! You're just saying what you heard grown-up people say."

"And what are you saying?"

"I'm saying I don't know. That's all."

"Well, whatever, we do know what happened after Margat Navook was going about with her fellow—up in the woods. Whether she killed it or not, she *had* it."

Bill had at last got his oblique shaft home, and knew it. So he immediately laughed and looked about. "What if anyone was hearing us!"

Hugh gave a constrained smile.

Bill became confidential and friendly. "Judging by the sun," he said, "it should now be about six. What do you think? Have a look."

Hugh looked.

Bill talked of rabbit snares. He had been at them this morning. He had twelve ready, beauties, and suggested nine o'clock as the best time to set them.

"I'll see," said Hugh, on his feet. "My mother is ill. But she may be easier. If she is, I'll come."

"Right you are!"

"So long."

And without another word or look, Hugh walked leisurely away, the grilse rolled in his jersey. He had meant to offer Bill part of it. If Bill had caught the fish himself, they would have been running and hiding and gloating over it all the time. Bill didn't want it to appear to be a great thing, and so—they had talked about Margat Navook and her fellow. . . . And Bill had made it seem in a way as if it was Kirsty and Charlie. He had meant that.

Hugh's face was pale with a sensitive intolerance and hurt. It would have been lacerated by the hurt had it not been for the memory of the fight. Bill had been frightened of him!

The cold exquisite assurance suffused him again. It compensated for the horrible accusation of spying —on his own sister. On Kirsty! . . . Kirsty and Charlie—in the trees—like yon.

A hot discomfort came over him. He walked more quickly. The colour of Margat Navook's hair came flashing into his mind. In a revulsion of feeling he hated—hated—hated all that. From the edge of the trees, he looked over the fields. No one. He would slip home quickly.

As he drew near the house, he saw a woman with her hat off on the doorstep. It was Elsie. Because of the anxious way she stood, his heart sank in him.

IV

"Oh, Hugh," Elsie said in a low voice, taking a step to meet him, "where have you been?"

"I was up the river."

"Did you see Kirsty?"

"Yes."

"Where was she?"

"Up the river. Is mother worse?"

"Yes. Was Kirsty coming home?"

"I don't know. I think so. Is she very bad?"

"Yes." Her eyes were full of pain and indecision— and fear. "I don't know what to do."

"I'll run for the doctor."

"Yes, you'll have to go at once. I wish Kirsty was at home." She stared away over the fields. "You'd better run."

"All right. I'll shove this fish in the back-kitchen first."

"Don't make a noise."

When Hugh stole out again, the front door was shut.

He started running, quietly as it were, on his toes, and at a great speed.

His mother must have taken a turn for the worse. She must be pretty bad. Elsie was frightened. Elsie wouldn't be frightened easily. She was always so pleasant and reserved.

Perhaps his mother was sinking.

Even when his breath was gasping and raw in his throat, he kept running. Nor did he pause when a man cried to him:

224

"Surely you're in a great hurry, boy!"

But he couldn't keep it up, and the doctor's house was on the other side of the glen, beyond the school. As it was his wind made loud noises in his throat. These noises helped to keep him from crying at the sheer impotence of his body. The doctor might be five minutes too late, or even one minute. He might walk in at the door—a second too late.

If he had been at home, he would have gone for him earlier, in plenty of time. That would have made all the difference. His mother would then have been safe.

This feeling that he would be to blame if the doctor was too late obsessed him. The responsibility, the guilt, terrified him. He gave it full play—because hidden out of sight in his youth was a profound disbelief in death, death that could touch his own home.

But to say, even to think, that his mother would not die, would be a temptation to death. She could! she could! (so that death, appeased, might wander by).

He was soon altogether taken up with the weakness of his body, and cunningly set the remnant of his strength to a jog-trot.

Some boys and men were on the bridge. They watched him coming with his lean boyish stride.

"Hullo, Hugh! Practising for the Games?"

"Entries for the mile race!"

"Keep it up! Go on, Hugh!"

And one freckled youth, stepping out a pace, swung his arm up and down, shouting:

"Ting-a-ling! Last lap!"

This sally provoked delighted laughter.

The embarrassment brought a tremor to his weakness. But he kept going grimly, until the uprising of the road finished his strength, and he dropped to a slow walk, mouth open, head lolling a little from side to side.

225

In a minute the dizzying air cleared again. By the time he reached the school, he was pushing himself into a trot. As the doctor's old house stood up before him, he gave of his last ounce, so that for a second or two he could not speak to the maid.

She replied, however, in a perfectly normal voice: "He's not in."

He stared at her, breathing hard.

"What's wrong?" she asked, her not unkind eyes searching his face. "Who is it?"

"My mother."

"Well, he's not in. He left word that he wouldn't be back until after eight. Is there anything awful wrong?"

He nodded. "She's very ill."

Her plump young face became thoughtful in a dubious way. "Wait a minute."

But she came back with the same look.

"We cannot say for sure where he is now. But it's not so long until eight. I'll give him the message to go over at once."

Hugh stood unmoving, his face averted.

"Is it the same trouble as before?"

"Yes." He nodded politely, with an odd little smile, and walked away, quite steadily, his head up, all his face drawn rigid about his closed mouth.

He kept on walking, unable even to think, damming back the bitter surge of his disappointment.

When the hollow of the valley came in sight, he saw the folk still on the bridge and, up the glen road, Kirsty and Charlie Chisholm. Even as he looked, they parted, Kirsty taking a roundabout path to avoid the bridge, Charlie turning back.

He would overtake Kirsty by the birch wood.

As he crossed the bridge, walking, a boy shouted:

"First prize, Hugh!"

226

A man flung, "Shut up!" at the boy.

Then they were all silent.

Hugh began to run. Nobody shouted anything. They had now all guessed he'd been for the doctor.

Kirsty, hearing his padding feet, turned and waited. Her face was flushed, her eyes shining. She was smiling in a strange shy way.

"Well, Hugh!"

He looked past her as he stopped, and said in an even voice:

"I've been for the doctor."

In the silence he felt her body contract. He glanced at her face. It stared at him out of an intense dismay, the eyes round, the lips apart. Her breast caved in a little as if she were shrinking from the thought which she put upon his face.

"What's wrong?"

"She's worse. Elsie is frightened."

She let out a small animal cry and, turning, began to run. Very soon she was out of breath. She muttered to herself every now and then, "Oh, Mother! Mother!" but the anguished words only acted as a whip, quickening her feet for a few steps.

"Did you see her?"

"No," answered Hugh. "I was out, too—and only just came back."

"We shouldn't have both been out! We shouldn't!"

They came in full sight of the house.

"Oh, Hugh!" she choked, looking at it.

"The doctor wasn't in," he said almost coldly.

She stopped.

"He won't be home till after eight."

"Where is he?"

"They don't know."

From a sidelong glance at her face as they hurried

227

on, Hugh knew that she was blaming herself bitterly for having left her mother so long. Perhaps she was thinking that all the time she was—up yonder—her mother was suffering more and more. At the same time. Her eyes were bright, but haunted.

"There's Elsie at the door!" she cried, and put forward her last strength.

Elsie came towards them, saying. "Oh, I'm glad you've come, Kirsty." And in answer to Kirsty's look: "She's very weak. I have never seen her like that. I didn't know what to do."

They spoke in whispers. Kirsty collected herself in a wonderful way. She nodded, she smoothed back her hair, she put her dress straight.

"When I left her I thought she had taken the turn," she said.

"She grew restless and very tired. Then I don't think she wanted anyone with her," murmured Elsie earnestly. "She seemed to want to be left alone. I didn't know what to do. I daren't leave her. And when I came to the door I couldn't see anyone. She asked for you twice."

Kirsty nodded, her whole mind seeming to listen not merely to Elsie, but to her own thought.

"We'll go in," she said.

Hugh followed them and, closing the door, stood beside it, listening intently.

"Well, Mother, how are you?" Kirsty's seeking voice was bright and cheerful.

"Very tired." The burden of the whispered weariness caught Hugh's breath.

"And I thought you had taken the turn! Are you feeling a little weaker, then?"

"A little, yes."

"That will never do, Mother! We mustn't have you
228

weaker on any account. Is there anything you would like?"

"No."

"Come now, Mother; you'll just take your tea-spoonful of whisky."

"Never mind, lassie."

"Yes, we'll mind, Mother. She's merely frightened, Elsie, that people will think she's taking to the drink."

"If only I had known!" murmured Elsie.

"Our dear mother wouldn't tell you, Elsie, for worlds. Now, Mother, here you are. Take your medicine. Steady now! . . . that's you! Now!"

There was silence for a little while.

"I'm a trouble to you."

"We know that, Mother dear; but we'll have to put up with you as best we can. There's nothing else for it!"

"Well. . . ."

"You're sounding better already. Wouldn't you try to take a little sleep?"

"Very well, I'll try."

"Elsie will have to run."

"You've been very kind to me, Elsie," breathed the weak voice. Its friendliness was heart-searching.

"I was only sorry," replied Elsie, "that I could do nothing for you."

Hugh opened the door noiselessly and slid out. His face was stilled and bright. Kirsty was great! She always knew what to do, how to make things cheery and hopeful. His mother wasn't so bad after all. Elsie had merely been frightened because she didn't know. He would have been frightened himself. It was an awful thing not to know what to do with a sick person.

Presently they came out. Kirsty closed the door silently and stepped to the corner of the house.

"She's very low," were her first words.

229

Hugh's startled eyes opened wide upon her.

"I have never seen her so weak," she added. Her quiet face exhibited a curious thoughtful resource. Her steady glance seemed fixed on a far imponderable balance of life and death. All at once her throat went through the motion of swallowing. "Poor Mother!" she said, but with a strange detachment, as if no one was there.

A soft weight came pressing over and about Hugh. He could not move. The world all around grew silent and fatal.

"I had a queer feeling—" began Elsie, but stopped and added, "Perhaps when the doctor comes—he can't be so long now—"

"No." Kirsty shook her head. "He can't do anything. It's her heart. The doctor says she must have strained it or something. She was always lifting that big tub of fish. But it's not a real heart trouble: it's false. It's not the same as Mrs. Macrae died of. But it's like it. What's aggravated it, you see, is that terrible chill she got—just after Alan left in the spring. Remember? And she wouldn't lie up."

Kirsty's gentle voice was remorselessly clear. There was no appeal against it. Fatality was closing in.

"Still," struggled Elsie, "she may come round."

"Yes," said Kirsty, "if only she would take the turn. But she's growing weaker. That's the danger: that she'll sink too low. The whisky revives her for a little, but when the effect of it wears off she'll be weaker than ever—unless she has come round. That's what I'm frightened of."

They were all silent.

"I thought," Kirsty added in a lower personal voice, "that she had taken the turn before I went out. She was brighter—she told me to go—but perhaps that was because—she thought I wanted—to go."

230

Hugh drew his body out. His legs answered him awkwardly. The consciousness of his body was almost unmanageable as he disappeared round the other end of the gable towards the back door. He stared at the door, seeing the dark red colour as for the first time. But he could not go in. Not into the kitchen—that strange chamber where his mother lay, weakening, in the shadow.

As he went down to the byre door he saw Kirsty and Elsie walking slowly away from the house. They stood and spoke together. He wondered what they were saying. From their leaning attitudes he knew that they were dealing in the strange intimate secrets that women seemed to have. Then they parted, Kirsty running back in a burst of energy to the house.

The summer evening glowed. Hugh noted the outline of things far away, particularly the outline of a cottage against the sky. It was like a toy cottage, so clean-cut it was. The beams of the sinking sun came through a vague bank of cloud, piercing shafts of light that turned its darkness to a luminous core, that touched sea and hill-crest with a fiery mist. It was like a light he had seen in a picture of the Crucifixion.

He leaned a shoulder against a door jamb, staring at the light, getting lost in it, but every now and then pulling himself back and regarding it with detached eyes, curious but vaguely hostile: a loss and regaining of personality that was like the flux in his mood, in his emotion, where there was no violence any longer, only a passionless uprising and sinking, a rhythm of controlled misery.

For there was that element of control left, caught in the fineness of the features, in their sensitive capacity for quick and passionate rebellion. The eyes might be afraid of the apocalyptic light, but they were sceptical of it, too;

in a final surge would dare it and not care. Even if the light had the power, the final power—of death.

And of what came after death. Which was the most awful and terrifying power. The piercing lean shafts of light from that molten core, not of the earth but of heaven—or lifted from beneath the earth for men to see—and sinking back again.

Against that power rebellion could only be not a passionate disbelief, but a passionate denial. One could beat one's hands against that power and flail one's soul to tatters. It was the power of death and hell. It was cruel and alien, and took no account of man's love and compassion. It was against man, against men and women and children, living their lives of work and feeling and happiness. It stared at them, with its broad swords of light, uncaring and terrible, and men hid from it, turned away and doubled up, their cloaks over them, like the men in the picture of the Crucifixion.

And, sinking, it took life with it—leaving behind the cold body of death and lamentation and woe.

The hand of God the Father, sinking slow and inexorable, of God the Terrible.

The fear of God.

The fear of God, to which men cried, praying desperately for salvation. "We beseech Thee, O God, to remember us here at Thy footstool!" were his father's words as they knelt at prayer in the kitchen. To remember us all—and to save.

From the swords of light there in the west, streaming from a molten core, from a core that declined in its uncaring majesty, like a slow hand whose palm was as white fire, whose streaming fingers closed upon it even as it sank.

From that gripped sunken hand there spirted across

232

the sky streams of red. The dye came upon a cloud as blood upon a bandage, tinged it and spread, growing deeper, until the whole hung penetrated and soaked.

Yet still was there light in the red, as if it cried. The whole west was full of this crying. But as the red darkened, the sound lost its individual note and became like thunder, and rolled there, trumpeted and echoing, its banners and crests going down in august marching order into the chasm.

And the bruised sky, blue-grey, was left cold and mute.

V

A foraging rat came past Hugh's stiff body. It was going to have entered the byre when its beady eyes saw him and it scuttled off. In a moment Hugh was after it and, picking up a stone, let fly. But already the rat had disappeared.

The sudden action made Hugh's heart beat painfully. Looking up at the house, he saw its quiet shape untouched by the rattle of the stone. It drew him despite himself, and he went slowly round to the back door. Listening, he heard no sound, and with infinite precaution he lifted the latch and entered.

No one was speaking within the house, no one was moving. His eyes rested on the grilse. Its silver had dulled to a blue-grey. Its sheen was tarnished. Yet in the faint gloom its shape was swift and beautiful; glazed and dead, but still of the river and woods, the secret world yonder where one raced and thrilled. Here it was now. Here he was. And through in the kitchen— the terrible and greater thing that imprisoned them— giving no sign.

Softly the communicating door opened and Kirsty was there. Hugh looked into her face.

She shook her head.

"She is weaker."

Hugh looked away.

"Where have you been?"

"I was down about the byre."

"You didn't see any sign of the doctor?"

"No."

There was silence.

"Hugh, wouldn't you like to see mother?"

He turned away a step. "No." His impatient whisper sounded harsh and distressed. "I'll see if I can get the doctor." And he went out, drawing the door to behind him.

He set out walking for the doctor, down moodily through the fields, thinking to himself that he could not go in to see his mother. A fear, a shrinking—but he couldn't help it. What was he frightened of about his mother, his own mother, whom he knew so well?

He hated her being at the point of death. That was it. He hated this gloom, this death. He could not face up to it. He hated it rebelliously—and hated himself for hating like that. But he couldn't help it. He would not know what to do or say. . . .

Gloomily he walked, his eyes straight ahead. The world was empty, a great grey place in a grey light. All in a moment his mother's face came up through the grey cover set over his mind. His fist jerked, and he shouted under his breath, "No!" It was as if a rent had been made into the seething passion and pain beneath, and the "No" gripped at it. Three times and quickly he repeated it, then went on securely.

Every now and again he resorted to some such trick of physical convulsion. And once shouting, "No!" out loud involuntarily, he repeated it less loftily and with a singing rhythm, so that no chance listener might think him mad. He could even forecast when the apparition or vivid emotional surge was about due and counter it before it started.

In this way his whole body grew gradually colder and keener, stronger and fiercer, until at last he was running. What he had to do was to get the doctor, who should have been over already, for he was bound to have been back home by this time. Perhaps he never meant to come. He might be in that mood.

Hugh's thought got directed on the doctor in a fugitive visual way as he ran, the man appearing in disconnected images that yet were each clear and alive, to the point of being resented or feared. The occasional abrupt coarse manner, the gruff voice, the way of saying what he thought brutally—even to a patient. His reputation for doing as he liked, no matter who wondered. All gathering into an image of strength, so that persons who criticized yet feared—even secretly admired. "He's a great woman's doctor" . . . lucky with the women who were having babies, it meant. . . .

Until Hugh finally arrived at his door and found that he was in.

The maid said that she had given the message, and that no doubt he would be across when he finished supper.

"Tell him—she is very ill," he stammered, unable even at such a crisis—for he sensed the unwillingness of the doctor to start out again—to use the word "sinking".

On the way back he forgot to have resentment against the doctor because of the fear that he wouldn't come, and he wondered what more he could have said or done to have made the case imperative.

Kirsty was at the front door, her face white in the gloom.

"He's at home now. He's coming when he's finished his supper."

"Oh, I wish he would hurry," rushed her voice on a strained undernote.

"Is mother no better?"

"No, no."

They stood there in the deep twilight.

"I must light the lamp. Come away in, Hugh."

Kirsty's voice made hesitation impossible now, and, entering, he sat down on the chair by the table. When Kirsty had lit the lamp, he lifted his face with an effort and looked at his mother.

The curtains had been taken off the bed, and his mother's face lay death-pale on the pillows, her eyes closed. Already she looked removed and uncaring. The familiar features had taken on an austere difference that startled him to the fear and terror which he knew had been waiting for him.

Then her eyes slowly opened and looked at him; glimmered into a smile of welcome. She whispered:

"Is that you, boy?"

"Yes."

"Where have you been?"

"Did you not see the salmon he got, Mother?" interposed Kirsty.

"Did he?" And her eyes slowly uprolled to command Kirsty.

"Yes. You wait until I show you."

Hugh twisted in his chair, his face smiling and confused, his throat choked.

"Look!" exhibited Kirsty. "What do you think of our Hugh now?"

"Well, well!" said his mother with a mock air of

resignation before the wonders of her family, and let fall on the coverlet the hand she had but raised from the wrist.

"A beautiful fish, Mother, isn't it? You'll have a small piece cold—the day after to-morrow. Not a moment before." And Kirsty returned to the back-kitchen.

Her mother closed her eyes, then slowly opened them again.

"Did anyone see you?"

"No," he answered. "I was by myself."

"You must be careful—that nothing happens to you."

There was a faint resignation in this note, as though he would now have to be specially careful in a world where she could no longer look after him. Her deeply lit eyes took him all in and saw his face, his embarrassed expression, as merely the veil, hardly saw his face at all except in its permanent lines and aspects, so concerned was her regard for his abiding self, for the boyish being that was but the incarnation of her mother's love.

"Oh, Hugh, I'm tired," she said in the friendliest weariness.

He started from his chair, took an indecisive step or two towards her, paused, looking round at the window, wrung his cap slowly in his hands.

Kirsty, watching him, smiled unknowingly out of her pity.

"Hugh," said his mother, her look drawing back to the surfaces again, her smile alight, "you wouldn't like to—lose me?"

"No." The word was wrung out of him. A sob came growling from his throat. He started for the door.

"Poor boy!" murmured his mother, "I shouldn't

237

have said that to him." And her eyes closed, leaving her face grey, with deep-sunken, blue-dark eye-sockets.

Kirsty stared at the face, and listened to the outside world. Her mother's body, lying flat and still, floated on the world . . . up through which there came the tramp of footsteps.

Hugh noiselessly followed the doctor in, and stood by the door.

"I'm glad you've come, doctor," Kirsty greeted him gently.

There was a moment's silence, then his gruff voice cried in downright astonished abruptness:

"Good God, woman, you're blue!"

It was a terrible way to accost his mother. It not only killed hope, but brought within its shattering violence the commonness of mortality.

A weakness came over Hugh, a deep trembling. With all his body wanting to sink down through itself, he had nothing to hang on to.

The doctor's feet went to the bedside. "Hm . . . hm . . . let me feel your pulse. . . ."

Silence.

"Are you feeling weak?"

"Oh, yes, doctor."

Hugh went and sat down on the stairs. The door to the kitchen swung noiselessly shut. It was quite dark here except for the grey light above the door. He lay back against the stairs. The doctor's voice came throaty and indistinct. He sat up at once, listening for it breathlessly. But he heard nothing . . . nothing but an odd ominous muffled sound. He would tiptoe to the door and put his ear to the keyhole.

He did this, but caught nothing except a "hm . . . yes . . . " grunted by the doctor. Then the doctor's feet moved, and Hugh slipped back to the stairs.

But it was several minutes after that before the doctor came out followed by Kirsty, who pulled the kitchen door after her and found the front door latch for the doctor's fumbling hands.

"She's very low," he said clearly.

"Is she, doctor?"

"Yes. I doubt if she will see the morning. She may —but it doesn't look like it."

"Oh, doctor!"

"I can't do anything for her—if she can't pull through of herself. The injection will help her heart for a while."

He was now on the doorstep.

"Oh, doctor, can we do nothing for our mother?" pleaded Kirsty, as she slipped after him.

Hugh knew that voice. It turned his heart to darkness.

But the doctor could do no more.

"If you see her sinking, you can give her a drop. I've got to go out yet to-night. Good-night."

Kirsty watched him dwindle away. His stumping figure disappeared. She was alone, the new night about her, the far horizon beyond Barrostad divinely clear in a faint afterglow.

So this was the end of her mother, on this night. The time had come. The remote horizon light was hardly of this world; its strange beckoning serenity, so pure, so thin, understood and waited. Kirsty gazed at it for a long time; then suddenly shivered and drew a quivering breath. The light was cold and unearthly. She feared it, wanted to run from it and cover herself.

For a blinding moment she rebelled, and a low whimpering came into her throat. She was not reconciled. No, no! Not, not—to that!

She turned to run, but steadied herself, drew a slow

239

deep breath, her skin shivering cold, and walked quietly in at the door.

Hugh, crouching in the dark stairs, hid the whiteness of his face.

Kirsty went into the kitchen.

"Well, Mother," she said, in a bright but gentle voice, her eyes hidden and searching.

Hugh waited on the silence.

"I heard what he said," came the weak voice calmly.

"What was that, Mother?" dissembled Kirsty.

"That I would not see the morning."

"But, Mother," said Kirsty.

And then there was silence.

VI

Kirsty did not move from the middle of the floor, but closed her mouth and swallowed her emotions. The time for dissembling had gone. A quietude came upon her spirit.

"Kirsty."

"Yes, Mother."

"I would like you to read a chapter."

"Very well, Mother."

She went and got the Bible, fixed the lamp, then came and sat on a chair by the bed.

"Where will I read, Mother?"

"In Ecclesiastes."

Kirsty found the place and started reading:

Cast thy bread upon the waters; for thou shalt find it after many days.

Give a portion to seven, and also to eight; for thou knowest not what evil shall be upon the earth.

Kirsty's voice was the voice of legend. It penetrated the years, going back into far time and to distant places of the imagination. It moved with a haunted loveliness, for light went with it and a remembering.

This storied voice fell upon Hugh, and he turned over and pressed his face into his arms. He pressed his wrist into his mouth and his teeth bit on it so that the pain was sharp and pierced his memories.

Cast thy bread upon the waters.

So did his mother love charity, giving of what she had with an open hand, and when rebuked, adding "for thou shalt find it after many days".

Her quiet wise smile, glad of the authority that could justify her giving. In Ecclesiastes where dark wisdom was and all the ways of life. And where all the ways of life are vanity. *Vanity of vanities, saith the Preacher, all is vanity.*

> *I returned, and saw under the sun, that the race is not to the swift, nor the battle to the strong, neither yet bread to the wise, not yet riches to men of understanding, nor yet favour to men of skill; but time and chance happeneth to them all.*

So was life on this bare land and on this wild sea. To her own generations and to the children of her blood. Time and chance had happened to them all.

> *The wind goeth toward the south, and turneth about unto the north; it whirleth about continually; and the wind returneth again according to his circuits.*
>
> *All the rivers run into the sea; yet the sea is not full: unto the place from whence the rivers come, thither they return again.*
>
> *All things are full of labour; man cannot utter it: the eye is not satisfied with seeing, nor the ear filled with hearing.*

241

> *The thing that hath been, it is that which shall be; and that which is done, is that which shall be done; and there is no new thing under the sun.*

There is great beauty in the truth. It comforts the breast, and the heart rejoices in its knowledge of the abiding things that are as the features of truth's face. The wind and the rivers, labour, the sea and the sun. The eye has seen them, and the ear heard, and they are known of the body and of the hands. Even now as in the immemorial ages. Nor is the eye ever satisfied with seeing, nor yet the ear with hearing.

There is no time, but only the face of truth. All the rest is vanity. Why then mourn and cover up your head? What does it avail you before God? Be glad, rather. *Be merry*, saith the Preacher.

> *Then I recommended mirth, because a man hath no better thing under the sun, than to eat, and to drink, and to be merry; for that shall abide with him of his labour the days of his life, which God giveth him under the sun.*

For the great Preacher preaches not dogma at the understanding, but tells of that which he has found in his experience and in his heart, and in a moment that which he has found is quick in the understanding of his listener.

Love then springs up and charity, and the understanding grows glad.

And because it is thus with the Preacher and with one's own mind, so may it be with God.

For the churches' preachers have grown to tell of a jealous God and of hell and of hell's torments, of doctrine, and of things difficult and dark and full of fear.

But with the old Preacher and with God Himself

surely it is easier. Wind and river, labour, land and sea, under the sun. Life is a vanity that dies, a shadow that passes, a smile that fades. How sweet it is in the sun, where the eye is never satisfied with seeing nor the ear with hearing! *Truly the light is sweet.*

So are things opposite appeased, and out of vanity comes gladness. For it is the mind that sees vanity, and finds gladness in its vision.

For truth is not of words, but of vision. Thus many things that are spoken contradict one another, but in the vision there is no contradiction. *A time to weep and a time to laugh, a time to kill and a time to be at peace.* All these things are comprehended in vision. And there, too, is the Preacher understood in fellowship of the spirit, in gladness and in travail. For he is even as I am. Seeing as I see, feeling as I feel, uncomprehending, even as I do not comprehend, the encompassing mystery of God.

For we may not look at God, not even as in a glass darkly, but as that before which we veil our foreheads.

Life is an adventuring to which time and chance happen. On this bare land and on this wild sea, if poverty happen, then shall we make of poverty a fellowship, with charity its flower.

And our name for charity will be hospitality; and for chance, courage; and for time, vanity; and for vanity, gladness.

What more can be done—under the sun?

What more from us, O God, who are without learning and ignorant?

For hospitality has moved in us not as a duty, but as a sweet need, yea, even a gladness. How profound then is the mystery of Thy hospitality, so that we tremble before that which may overwhelm us, *when the silver cord be loosed, the golden bowl be broken.*

When Kirsty had finished reading, her mother told her to turn to the Forty-sixth Psalm.

> *God is our refuge and our strength,*
> *in straits a present aid.*

As Kirsty lifted up her voice in the old slow tune, Hugh could not bear the sharp tumult of his emotion. The singing voice pierced him so that his body writhed together, forcing the blood to his ears to dull the sound, not merely of the sweet voice in its simplicity, but of words and melody brought to him from all the Sundays of his life.

He went out at the front door, closing it behind him, and faced the darkness. The singing reached him. He moved away from it, but not out of earshot, not out of sight of the lighted window—which slowly drew him with a curiosity that was not so much within himself as within life's strange detachment.

Through an angle of the scalloped lace fringing the foot of the yellow blind, he saw their faces. The Bible lay open on Kirsty's knees, but her eyes gazed straight in front of her in a wrapt dreamy sightlessness. They were bright as if hypnotized. Her mother's eyes were uplifted, as though the weight of the eyelids had been rolled back. They saw far beyond the veil of the roof, and something of the burden of her travail remained in them like holiness.

Kirsty's mouth opened round and red at each syllable. Her mother's pale lips opened also. Listening with a dreadful intensity, Hugh caught the thin frail sound of his mother's voice.

His body went shivering cold. His hair moved on his head. Turning from the window, he walked away into the night.

Usually life's emotions came to him in spasms. In

the midst of mild amusements or active games, or within the long hours of every day, his normal self-forgetfulness would suddenly be stung. Fierce and swift, emotion would rage and then pass.

What he had seen through the window should have wrung him with a blind agony. But he had come through too much already that night, and as he now walked on, bare-foot, the chill of his body drew taut the skin on his face.

This in a ghostly way released his mind. It found a strange uplifted freedom in the taut shell of his body, which walked on with a tall grace, head high.

No one could see more than he had seen. Even Kirsty was no longer brave and wonderful so much as set in the inexorable ways of life.

And if he hid even now from his thought that his mother was about to die, fearing in the dark night the effect upon him, yet was he merely gaining man's power of recognizing an event like death without the need for seeing it.

And presently a staring weariness came upon him wherein all feeling died. When the lighted window was once more before him, he hesitated to look in, as if the action would be a burden. He stooped, however, and for a long time gazed at his mother's rigid features and closed eyes and Kirsty's motionless body with its face buried in the bedclothes just below his mother's spent hand.

Before he knew that he was giving way, his fore-head hit the stone ledge of the window. When he pushed himself erect, he was giddy. His teeth shut on a dissolving sickness.

He fought it to the door. Drawing his hand across his cold brow, he summoned all his strength to force himself to open the door and enter.

In the dark passage-way, he stood listening. The door to the kitchen swung upon the light, and Kirsty looked at him. The sight of his deathly pallor made her face fly open.

"Where were you, Hugh?" she whispered, coming towards him.

"Out."

Her hand caught her breast:

"Mother is asleep."

He looked his terrible question.

She was silent for a moment.

"No, Hugh," she whispered on a compassionate breath.

But he hadn't had any food since some brose he had made for himself at midday. His belly was empty and the weakness went into his legs. His teeth suddenly began to chitter.

"I'm cold," he murmured indifferently.

"Come in to the fire."

He had wanted to go upstairs, to be alone, to lie down.

"Why are you frightened of Mother, Hugh?"

"I'm not." She had no right to say that. It wasn't fair. Not now.

He went into the kitchen and sat down by the fire, without looking at his mother. Kirsty could hardly take her eyes off him. After a little she beckoned him out of the kitchen, and made him follow her upstairs to his bedroom.

"I'm frightened we'll wake Mother," she explained. "I think she's sleeping. Sometimes I'm not sure— she may be just too weary to take notice." Then she continued, in the dark, "This is what I think, Hugh: I'll watch for the first bit of the night and you'll go to sleep. In the early morning I'll call you for a turn.

Meantime I'll bring you up a bowl of hot milk and a little water in a basin for your feet."

Her soft breath was a conspiracy. It drew him out of his indifference. But he would not relax externally, not even answer, and stood quite still until she withdrew. Then he went and sat on his bed.

She came first with the candle and the milk. "Drink that, and I'll bring the water. It'll warm you." She felt his hands. "How cold you are!"

When she brought the water, she knelt before him. "I'll do it myself," he said.

For answer, she lifted his feet into the basin.

"I'll do it," he insisted.

She washed in between his toes, about his ankles, smoothly up his legs, and round and round his kneecaps. Then lifting each leg into the towel, she dried it, giving him a smiling glance as she did so.

"Now, isn't that better?" and she removed basin and towel. "Drink up your milk and get into bed."

But he sipped his milk slowly, waiting for her to go out.

"Hurry up," she whispered.

Reluctantly he skinned off his jersey. Then, standing by the window, she turned her back to him.

With a certain calm, he kicked off his trousers and slipped under the clothes. She did not move, as if, while respecting his privacy, her mind had got caught unawares by the night and the stars.

Watching her standing there, he grew uneasy. All at once she stole from the window out of the room. He knew she was listening on the stairhead. But no pulse touched the taut ear of the house. She came back and sat by him on the bed. For a long time she looked over his head without moving.

Once he glanced at her eyes, but then no more. Her

silence stifled him. He wanted to move restlessly, but
dared not. Not that he felt inferior to his sister's mood,
but that he had not the heart to break its shining silence.

"She asked for you to-night," she said suddenly.

He made no response.

"I think she was wondering where you were—and
why you weren't in." Her tones were inward, hypnotic. After a little, she asked: "Did you hear us at
the books?"

"Yes," he muttered.

"When she asked me to read a chapter, oh, Hugh,
my heart fell out of me." She stirred. "Then strength
came to me. I do not know from where. I felt calm.
And I read in Ecclesiastes. I knew the portions she
liked . . . and I read here and there. I got a strange
meaning out of it. I always thought before that that
sort of reading was dry—you know, that it was a sort
of minister's language. But she knew it—she's clever,
mother—she had been thinking over it for long and
long—she had got the sort of queer light that—that. . .
I don't know." Her story-teller's voice was coming
upon her. Despite himself, Hugh was moved. "Often
when mother had been sitting alone by the fire, I
would come on her unbeknown, and would look at her
and wonder what she was thinking. You have seen her
like that. And then when she knew you were there she
would look round and smile. She was always so pleased
to see you then. There was nothing ever sad or sorrow-
ful about mother. She was never like the wifies who
go about mourning at the communion times. Have
you ever thought of it, Hugh, that mother was never
very religious. And yet—" Kirsty's low voice came
with a rush of conviction—"I would sooner have her
mind than all the religions in the world! Oh, Hugh,
mother was so quiet and wise. She did not cry, 'Lord!

Lord!' . . . she *knew*." She was silent a moment, then continued in a reflective way: "Sometimes when I'm away from mother I see her, Hugh, not so much like our mother, but like a woman . . . I don't know, I can't explain it . . . I don't mean set apart or that . . . I don't know what I mean . . . but like a woman sitting alone . . . and going back and going back and going back . . . she is like a great mother of great peoples . . . do you think I'm silly, Hugh?" And she looked at him with a faint sweet smile.

He stirred, but did not answer.

"You know, away in the time of the Preacher and in these strange places, mother would be a woman amongst them wise and calm, smiling and hospitable and welcoming them. Our mother. She would. In some way the world here is little, and the people are little. We are all—I don't know—we seem to be passing away. And these wifies who go moaning about their religion—they don't understand mother, they don't see the greatness of her spirit. Her spirit is old and great; it is restrained; it doesn't gush forth and lament, crying, 'Ow! Ow!'" Her face steadied from the distasteful expression, her eyes flashed through their smile; then her words came dropping from a distance: "I know what religion is now," and her glance fell on him, half-wondering, half-searching.

He could see that she was overwrought, but he could see also that she was in love with her vision because it satisfied her in a profound way, going far back. And because of all that, her mother in the bed down below was forgotten. This immersion in her own mood was too much, was overdoing it. He felt his spirit bathe in it and grow weak and tremulous. It was the final truth—but it was too emotional to be borne. He would not give way. Kirsty should not remember the truth like this. The desire to give way was over-whelming. But he was the only man in the house.

"And then," began Kirsty again (his soul crying out against this new assault), "when we had read and sang—there was no more to do. She closed her eyes. Oh, Hugh!" She lowered her head in a sudden blind-ing pain, and raised it again. "She opened her eyes and looked at me. And—and—do you know what she said? She said, 'Kirsty, you may think that I'm an old woman. But I don't feel old.' Oh, Hugh, as if we thought her old! She's not sixty!"

Now Hugh thought that even Kirsty was old.

Kirsty could hardly control her voice. "It was terrible," she said. "I didn't know what to say. For—you see—it means—mother doesn't want to die. Oh, Hugh, she doesn't want to die! I—I said to her that we didn't think her old. Oh, Hugh, I couldn't say it calmly or brightly. I broke down. It all came over me. I couldn't help myself. I cried to her, 'Oh, Mother, don't die! don't die!' I fell on the bed. I cried to her, 'Don't leave us!' I was beside myself. I'm sorry. Oh, I couldn't help it. I felt her hand on my head." Kirsty suddenly buried her face in the bedclothes.

The muscles of Hugh's face contracted to a fixed rigidity, over which tears rolled from staring glittering eyes. Kirsty's stifled sobbing made the bed quiver.

She sat up slowly, wiping her eyes, and gazed side-ways at the window for a long time, her body so still that it did not seem to breathe.

"Though I'm not really sorry I said that now." came her remote voice. She turned to him. "I'm frightened even to whisper what's in my mind."

He refused her look. But all the meaning of her talk, the spirit prompting it, became clear. His eyes held a light so burning bright that it suggested pain. What had been driving Kirsty on to speak of her mother, almost as of someone gone, was the beginning of an assurance that her mother would not die. It was far away yet, like the sound of a wave on a shore that the ears caught doubtfully in a great silence. So that, by a strange deception, her voice had had at times the air of remembering an event already over.

"It was when—"

But he stopped her, on an abrupt note almost of hostility.

She looked at him and saw that he understood. The pale reserve of his face, the troubled intolerance, went to her heart. She had to turn away from him to keep her hands from fondling, her mouth from kissing him.

She got up, but did not move away.

"Oh, Hugh, if only!" she dared hope. She had no fear of offending the jealous powers, though she, too, felt there was something fatal in too great an optimism.

He made no response, and at last she added: "Well, I'll go down. The turn won't come likely until near the dawn. That's when the body is weakest and the spirit—" She hesitated and turned to him. "I'm away, then. Go to sleep. I'll waken you—when need be."

She smiled to him lingeringly, and with that oddly considering look. He smiled back awkwardly, and turned his face to the wall. He heard her pull down the blind. When the door closed, he lay over on his back again and listened. No sounds came from below. No voice. No whisper. The last waiting had begun.

The fire in his head made it restless. He rolled it from side to side on the pillow. The eye-sockets were burning hot. He steadied his head, let his body and limbs lie dead, and breathed heavily. Sometimes he moaned a little under his breath, a tiny whimpering sound protesting that he was too tired. The sound helped to blot out thought. Raising himself, he put out the light as he turned over and lay on his face. "I'm tired!" he cried into his pillow. "I'm too tired!"

Then exhausted, and breathing in gulps, he lay still. Though his eyes were closed he was conscious of the darkness, felt it pressing down on him. Putting out the light had been a sudden action that he would not allow himself to think about any more than about the dark. He was not going to sleep. Never would he sleep while down below. . . . His protestations, smothered by the pillow, dulled thought and feeling, eased the peril of the dark. The terrors encompassing him were too many. His head rolled again from side to side. His mind swayed and through the smothering warmth of his breath sank into sleep.

VII

But some part of his mind must have remained alert, for at the mere opening of his door he became wide awake, knowing in a moment where he was.

Some one had entered and was standing invisible against the darkness of the clothes that hung on the back of the door. The room was full of a dim light and the window blind was luminous. The person who had entered was listening. Hugh held his breath against the uncoiling of terror.

The person crossed quietly to the blind and pulled it up. It was Kirsty. She stood looking out on the grey dawn.

Nor did she move. The suspense became intolerable. The pulling up of the blind was for the living, but her quietude had surely the gaze of despair. Looking out on a lost world, a still grey world, where no life moved, only the wind in a faint sigh, *ssh-h-h.*

His griped body moved. The bed creaked. Kirsty turned round, and after a moment came over.

She stooped and saw his straining eyes.

"Mother is better," she said.

All his face strained upward, the smile disfiguring it.

This, then, was the news. This was the final dread word that had to come. The veil, the blind, had been raised—to let in the daylight of life.

Kirsty sat down and in a casual way nodded, "Yes." Her tone was amused. It was slow and happy and amused. She studied Hugh rather reflectively.

"A wonderful woman, our mother, isn't she?" Her assurance had a mild grandiloquence. A serene pride was hidden in her voice. This was the mother they thought was going to die! "Won't the doctor get a shock!" She regarded Hugh ponderingly, her face flushed and full of light.

Hugh was now trembling with excitement. The short but profound bodily sleep had restored his vigour. His mother was better. They were free! The awful weight, stiffening the flesh, gripping at the bones, slid down past the feet, and body and soul rose up.

"Do you know what happened?" Kirsty asked largely.

"No."

His tremulous eagerness caressed her.

"Well—about an hour ago. Not more." She was inclined to a fastidious estimate. "Just about an hour ago—she woke up."

"Did she?"

Kirsty nodded. There was no hurry. "I was sitting in the chair. I wasn't feeling too good. It couldn't have

253

been five minutes before that I had gone and listened for her breathing. I thought—once—it had stopped. I was sitting in the chair wondering about what I might have to do in the morning. I was making up the telegrams in my mind. It's queer the things you'll do at a time like that. My mind was counting the words! And because it couldn't get them right I couldn't stop it! And I daren't use my fingers. Funny, wasn't it?"

"Yes," said Hugh.

"Well, in the middle of that I heard a voice saying, 'Kirsty.' I looked up. It was our mother! And her pale worn face was smiling. . . . Oh, Hugh, my heart leapt! . . . However, I got up and went to her. 'Hallo, Mother,' I said; 'feeling a little better?'"

"'Yes,' she answered.

"'That's right!' . . . Oh, Hugh, I could have thrown myself on the bed! . . .

"'Did you sit up all night? Poor lassie, you must be tired.'

"'What was I going to be tired for, Mother?'

"'Kirsty,' she said.

"'Yes, Mother.'

"'Do you know what I would like?'

"'No, what?'

"'A cup of tea.'"

Kirsty rose from the bed and sat down on it again. A cup of tea! Wasn't it a superb joke? "And quite the thing—as if nothing had happened!"

Hugh laughed huskily.

"And she took it, too—with a piece of oatbread and butter—nearly as big as your palm. That's your mother for you!"

The humour was irresistible. It put them a little beside themselves. They did not know right what to do or to say. Kirsty's bravado, too, was wearing a trifle thin.

"If you lie down now for a little, then you'll be fresh to go off to work," Hugh suggested.

Kirsty turned and looked at him. Her voice came strangely gentle.

"Hugh, are you glad?"

"Oh, yes, Kirsty." His voice quivered with gladness.

"Hugh, I'm—I'm so glad." And as she said it in a breaking voice, she lay over and buried her face in the bedclothes.

He slipped over her body and pulled on his trousers and jersey. Then he covered her with the patchwork quilt as well as he could. She was crying quietly and steadily, utterly spent.

On bare feet he went downstairs and stole into the kitchen. His mother's face met him. Out of the shrunken frailty of its pallor, its new life was shining.

"Is that you, Hugh?"

The weak thin voice was also alive.

For the moment he could not find his tongue.

"What are you doing up at this hour?"

"I just came down to see you. Kirsty is resting."

"You should be asleep, you rascal."

"I'm glad—you're better."

Then her eyes looked at him with such a quiet shining, that his own filled and he hurried away quickly.

Nor could the closed house hold him. The front door was unlocked. Round by the gable corner he paused and looked on the world. The fields, the crofts, every known thing, asleep in the grey of the dawn that was turning to silver and brightness. The sea glittered, and even as he looked, away north-east, the red rim of the sun pushed itself slowly up beyond the horizon. Soon the water between threw off flakes of vivid colour as big as moons. The ocean rippled in spangled loveliness. The great sea-serpent was casting its scales of every colour, was lashing its morning bath in sheer delight.

And on that sea his father would be under way, or perhaps hauling in the last nets laden with the flashing silver of a great shot of herring. If ever there was a morning for luck, surely this was it! And Alan, on horseback, would be swinging over an endless plain. . .

This sense of exquisite motion got into Hugh's body. He wanted to run. And all at once he thought of Bill and his snares. A cunning laughing look came into his eyes. If he did a circle up round where the rabbits would be feeding and rushed them down their little hopping paths into the snares, he would be sure to get a couple! Though probably Bill had been frightened to set the snares without him! He blew the air out noisily through his lips and trampled the earth in dancing steps. The round rusted end of a little tin a stone's throw away caught his eye. Picking up a pebble, he let fly, and hit the tin, making it give a ludicrous jump. Thrilled by the unexpected accuracy, he crouched under the sound. His mother would have heard that. Embarrassment made him blush. His mouth fell open as he listened. The lances of the new morning came about him and he challenged their leaping ecstasy, his eyes flashing hither and thither in his still head as he thought of his mother who had been given up for dead but was alive and would be wondering at this moment what he was doing knocking tins about! When he would go in at the door in a minute, she would call him! . . . Unless he went to the woods—for an offering? His head turned. And all at once he started running, his body light and fleet, his bare legs twinkling across the fields of the dawn.